A MacCallister Christmas

*Look for these exciting Western series
from bestselling authors
William W. Johnstone and J.A. Johnstone*

The Mountain Man

Preacher: The First Mountain Man

Luke Jensen: Bounty Hunter

Those Jensen Boys!

The Jensen Brand

Matt Jensen

MacCallister

The Red Ryan Westerns

Perley Gates

Have Brides, Will Travel

The Hank Fallon Westerns

Will Tanner: U.S. Deputy Marshal

Shotgun Johnny

The Chuckwagon Trail

The Jackals

The Slash and Pecos Westerns

The Texas Moonshiners

A MacCallister Christmas

WILLIAM W. JOHNSTONE
and
J.A. JOHNSTONE

KENSINGTON BOOKS
www.kensingtonbooks.com

KENSINGTON BOOKS are published by

Kensington Publishing Corp.
119 West 40th Street
New York, NY 10018

All Kensington titles, imprints, and distributed lines are available at special quantity discounts for bulk purchases for sales promotion, premiums, fund-raising, educational, or institutional use.

Special book excerpts or customized printings can also be created to fit specific needs. For details, write or phone the office of the Kensington Special Sales Manager: Attn.: Special Sales Department. Kensington Publishing Corp, 119 West 40th Street, New York, NY 10018. Phone: 1-800-221-2647.

Kensington and the K logo Reg. U.S. Pat. & TM Off.

Library of Congress Card Catalogue Number: 2020931316

ISBN-13: 978-1-4967-1852-5
ISBN-10: 1-4967-1852-6

First Kensington Hardcover Edition: July 2020

10 9 8 7 6 5 4 3 2 1

Printed in the United States of America

Prologue

" 'Tis because o' that television show that yer here, isn't it, lassie?" the old woman asked as the young American couple came up to the counter to pay for the lunch they'd enjoyed in this picturesque little café.

The young woman smiled and said, "Is it that obvious?"

"Ye look a wee bit like the girl who plays the daughter, ya ken."

"You really think so?" The young woman blushed, obviously pleased by the comparison.

"Oh, aye. In fact, ye look as if ye have some Scots blood a-flowin' in yer veins."

"I do! A little. I don't really know how much."

"Enough that I'd consider ye a good Scottish lass. We need to figure out what clan. Once we ken what yer colors are, ye can go next door to me sister's shop, where she sells all sorts o' goods decorated with all the clan colors . . ."

While that conversation was going on, the young man had handed over his credit card. He took it back from the old woman now as she handed him his receipt, along with it. His wife said eagerly, "I don't really know anything about the clans. Well, other than what I've learned from watching TV."

"Then ye've come t' the right place. I'll teach ye everything ye need to ken. What is't ye Americans call it? A *crash course?*"

"Yes, that's right."

While his wife leaned over the counter to continue the spirited conversation with the woman who ran the café, the young man stepped through the door to the narrow cobblestone street to wait for her. He had a hunch it might be a while.

"Snagged another'un, did she?"

The voice came from the young man's left. A burly older man sat there, puffing on a pipe, bundled up against the day's chill with his cap pulled down on his gray hair.

"I beg your pardon?" the young man said.

The older man took the pipe out of his mouth and pointed with the stem at the café entrance. "Aileen in there. She can spot the tourists and the TV fans and manages to send about half of 'em in her sister Isobel's shop. 'Twouldn't surprise me if she gets what you Americans call a *kickback.*"

"Annabel really does enjoy that show," the young man said with a smile. "We've been all over the Highlands during the past week. Saved up to take this trip for a couple of years."

The older man moved over on the bench and nodded curtly to the empty space. The young American sat down and held out his hand.

"I'm Richard van Loan."

"Is that an English name?"

"Dutch, I believe. I've never been into genealogy all that much."

"I've nothin' against the Dutch, so I'll shake yer hand. Graham McGregor is me name. 'Tis a pleasure to meet ye, lad."

"Likewise," Richard said. He looked around at the old buildings that fronted the narrow street. Eastward, between some of those buildings, a narrow slice of the Firth of Clyde was visible, the water a deep, deep blue on this cloudy day. "You have a beautiful city here."

" 'Twas not always so large. Me grandfather told me it grew like wildfire after the port was put in and the steamers began comin' up the firth, and James Ewing built Castle House next to old Dunoon Castle. A'fore that, 'twas just a country town, Dunoon, spelled a bit different than today. Me great-great-grandfather Ian McGregor had a pub here, the White Horse."

"Sounds like it would have been a wonderful place to visit," Richard said.

"Dinna ye go talkin' about such things! Ye would never believe how many tourists show up in the Highlands searchin' for some magical place where they can go travelin' through time!"

Richard laughed. "Really? Well, people take these things seriously, I suppose."

"Aye, they do. Yer wife . . . I'd wager she's a wee bit in love wi' tha' braw laddie on the TV."

"Oh, I don't know about that—"

"But he's not the only hero t' come from Scotland, ye ken. Why, there was once a lad from right here in old Dunoon who was every bit as big and bold and handsome, an' even better in a fight! Me great-great-grandfather Ian was his friend, ye ken, before he left to go t' America and become a famous frontiersman, like in yer Western movies."

"Your great-great-grandfather became a frontiersman in America?"

"No, th' lad I'm tellin' ye about! Duff MacCallister, tha' was his name. Duff Tavish MacCallister. Did ye ever hear of him?"

Richard shook his head slowly and said, "No. No, I don't think so."

Annabel came out of the café, pointed at the shop next door, and said, "Richard, I'm going to be in there for a while looking around. Are you all right out here?"

"Yes, I'm fine," he told her. "Take your time."

"She will, ye ken," Graham McGregor said after Annabel had vanished into the shop. "Take her time, that is. Lassies always do."

"Yes, I've been married long enough to know that. You were saying about this fellow Duff... Tell me more about Duff MacCallister."

"I reckon I can do that," Graham said, nodding. "Old Ian filled me grandfather's head wi' stories, and he passed 'em on to me when I was naught but a tyke." He paused, obviously thinking about which story to tell, then went on, "I know a good one. Lots o' ridin' an' shootin' an' fightin', like in them movies I was talkin' about. It started in th' month o' December, long, long ago, in a frontier settlement, Chugwater, Wyomin'..."

Chapter 1

Chugwater, Wyoming . . . back then

Duff MacCallister took off his hat and raised his arm to sleeve sweat off his rugged face.

"If I dinna ken what day 'tis, I'd say 'twas the middle o' summer, not December!"

"Not that long until Christmas," Elmer Gleason agreed. "It's unseasonably warm, that's for sure."

The two men had just finished loading a good-sized pile of supplies, including heavy bags of flour, sugar, and beans, into the back of the wagon they had brought into town from Sky Meadow, Duff's ranch farther up the valley. Both were in shirtsleeves, instead of the heavy coats most men normally wore at this time of year in Wyoming. In fact, Duff had rolled up the sleeves of his shirt over brawny forearms.

He was a tall, broad-shouldered, tawny-haired young man, originally from Scotland, but now, after several years here in Wyoming, a Westerner through and through. He had established Sky Meadow Ranch when he arrived on the frontier, brought in Black Angus cattle, like the ones he had raised back in Scotland, and built the spread into a large, very lucrative operation that took in thirty thousand acres of prime grazing land.

Elmer, a grizzled old-timer who had lived a very adventurous life of his own, had been living on the land when Duff bought it, squatting in an old abandoned gold mine at the northern end of the property. People believed the mine was haunted, but what they had seen was no ghost, just Elmer.

Since Duff had made that discovery, the old-timer had become one of his most trusted friends and advisors. He worked as Sky Meadow's foreman, and Duff had even made him a partner in the ranch with a 10 percent share.

Now, with the supplies Duff had purchased from Matthews Mercantile loaded, Elmer licked his lips and said, "I reckon we'll be headin' down to Fiddler's Green to wet our whistles before startin' back to the ranch? A cold beer'd taste mighty good on a day like today."

"Aye, the same thought did occur to me," Duff said. "Go ahead, and I'll catch up to ye. I'll be makin' one small stop first."

"At the dress shop?" Elmer asked with a knowing grin.

"Perhaps . . ."

"Go ahead. I'll be down there yarnin' with Biff when you're done. We can talk about the weather, like ever'body else in town is probably doin'."

Duff lifted a hand in farewell and turned his steps along Clay Avenue toward the shop where Meagan Parker sewed, displayed, and sold the dresses she made, which were some of the finest to be found anywhere between New York and San Francisco, despite the unlikely surroundings of this frontier cattle town. Meagan's talents were such that she could have been in high demand as a designer and seamstress anywhere in the country, but she preferred to remain in Chugwater.

Duff MacCallister was a large part of the reason she stayed.

Duff and Meagan had an understanding. Neither of them

had a romantic interest in anyone else, and because of financial assistance she had rendered him in the past, she was also a partner in Sky Meadow.

The ranch was named after Skye McGregor, Duff's first love back in Scotland. The young woman's murder had been part of a tragic chain of circumstances that resulted in Duff leaving Scotland and coming to America. A part of Duff still loved her and always would. Meagan knew all about Skye and Duff's feelings for her, and she accepted the situation, so it never came between the two of them.

Someday they would be married. Duff and Meagan both knew that. But for now, they were happy with the way things were between them and didn't want to do anything to jeopardize that.

Now that Duff wasn't lifting heavy bags and crates into the wagon, the day didn't feel quite as warm to him, although the sun still shone brightly in a sky almost devoid of clouds. A couple of times earlier in the fall, a dusting of snow had fallen, but it wouldn't have been unusual for several inches to be on the ground by now.

A little breeze kicked up as Duff walked toward Meagan's shop. He lifted his head to sniff the air. There was a hint, just a hint, of coolness in it.

Maybe that was a harbinger, Duff thought, an indication that the weather was going to change again and become more seasonal. Even though a man would have to be a fool not to enjoy the pleasant weather—it wasn't a raging blizzard, after all—with Christmas coming, it needed to *feel* like winter. That little tang he had detected put some extra enthusiasm in Duff's step. He was in a good mood, and he didn't think anything could change that.

Four men reined their horses to a halt in front of the Bank of Chugwater, swung down from their saddles, and looped the reins around the hitch rail there. Hank Jessup, the oldest of the group, turned to the other three and said, "All right, Nick, you'll stay out here with the horses."

They all had the same roughly dressed, rawboned appearance, and their facial features were similar enough that it was obvious they were related. Hank, with his weather-beaten skin and white hair, could have been father to the others, based on looks, but in actuality he was their older brother. Half brother, anyway. Late in life, their father had married a much younger woman and somewhat surprisingly sired the other three— Logan, Sherm, and Nick.

They had willingly followed Hank into the family business of being outlaws, and they had come to Chugwater to help themselves to an early Christmas present of however much loot was in the bank's vault.

"You said I could go inside this time, Hank," Nick complained. "I always have to watch the horses."

Sherm said, "It's an important job, kid."

"You're our lookout, too," Logan added. "You've got to warn us if any blasted badge-toter comes along and starts to go in the bank."

"Yeah, yeah," Nick muttered. "I guess so."

Hank said, "And you're watching the horses because I say so, that's the most important thing." He squared his shoulders, nodded to Logan and Sherm. "Come on."

The three of them stepped up onto the boardwalk and headed for the bank's front door. They didn't draw their guns yet, because they didn't want to alert people on the street that anything unusual was going on.

Nick lounged against the hitch rail, handy to the spot where the reins were tied so he could loosen them in a hurry if he needed. This wasn't the first bank robbery he and his brothers had pulled. Sometimes the boys came out walking fast, still not wanting to draw attention, and sometimes they came on the run, needing to make as rapid a getaway as they could.

Inside the bank, Hank glanced around quickly, sizing up the

situation without being too obvious about it: two tellers, each with a single customer, one man and one woman. A bank officer, probably the president, was seated at a desk off to one side behind a wooden railing. The man had a bunch of papers spread out on his desk and was making marks on one of them with a pencil, pausing between each notation to lick the pencil lead.

No guard that Hank could see, but it was entirely possible those tellers had guns on shelves below the counter, and the bank president probably had an iron in his desk drawer, too. Question was, would they be smart enough not to try to use them?

Hank wouldn't mind gunning them down if it came to that. Wouldn't mind at all.

He exchanged a glance with his brothers and nodded. No time like the present.

Hauling the gun from the holster on his hip, Hank yelled, "Stand right where you are! Nobody move, or we'll start blasting!"

Meagan was sitting at a table with several pieces of cloth in front of her when Duff came into the shop. She had three straight pins in her mouth, taken from a pincushion close to her right hand. She looked up at him and smiled.

"Careful there, lass," he cautioned. "Ye dinna want t' be stickin' pins in those sweet lips o' yours."

Deftly Meagan took the pins out of her mouth and returned them to the pincushion, which allowed her to smile even more.

"I certainly wouldn't want to hurt my lips," she said, "when I have such an important use for them."

"Oh? And what would that be?"

Meagan stood up and came toward him, a sensually shaped blond beauty. Because of the unseasonably warm weather, she wore a lightweight dress today that hugged her figure, instead of being bundled up.

"This," she said as she put her arms around Duff's neck and

lifted her face so he could kiss her. He did so with passion and urgency.

After a very enjoyable few moments, Duff stepped back and said, "I have some news this morning. Elmer and I stopped at the post office on our way t' the mercantile, and a letter was there waiting for me."

"Well, don't keep me in suspense," Meagan said. "Who is it from?"

"My cousin Andrew. Ye've heard me speak of him many times."

"Of course. He's the famous actor. He and his twin sister, both."

Duff nodded and said, "Aye, Rosanna. The pair o' them were actually the first of my American cousins I ever met, when they came to Glasgow to perform in a play called *The Golden Fetter*. Andrew had written to me then, introducing himself and asking me to come see the play and meet him and Rosanna. Fine people they are."

"Being MacCallisters, how could they be anything else?"

"Aye, 'tis true, we are a fine clan. I've seen them a number of times since then, in New York and elsewhere, and back in the summer, I wrote to Andrew and invited him and Rosanna to spend Christmas at Sky Meadow if they could arrange their schedule to make it possible. In his letter I received today, he says they've been touring, but they're ready t' take a break from it and pay me a visit for the holidays."

"Duff, that's wonderful news," Meagan said. "I'm looking forward to meeting them. When will they be here?"

"Andrew is no' sure yet, but 'twill not be for another few days, at least. He assures me they'll arrive before Christmas."

"And what about your cousin Falcon? Didn't you tell me that he's coming for Christmas, too?"

Duff grinned and said, "Falcon told me he would *try* to make it. Wi' Falcon, ye never can tell what wild adventure might come along an' drag him away. So if he shows up, I'll be mighty glad t' see him, of course, but I willna be surprised if circumstances prevent that."

"Well, I hope he's able to come," Meagan said. "It would be almost like a family reunion. Isn't he Andrew and Rosanna's brother?"

"Aye, youngest brother. Falcon is the baby of the family, although I doubt he'd appreciate bein' referred to as such. Andrew and Rosanna are ten years or so older than him."

"Aren't there other brothers and sisters?"

Duff waved a hand and said, "Aye, spread out all over the country, they are. One o' these days, they need to have a proper MacCallister family reunion."

"I'll bet that would be exciting," Meagan said with a smile. "There's no telling what might happen."

"Och, lass, are you for sayin' that th' MacCallisters attract trouble or some such?"

"Well, now that you mention it . . ."

Duff chuckled and pulled Meagan back into his arms for another hug and kiss. He stroked a big hand over her blond hair and said quietly, " 'Tis something else I'd rather be attractin'."

"Oh, you do, Duff. You definitely do."

He was about to lower his lips to hers for another kiss when gunshots suddenly rang out somewhere down the street. The sounds shattered the warm, peaceful day and made Duff jerk his head up again.

Those shots were concrete proof of what Meagan had just said. No MacCallister could go very long without running into a ruckus.

"I'll be back," Duff said over his shoulder as he charged out of the dress shop.

Chapter 2

As president of the Bank of Chugwater, Bob Dempster's job usually involved making sure all the numbers added up and all the other day-to-day details were attended to. But as a frontier banker, he knew that sometimes he might be called upon to perform other tasks as well.

For that reason, a .45 revolver rested in the middle drawer of his desk. As the three rough-looking strangers entered the bank, Bob took note of them and carefully eased the drawer out so that the gun came into view.

When the three men pulled their guns, and the oldest one shouted for everybody not to move, Bob reached for his own weapon and closed his hand around it.

Unfortunately, the boss outlaw swung sharply toward Bob and lined his revolver on him.

"When you take your hand outta that drawer, mister, it better be empty, or I'll put a bullet right through your brain."

Bob wasn't going to throw his life away by betting on his own rudimentary gun-handling skills. Slowly he opened his hand and lifted it away from the drawer. He raised his other hand at the same time.

"Now you're bein' smart," the outlaw said. "Stand up and move over here, careful-like."

While Bob was doing that, another of the robbers herded the two customers away from the tellers' windows at gunpoint. The third man menaced the tellers with his gun and told them, "You fellas come out of those cages. We want everybody together. And make it pronto!"

Soon the robbers had the five people in the bank lined up along the railing in front of the president's desk. The leader jerked his head toward the counter and told his companions, "Get everything in the tellers' drawers, and then we'll clean out the vault."

"You got it, Ha—"

The man who started to reply cut it short just as he started to say the leader's name. Looking a little embarrassed by his near slipup, he hurried to carry out the orders.

Bob Dempster looked at the others and nodded confidently, hoping they would take his meaning that they should cooperate with the bank robbers and maybe they would all come through this all right. Bob hated to think of the monetary loss, but it was more important that these innocents survived.

The female customer was an elderly widow named Mrs. Hettie Richardson, who raised chickens and made a small but livable income by selling their eggs. Cloyd Nelson was the other customer, who had driven a freight wagon for R.W. Guthrie in the past, but currently worked in Guthrie's building supply warehouse. He was a short, brawny, middle-aged man known to have a bad temper, and if anybody was going to fly off the handle and cause a problem, Bob knew it would be him.

Unfortunately, Bob was wrong about that, because while he was watching Nelson warily, Mrs. Richardson reached into her bag and hauled out an old cap-and-ball pistol that had been converted to percussion. She held the gun in both hands, hooked bony thumbs over the hammer, and hauled it back to full cock.

"You scoundrels, get away from my money!" she cried, and the next instant she pulled the trigger.

The booming report was thunderously loud inside the bank. The boss outlaw's hat flew off his head. The gun in his hand came up toward the five people gathered along the railing.

Cloyd Nelson yelled, "Mrs. Richardson, get down!" and lunged at her, apparently intending to grab her and pull her to the floor, out of the line of fire.

That put his back toward the outlaw, and the shot the man fired struck Nelson squarely between the shoulder blades. The slug's impact threw the man forward into Mrs. Richardson. Both of them toppled over the railing and sprawled on the floor behind it.

The two tellers dived for the floor, no doubt thinking that now the shooting had started, the air would be full of flying lead. That was highly probable.

Bob Dempster turned and dashed back through the gate in the railing. Another shot boomed. He heard the ugly, high-pitched whine of a slug passing close beside his ear.

After the outlaws had gotten the drop on him, Bob would have cooperated in the hope that no one would be hurt. Now, with the fat in the proverbial fire, his best chance seemed to be to fight back.

He flung himself behind his desk, snatched the .45 out of the still-open drawer, and triggered twice in the general direction of the bank robbers. His two employees were on the floor, as well as Mrs. Richardson and Nelson, so he didn't have to worry about hitting any of them.

Return fire blasted at him. He heard the bullets thudding into the desk, but the heavy piece of furniture stopped them. He stuck the gun up and risked another shot without having any idea if he'd hit anything.

"Hank's hit!" one of the outlaws yelled. "Let's get outta here!"

"I got the money from the drawers!" another man shouted.

Boot soles slapped the polished wooden floor as the men rushed out of the bank.

Bob Dempster waited a couple of heartbeats to make sure they were gone, then looked over the desk. A haze of powder smoke floated in the air. Bullets had shattered the frosted glass that flanked the tellers' windows, and there might be other damage he couldn't see yet. He pushed himself up and called, "Mrs. Richardson! Are you all right?"

"Get this big ox off me!" the old woman wailed.

That *big ox* probably had saved her life, Bob thought, but with Nelson's considerable weight pinning her to the floor, she wasn't thinking about that. She had to be worried that he would suffocate her, which he just might. Bob hurried around the desk and called to the tellers, "Give me a hand here!" Both young men appeared to be unhurt.

They were trying to lift Cloyd Nelson's limp form off Mrs. Richardson when more shots roared outside.

When Duff reached the street, he could tell the shots were coming from the direction of the bank. He pulled his gun from its holster and started running along the street toward the impressive brick building.

As he approached, he saw Thurman Burns, the deputy town marshal, hurrying toward the bank from the other direction. A young man stood near four horses tied at the hitch rail in front of the building. He didn't seem to have noticed Duff, but he had seen the deputy. Using the horses to shield his movements, he drew his gun and aimed over the saddles at Burns.

"Look out, Thurman!" Duff shouted. The warning caused Burns to veer to the side just as the man behind the horses fired. Burns didn't appear to be hit.

Duff paused to line up a shot of his own. He wasn't a fast draw, but he was remarkably accurate in his aim. Not even

Duff could hit every mark, though. Just as he squeezed the trigger, the man pivoted, so Duff's bullet missed narrowly and struck one of the saddle horns instead, blasting it to pieces and spooking the horse on which the saddle was cinched. The animal started to caper around and pull against the hitch rail. That made the other mounts skittish, too.

The young man snapped a shot at Duff that kicked up dirt in the street a good twenty feet to Duff's right. He grabbed the reins and tried to get the horses under control as three more men came barreling out of the bank, throwing shots behind them. One of the robbers was unsteady on his feet and had blood on his shirt.

Duff dropped to a knee behind a water barrel and leveled his revolver. Confident that the men had at least attempted to rob the bank and might have committed who knew how much mayhem inside, as well as taking shots at him and Deputy Burns, Duff felt no hesitation in shooting to kill. He squeezed the trigger as one of the outlaws tried to swing up into his saddle. The gun roared and bucked in Duff's hand.

Blood and brain matter sprayed in the air as the bullet blew a fist-sized chunk out of the man's head. His momentum carried him on over the horse's back, where he spilled into an ungainly heap in the street. The horse broke away and stepped on him a few times in stampeding away with reins trailing in the dust.

Thurman Burns had taken cover in an alcove, where a doorway was located. He fired around the edge of that alcove, not hitting any of the outlaws but coming close enough to distract them. That gave Duff an opportunity to aim again. His best shot was at the man who was already wounded, but still on his feet, and spraying lead around. He was hatless and had striking white hair, although he didn't move like an old man.

Duff triggered two rounds. Both bullets pounded into the outlaw's chest and drove him toward the boardwalk. The back of his boots hit the edge of the walk. He sat down, but didn't fall over. Slowly his head slumped forward and he bent over until it looked like he was going to fall on his face, but he didn't.

"Hank!" one of the remaining two outlaws shouted. "Hank, no!"

"Come on!" the other one urged. "Let's go!"

They leaped into their saddles despite being caught in a cross fire between Duff and Burns. Desperation had given them wings. Bending low, they slashed at their horses with the reins and sent the animals charging into the middle of the street. Wild shots flew from their guns. All the bystanders on the street and the boardwalks had scurried for cover as soon as the shooting started. Duff hoped none of that flying lead found any of them.

The fleeing men were bouncing around so crazily in their saddles and the horses ran in such a jerky fashion that drawing a bead on them was next to impossible, even for Duff. He fired a few more times, then grimaced in disgust as the two outlaws galloped out of Chugwater without ever slowing down. He straightened from his position behind the water barrel and walked toward the two fallen outlaws, keeping his gun trained on them, just in case.

The man Duff had shot in the head was clearly dead. Nobody could survive having so much blood and brains leak out of his shattered skull. The other man, the white-haired hombre, hadn't moved since sitting down on the edge of the boardwalk. He had dropped his gun, which now lay between his feet.

Duff kept his gun ready while he reached out cautiously with his other hand and prodded the outlaw's shoulder. That was enough to make the man flop over backward onto the boardwalk. The glazed, unseeing look in his eyes was unmistakable as he stared up at the awning over the walk.

"Are they both dead?" Deputy Burns called from the alcove.

"Aye," Duff replied. "Dead as ever can be."

Burns emerged from cover and blew out a relieved breath.

He said, "That was some mighty good shooting, Duff, as usual."

Duff ignored the compliment and asked, "Where's Marshal Ferrell?"

"Rode down to Cheyenne on some business and left me in charge." Burns rolled his eyes. "Sure enough, that's when somebody tries to rob the bank." He paused, then said, "The bank! Has anybody checked in there yet?"

"Just about to," Duff said.

"No need," Bob Dempster said as he stepped through the open doors. He was pale and obviously shaken, but didn't seem to be hurt. "They killed one of the customers, Cloyd Nelson, and the other customer who was inside, old Mrs. Richardson, may have a broken rib from Cloyd falling on her, but the tellers and I are all right."

"Did they get away with much money?" Burns asked.

"Just what was in the tellers' drawers. A few hundred dollars, more than likely. I'll have to make an exact count, to know for sure."

"So, three men dead and an old woman hurt, all for th' sake of a few hundred dollars," Duff said.

Dempster nodded and said, "I'm afraid so. Greed has a high price."

"Aye, 'tis true." Duff looked at the white-haired outlaw with the empty stare and thought about poor Cloyd Nelson. "And all too often, 'tis the innocent who have t' pay."

Chapter 3

Nick Jessup struggled to hold back tears. He couldn't allow himself to cry. He was a grown man. He had turned twenty-two his last birthday. Besides that, he was an outlaw. A bank robber and hardened criminal. Hombres like that didn't bawl like babies.

But two of his big brothers were dead, and Nick had heard hot lead whispering past his ear. He would never forget the sight of Sherm's head flying apart like that, blood and brains spraying in the air. Nick wasn't sure, but thought some of it had splattered on him.

Even worse, Hank was dead. As far back as Nick could remember, Hank had been there, already grown, advising and protecting his younger siblings, more like an uncle or even a pa than a brother. Nick just couldn't bring himself to believe in a world that didn't have Hank in it.

It was that big fella who'd done it. The one who was such an eagle-eyed shot with a handgun. Nick suddenly wondered if that was Duff MacCallister, the man that Kent Spalding had warned the Jessup brothers about.

"They say he's Falcon MacCallister's cousin, but he's not a fast-draw artist like Falcon. Deadly accurate with a handgun or a rifle, though, and hell on wheels in a hand-to-hand fight. Gangs have ridden into Chugwater to rob the bank in the past, and they've always come out second best when they tangled with Duff MacCallister."

Kent Spalding had spoken those words in his gravelly voice as he stood next to a roaring fire at the outlaw encampment in Badwater Canyon. Long riders from all over Wyoming, Colorado, Montana, Idaho, and the Dakotas knew about Badwater Canyon and made use of it as a hideout from time to time. Located deep in the rugged Grabhorn Mountains, the place would never be found, unless a person knew the mazelike trail in, which, therefore, made it a good spot to lie low.

Many years earlier, some stubborn cattleman had tried to establish a ranch in the canyon and had even gone so far as to build a stone house. He had failed because the springs from which flowed a stream that watered the rest of the canyon produced bad water, hence the name. The cattleman had abandoned the spread, but the house still stood, although somewhat worse for wear from the elements by now.

Eventually an outlaw who had studied geology and such things before going over to the wrong side of the law had wandered in here and decided there was good water to be had if a man knew how to blast down to it. He knew, and a few sticks of dynamite later, he had a pure artesian well flowing and a good place to hide from the law. Word had spread along the owlhoot trail.

The man who'd been responsible for establishing this outlaw haven had met a bad end, shot to doll rags by deputies up in Miles City, Montana, when he'd tried to rob the bank there, but his legacy lived on in Badwater Canyon.

The Jessup brothers had drifted in there a week or so earlier and found the canyon occupied by Kent Spalding and his gang of hard cases. The rules were simple: You got along, or you were banned from the hideout. Any grudges you had against somebody else using the place had to be put aside. Anybody who broke that truce could expect trouble in a hurry, a lot of it.

As it happened, the Jessup brothers had never crossed trails with Spalding and his bunch before, but as two longtime holdup men, Hank Jessup and Kent Spalding knew each other by reputation. They had gotten along well together, but when everybody had been gathered around the campfire cooking their supper, one night previously, and Hank had mentioned they intended to hit the Chugwater bank today, Spalding hadn't hesitated to warn them about the danger that might await them there.

Now, as Nick and Logan threaded their way through a narrow passage between high cut banks, Nick sniffled and fought back tears. He said, "You reckon that fella who killed Hank and Sherm was Duff MacCallister?"

"What?" Logan was riding in front. He didn't look back over his shoulder.

"Duff MacCallister," Nick repeated. "That big son of a gun who shot Hank and Sherm. You reckon it was him?"

"What does it matter who it was?" Logan asked bitterly. "They're still just as dead. Besides, it was that blasted bank president who winged Hank first. Blind luck, just like that old bat shooting the hat off his head."

"Hank wasn't hit that bad. He would have made it if that big fella on the street hadn't shot him again."

Logan shrugged. "Maybe. We'll never know . . . will we?"

He had a little catch in his voice. Maybe he was upset, too. He ought to be. With Hank dead, Nick didn't know what they were going to do next. The oldest Jessup brother had always called the shots.

A couple of hours later, they approached the narrow entrance to Badwater Canyon. A massive boulder blocked part of it and made it even more difficult to get into the canyon. Two guards were posted at the entrance around the clock, and two riflemen had scaled the steep canyon walls on either side, climbing up to ledges where they had excellent fields of fire.

One of the guards, a Mexican in a sombrero and crossed cartridge belts, stepped out from behind the huge rock as Nick and Logan rode up. He had an old Henry rifle in his hands.

"*Hola*, amigos," he called. He was one of Spalding's men. "Are the other two *hermanos* coming along later?"

"They won't never be coming," Logan said as he reined in. Nick came to a stop alongside him.

The Mexican let out a low whistle of surprise through the gap between his front teeth.

"My condolences, amigos. The lawdogs, they were waiting for you in this Chugwater?"

"We saw one badge, but he wasn't the one who killed Hank and Sherm. That was a civilian. We don't know his name."

"But we think it was Duff MacCallister," Nick added.

Logan finally looked at him again, jerking around in the saddle to glare at him and say, "Will you shut up about Duff MacCallister? I told you, it doesn't matter who killed them, they're just as dead!"

"I'm sorry, Logan." Nick was hurt, but tried not to show it.

"Did you at least get the money from the bank?" the Mexican asked.

Logan patted a canvas money bag he had tied onto his saddle. They had stuffed all the cash from the tellers' drawers in there during those hectic few minutes in the bank. The money hadn't filled the bag. They hadn't stopped to count the take, but it was bound to be disappointing.

"That's something, anyway," the guard went on. He jerked his head to indicate that they should ride on into the canyon. Logan and Nick heeled their mounts into motion.

As they rode past the Mexican, he said, "Señor Spalding warned you about Duff MacCallister."

Nick saw Logan's shoulders twitch, but his brother didn't say anything.

The canyon twisted and turned, too, but not as much as the trail leading here. After a few minutes, Nick and Logan came in sight of the old ranch house. A low stone wall off to one side surrounded the well and formed a pond. A series of pipes supplied water to several horse troughs in pole corrals. In front of the house was a stone fire ring, where a good-sized blaze could be built. The fireplace in the house itself had collapsed at some time in the past and was useless.

Spalding's gang had extra saddle mounts, as well as pack-horses, so more than three dozen animals milled around in the corrals. Some of the men had spread their bedrolls inside the house, while others had pitched tents outside. Nick had never been in the army, but the place resembled what he imagined a military camp might look like.

Men sat around on logs, stumps, and rocks. Some swigged from whiskey bottles, others played cards. One man mended a saddle. Several others were cleaning their guns.

One walked out to meet Nick and Logan. He was tall, with a thick waist and barrel chest. A thick, gray-shot black moustache drooped over his wide mouth, under a prominent nose. The high crown of his black hat had a pronounced Montana pinch.

"What in blue blazes?" he asked in a voice like a load of rocks rasping down a sluice. "Four ride out and two come back? Your brothers get delayed?"

"Permanently," Logan said dully.

Nick again felt the hot sting of tears in his eyes and blinked them away.

Kent Spalding shook his head slowly. "I'm sorry to hear that," he said. "Ran into trouble in Chugwater, did you?"

Nick opened his mouth to say something, but Logan shot an annoyed glance his way and shut him up. But then Logan himself said, "That fella MacCallister you warned us about . . . you happen to know what he looks like?"

"Big, blond-headed fella. Shoulders a yard wide. They say he's a Scotsman, and you can sure tell it from the way he talks." Spalding cocked his head to the side. "You exchange much palaver with the gent who gunned your brothers? Because I'm guessin' that's what happened."

"That's what happened," Logan agreed. He sighed. "And the fella who did it matches MacCallister's description, all right. Didn't you say he has a ranch somewhere near Chugwater?"

"That's right. Big spread named Sky Meadow, or some such. I recollect some boys who figured on wide-looping some cows from him." Spalding shook his head again. "They didn't live to tell about it."

"Then why wasn't he out on his ranch, instead of in town where he could ruin everything for us?" Logan asked plaintively.

"Just your bad luck, I reckon." Spalding looked at Nick. "You all right, kid? You look like you're about to bust out bawling."

Nick's jaw clenched tight for a second. "You just shut up," he snapped. "I'm fine."

Spalding's eyes narrowed in anger at being talked to that way, but after a moment, he shrugged and said, "Nobody would blame you for bein' upset about your brothers getting killed. What are you gonna do now?"

"Go back to Chugwater and blow a hole through that Duff MacCallister!"

"Not hardly," Logan said. "I'd do it myself if I ever got the chance, but going after MacCallister in his own stomping grounds would be loco."

Spalding said, "I'm glad to see you got some sense, Jessup."

Logan took a deep breath. "I was thinking that maybe we'd throw in with you and your bunch . . . ?"

"You were, were you?" Spalding considered. "I'll admit, the same idea crossed my mind. I can always use a couple of extra men, as long as they're good ones and know how to do what they're told."

"My brother and I can handle whatever you throw at us," Logan said with an emphatic nod.

"We'll get a chance to find out. There'll be a train coming through in a few days on that new Cheyenne and Fort Laramie line, and I'm thinking it'll be ripe for a holdup."

"You can count on us, Mr. Spalding."

"You'd better hope so." Spalding started to turn away, but then he paused to add, "Because if you foul anything up, I'll blow holes in you myself."

Chapter 4

The Cheyenne and Fort Laramie Railroad had been completed only a few months earlier. Several trains a week used the spur line, which traveled through several smaller settlements along its route, including Chugwater.

At one point several miles out of Chugwater, the steel rails curved around a large knoll topped with trees. Boulders dotted the slope leading up to that crest.

More than a dozen men sat on horseback among the trees. A single man stood out in the open with field glasses pressed to his eyes as he gazed off into the distance. After watching for a while, he lowered the glasses and trotted back into the cover of the trees.

"I see the train comin', boss," he reported to Kent Spalding. "It'll be here in a few minutes."

"All right," Spalding said. He made a curt gesture to several of his men. "Get those rocks loose."

Four men—including Nick and Logan Jessup—dismounted and hurried down the slope to a clump of boulders. The men put their shoulders to one of the rocks and started pushing, grunting with the effort as they dug in their heels and leaned into the task.

At first, the rock didn't budge and looked as if it never would. But as the men got red in the face from exertion and heaved harder, it began to shift, first just slightly, a fraction of an inch at a time, and then it lurched forward an entire inch. Two, three more inches, and then without warning, it tipped forward and began rolling down the slope.

The boulder crashed against other rocks and dislodged them as well. It wasn't a full-fledged avalanche, there weren't enough of them for that, but within moments, several tons of stone were rolling down the side of the knoll toward the railroad tracks.

Mixed with that rumble was the clattering roar of the approaching train. It was visible with the naked eye now as clouds of smoke belched from the locomotive's diamond-shaped stack.

Some of the rocks built up enough speed that they overshot the tracks, but most of them came to rest right where Spalding figured they would—covering the steel rails and blocking them so that the train would have no choice but to stop or derail. The slide had caused a cloud of dust to billow up. The engineer had to have spotted it by now and would be leaning on the brakes.

It took some time and distance to stop a train . . .

The men who had started the rock slide had already run back to their horses and leaped into the saddle. Spalding waved his arm to signal the whole gang to charge down the hill.

Some of the outlaws whooped and hollered in sheer exuberance as their horses pounded toward the slowing train. It approached from their left, skidding along the rails on locked drivers. From several windows in the passenger cars, frightened faces peered up the slope at the horsemen, who by now were brandishing guns.

Those people on the train knew they were in for trouble.

Aboard the Cheyenne & Fort Laramie Flyer,
ten minutes earlier

"It's all so vast," the beautiful redheaded young woman said with a note of awe in her voice as she gazed out the window beside her.

"It is, indeed," Andrew MacCallister said from the seat in front of her, where he had turned halfway around to rest his arm on the back of the seat. "People nicknamed Montana, the state north of Wyoming, *Big Sky Country*, but I believe the term applies equally well to this region."

"I've seen so much already on this trip," the young woman said. "These United States are huge, especially compared to Scotland."

"At least now there are trains to connect one side of the country to the other," Rosanna MacCallister said. She sat next to the young redhead. "Imagine what it must have been like setting out to cross such immense distances in a covered wagon, the way Jamie and Kate MacCallister did."

"Your parents."

"That's right," Andrew said. He smiled. "I'm not sure I would have had the courage they did."

"Nae, I'm thinking ye would have. The two of ye are Mac-Callisters, after all, and everyone where I come from knows what a fine, valiant clan they be."

"Go on wi' ye, lassie," Andrew responded with a touch of a Scottish burr in his own voice. Born and raised in America, talking like a Scotsman didn't come naturally to him, but as an actor, he could replicate many accents and sound like a native.

"Are ye makin' sport of me, Mr. MacCallister?" the redhead asked tartly.

"Of course, he isn't," Rosanna said. "My brother is just a bit of a rascal sometimes."

"And I've told you to call me *Andrew*," he added with a smile.

There was nothing flirtatious about the comment. In his fifties, Andrew was certainly still handsome and distinguished—for his age. But he was old enough to be Fiona Gillespie's father, and he wasn't one of those actors who had an unsavory habit of pursuing young girls.

Age didn't enter into any consideration of his twin sister's looks. Rosanna MacCallister possessed a timeless beauty that, if anything, grew more compelling as the years passed. For several decades, they had been leading lights of the American theater. Indeed, they were well known on stages around the world, and there were only a few civilized countries in which they *hadn't* performed.

They had toured in Scotland on several occasions, including the one during which they first met their cousin Duff Tavish MacCallister. Duff had become a good friend, and for a while, he had even worked at the theater in New York where Andrew and Rosanna were performing. Since he'd moved west and established his ranch in Wyoming, they had kept in touch with him through letters and also heard about him from their younger brother Falcon, who had also befriended Duff.

When Duff had written to them months earlier and asked them to spend Christmas at Sky Meadow, they hadn't hesitated to accept, providing they could work out their schedule to make it possible. As things had developed, the last leg of their current tour had finished in Scotland a couple of weeks earlier, leaving them free to take Duff up on his invitation.

But those last performances in Glasgow had held an unexpected development in the person of the beautiful young woman who was now their traveling companion.

Glasgow

Probably as a result of the American frontier legacy in their blood, Andrew and Rosanna had never been stuck-up and standoffish like some actors, who didn't like to mingle with the very people who made their careers possible. They didn't mind when someone came backstage to meet them after a performance. In fact, Andrew often left the door of his dressing room partially open as if to invite visitors.

So he wasn't surprised when someone knocked hesitantly while he was sitting at his dressing table, removing the makeup from his face.

He was just finishing up, so he wiped away the last of the cream and turned on his chair to call, "Come in."

The door swung open farther to reveal a young woman standing there. Andrew was accustomed to women wanting to meet him. Many of them were drawn to actors. Usually, he could spot them right away, because they had a certain worldly air about them and the bold look in their eyes made it clear what they wanted.

This young woman reminded him of a frightened deer about to bolt.

With her fresh, wholesome attractiveness and dewy-eyed innocence, she would have been an irresistibly tempting target for seduction for some men. Andrew just smiled and said gently, "Yes? What can I do for you?"

With a visible effort, she summoned up her courage and asked, "Are ye Mr. Andrew MacCallister?"

Still smiling, he said, "That's right."

She blew out an exasperated breath and shook her head. "Och, what a foolish question. Of course, you're Mr. MacCallister. Did I not just watch ye trod the boards for the past hour and a half?"

"I don't know," Andrew said. "Did you?"

"Oh, I did. And what a wonderful play it was. You and your sister were magnificent."

"Thank you," Andrew said solemnly. He smiled and went on, "Messrs. Gilbert and Sullivan deserve some of the credit, but I'd be happy to sign your playbill if you'd like, and I'm sure Rosanna would, too."

The young woman took a tentative step into the dressing room and said, "Actually, what I'd like to know if you're related to a lad named Duff MacCallister."

"Duff?" Andrew answered in surprise. "As a matter of fact, he's our cousin." He put things together in his head. "Do you know Duff? Or are you, perhaps, another of our Scottish cousins?"

The girl lightly touched her bosom. "Me? A MacCallister? Nae, I'm no relation, sir. Me name is Gillespie. Fiona Gillespie."

"I'm pleased to meet you, Miss Gillespie."

"But I am acquainted wi' Duff MacCallister. You see, 'tis the same village where we both grew up."

"Dunoon, in Argyllshire," Andrew said.

"Aye. Duff and me, 'tis old friends we be."

Andrew cocked an eyebrow. He had heard Duff speak at length of Skye McGregor, the young woman he'd been in love with and planned to marry, whose murder had caused him to become a fugitive for a while and eventually led to him going to America. The old hatreds had followed Duff even there and resulted in a violent showdown with his enemies.

Andrew had heard that story, but he didn't recall Duff ever mentioning anyone named Fiona Gillespie. To be fair, he didn't know all the details of Duff's life. For all Andrew knew, Duff and Fiona might have been childhood playmates.

Or there might have been other girls in Duff's life before Skye . . .

Those thoughts flashed through Andrew's mind in a matter of mere heartbeats, but before he could respond to Fiona's claim, a new voice said, "Excuse me. Am I interrupting anything?"

Fiona was inside the dressing room now, but blocking the doorway. She stepped aside hurriedly, turning as she did so. She said, "Miss MacCallister! 'Tis sorry I am for intruding—"

"Not at all, my dear," Rosanna said, just a touch coolly. She had removed her makeup and wardrobe for the play and now had a silk dressing gown wrapped and belted around her. She

looked at Andrew and went on, "If you'd prefer that I come back later . . ."

"Of course not," he said without hesitation, not wanting her to get the wrong idea. "Miss Gillespie just came in to say hello and tell me that she's an old friend of Duff's."

"Really?" Rosanna's attitude warmed up immediately. She extended a hand to Fiona. "In that case, any friend of Duff's is a friend of ours. Isn't that right, Andrew?"

"It is, indeed."

Fiona shook Rosanna's hand and said, " 'Tis honored I am to make the acquaintance of both of ye, ma'am."

"The pleasure is ours," Rosanna assured her. "When we see Duff again, would you like for us to tell him that we met you? Perhaps say hello to him for you?"

"Actually . . ." Fiona looked uncomfortable again. " 'Twas a bit more that I was hoping for, ma'am. I read in the newspaper that ye'll be returning to America after this tour is over. I'm planning to journey to the States meself, and I was hoping that . . . perhaps . . . the two of ye could see your way clear to letting me accompany you . . . ?"

Andrew frowned. "No offense, Miss Gillespie, but we just met you. We don't even know you."

"The idea strikes me as a bit unseemly," Rosanna added with that hint of coolness back in her voice.

"Oh, no, ma'am!" Fiona's fair-skinned face turned a bright red. "I assure ye, I meant nothing improper. I dinna explain the way I should have. I hope to work for ye . . . both of ye . . . as a . . . a maid and assistant and whatever else might need doing. And 'tis not charity for which I be asking, either. I've saved up enough to pay me own way to America. What I really need from you . . ." She took a deep breath and burst out, "I want to see Duff again!"

That impassioned plea struck a chord in both Andrew and Rosanna. They made no promises to Fiona that night, but over *the next few days, they spent time with her and got to know her better. After they had had dinner with Fiona twice, Rosanna later told Andrew, "That poor girl is in love with Duff, you know."*

"Then why did Duff never mention her? The only girl I remember him talking about was Skye McGregor."

"Well," Rosanna said, "just because she was in love with him doesn't mean that he returned the feeling. Duff may have courted her for a while and then decided that she wasn't the one for him. Or maybe that's when he met Skye and realized that she was."

"The one for him," Andrew said.

"Exactly."

"So what do we do?" he asked. "Do we help her reunite with Duff? He might not appreciate that, considering his apparently quite satisfactory relationship with Miss Parker. His letters make it sound like eventually they'll be getting married."

Rosanna pondered that for a long moment, then said, "The problem is that Fiona claims to have enough money for a trip to America. Even if we decide not to help her, I don't see any way we can stop her."

"Do you think she already knows where to find Duff?"

"He hasn't exactly hidden his light under a bushel since he's been in Wyoming," Rosanna said dryly. "During our travels, we've seen numerous sensational newspaper articles about his exploits, and it's entirely possible some of those stories made it as far as Scotland. Besides, she's from Duff's town. I'd venture a guess that some of his old friends keep up with him, like Ian McGregor, Skye's father."

"So it's entirely possible that even if we refuse her request, she'll turn up in Chugwater, anyway."

"That's how it seems to me."

Andrew looked dubious and said, "Would anyone go to that much trouble just to see an old flame?"

"'Was this the face that launch'd a thousand ships, and burnt the topless towers of Ilium?'" Rosanna quoted. "'Sweet Helen, make me immortal with a kiss.'"

"Fiona's a beautiful young woman, but she's not Helen of Troy."

"But Christopher Marlowe was right, sometimes people will do anything for love," Rosanna said. "When I listen to Fiona talk about Duff, I get the sense that she'd go to the ends of the earth to see him again."

Andrew sighed and nodded. "I've learned to trust your judgment about such things, my dear. If you believe that Fiona will pursue a reunion with Duff, anyway, perhaps the best thing we can do is stay close so we can keep an eye on her."

"I agree. It's settled, then. I'll tell her." Rosanna smiled. "She's pleasant company, and quite helpful. Having her come along with us won't be so bad."

"I certainly hope you're right," Andrew told his sister.

So far, that had proven to be the case. Fiona had accompanied them on the ocean crossing as they returned to America, and since Andrew and Rosanna had no financial worries, they had paid for her passage, as well as hotel accommodations during their brief stay in New York and the train tickets for the rest of the journey to Wyoming Territory. They had offered to pay Fiona wages for the assistance she rendered them, but she refused, insisting that they were doing enough for her already.

They were on a first-name basis with her. Fiona returned that with Rosanna, but she insisted on calling Andrew *Mr. MacCallister*. She seemed very concerned with everything being proper and aboveboard, which, of course, was a good thing.

Now, after he had told her again to call him by his given name, she said, "I wouldna feel comfortable doing that, sir. 'Twould seem disrespectful."

"Perhaps," Andrew said, "but we're in the American West

now, and I believe you'll find that things are more informal out here—"

The train suddenly lurched violently enough to throw all three of them forward in their seats. Rosanna cried out in pain as she used her arms to keep her from crashing into the back of the seat where Andrew was. Fiona exclaimed in surprise, too. Andrew said, "What the devil!"

The train was still moving, but they could feel it slowing down. Shudders ran through the cars. The engineer was doing his best to bring the train to a halt as quickly as he could.

Movement glimpsed through a window on the other side of the car caught Andrew's eye. His hand closed tightly on the back of the seat as he watched a number of men on horseback galloping down the side of a wooded knoll. He spotted several little white puffs of smoke and knew the men were shooting at the train.

"Brace yourselves, ladies," he told his sister and Fiona. "I believe we're about to experience something else that's common in the American West. *A train robbery!*"

Chapter 5

Andrew stood up and started to move across the aisle toward the window, where he had spotted the attacking outlaws. Rosanna caught hold of his sleeve and said, "What do you think you're doing?"

With his other hand, Andrew pulled back the lapel of his coat to reveal the butt of a small-caliber pistol in a shoulder holster.

"I'm sure some of the passengers are going to put up a fight," he said. "I thought I'd join them."

"And get yourself shot and perhaps killed? Besides, I doubt if that pistol has the range or the power to come anywhere near those men."

"I'm a MacCallister," Andrew said. "Are you asking me to stand by and just do nothing while those men rob us? There's no telling what sort of vile depredations they may carry out!"

Fiona paled, making the widely scattered, light-brown freckles on her face stand out more than usual.

"All I'm saying is don't waste your bullets," Rosanna said as she let go of Andrew's arm. "Save them in case you really need them."

Andrew grinned. "That's more like a real MacCallister talking."

The train had been shuddering and slowing since that first lurch, and now it came to a complete stop so abruptly that Andrew was thrown off-balance for a second. He braced himself on a seat back and told Rosanna and Fiona, "The two of you sit down. I'm not going to let anything happen to you."

"Be careful," Rosanna said. "Perhaps they'll just loot the safe in the express car and leave the passengers alone."

"That doesn't seem very likely, but we can hope, I suppose."

Nervously, Rosanna and Fiona settled back into their seats. Andrew stood in the aisle beside them. He started to draw the pistol, but then thought better of it. If one of the outlaws came in here, waving a gun around, and spotted a passenger who was also armed, the man might open fire instinctively. Andrew decided it was smarter not to draw his gun unless he had no other choice.

He couldn't see the gang of train robbers anymore. Shots sounded from somewhere else along the train. One of the female passengers in this car put her gloved hands over her face and began sobbing and wailing in fear.

"Be quiet, Miriam," a man who was probably her husband told her. "That's not going to do any good."

Neither did his admonishment. The woman kept crying.

A man who looked like a cowboy got to his feet and said, "Dang it, we can't let those varmints come in here and clean us out." He put his hand on his holstered gun. "There are enough men in here to make 'em pay in blood for tryin' it."

From the front of the car, a harsh voice said, "If anybody's gonna pay in blood, it'll be you, big mouth."

The man who had just stepped in from the platform appeared to be young, too. It was hard to be sure because he had a bandanna tied across the lower half of his face. He wore a long gray duster and a black hat and had a gun in his hand.

The cowboy who'd been urging the other passengers to fight jerked around and clawed at the revolver on his hip. The outlaw at the front of the car fired. The explosion was thunderously loud in the close confines of the railroad car.

The bullet slammed into the cowboy's chest and knocked him back and to the side. He fell into the lap of a female passenger who screamed in horror. The dying cowboy gasped a couple of times and then rolled off to land facedown in the aisle.

The killer charged a few more steps into the car and waved his gun around.

"Nobody move! Gents, hoist your hands, and they better be empty!"

Andrew made a slight move toward the pistol under his coat. Rosanna caught his eye. He could tell she was silently pleading with him not to draw and start a shoot-out with the robber. Andrew sighed and raised his hands as the man had ordered. He was not his brother Falcon or his cousin Duff. More than likely, trading shots with the outlaw would just get him killed. More important, with so many innocent people in the car, someone else might get hurt if lead started flying around.

Another masked desperado crowded into the car behind the gunman. This one carried a canvas bag. The killer, his voice slightly muffled by the bandanna, said, "Gents, we want your wallets and watches and rings. Ladies, all your jewelry and any other valuables go in the bag, too. Do as you're told, and nobody else gets hurt."

He kept his gun leveled and used his other hand to wave his companion forward. They began working their way along the aisle. The passengers cooperated, dumping their valuables into the canvas bag the second outlaw held open.

As they neared the spot where Andrew still stood beside Rosanna and Fiona, the outlaw gestured with his gun barrel and said, "Sit down, mister. You're making me nervous."

"Take it easy," Andrew said.

"You're not the one giving the orders. Now sit."

Andrew lowered himself onto the seat in front of Rosanna. The man with the bag held it out wordlessly. With his teeth grinding together in frustration, Andrew took out his wallet and dropped it into the bag.

"Your watch and ring, too," the gunman ordered.

With the revolver's muzzle practically in his face, Andrew had no choice but to comply. He was so furious he wished now that he had tried to fight back.

The man with the bag got a wallet from the passenger across the aisle, then turned to Rosanna and Fiona and said, "All right, ladies, let's have what you got."

He snickered, and it was easy to imagine that under the bandanna he was leering.

Coldly, Rosanna said, "You should be ashamed of yourself," as she dropped a ring and a bracelet in the bag.

"Is that it?"

"Would you care to search me?"

"Now that you mention it, I'd like that, lady, but I don't reckon we got the time." The man thrust the bag toward Fiona. "Now you, girl."

"I . . . I don't have anything," she said.

"You got a ring on your finger. I can see it."

Fiona closed her other hand around the one with the ring, as if to hide it.

"Please," she said. " 'Twas me dear old granny's—"

"I don't care who it belonged to, it's ours now. Hand it over."

Tears still shone in Fiona's eyes, but her face darkened with anger as she tugged the ring from her finger and all but threw it into the bag, where it clinked against other jewelry.

" 'Tis a terrible, terrible man ye be. I hope you're proud o' yourself."

The outlaw ignored that and moved on, to continue looting valuables from the passengers.

With narrowed eyes, Andrew watched the gunman. He hung back some from his companion and pivoted constantly from side to side so he could keep an eye on all the passengers. The gun in his hand swung back and forth as well. He worked his way along the aisle slowly, and eventually he stepped past the seat where Andrew sat tensely.

The wheels of Andrew's brain had been turning rapidly. He knew he couldn't try to draw the pistol from under his coat. He wasn't fast enough for a move like that. However, he was well-built and fairly strong for a man of his age. Trodding the boards for all those performances kept a man in reasonably good shape. He thought that if he jumped the gunman quickly enough, he might take the man by surprise and wrestle the weapon away from him.

It was the only chance he had to stop this outrage, so without agonizing over the decision any longer, he acted.

The outlaw had turned to look in another direction, and the gun in his hand had swung away from Andrew for a second. Andrew surged up out of his seat. He clubbed his hands together and smashed them against the right side of the outlaw's neck where it joined the shoulder. The heavy, unexpected blow drove the man a step ahead and dropped him to one knee.

Andrew tried to jump on his back and force him all the way to the floor, but the man reacted quickly despite being startled. He jerked his right elbow back just as Andrew leaped. The point of the elbow sank into Andrew's midsection and forced the air out of his lungs. The impact against his belly was enough to make Andrew sick.

He doubled over and stumbled back as he gasped for breath and tried to fight down the nausea. The outlaw sprang up and swung the gun in his hand. For a second, Andrew thought the man was going to shoot him, but then the barrel crashed against the side of his head. The gunsight opened up a long scratch. The blow made stars explode behind Andrew's eyes. He slumped,

serting himself. He had always been the little brother, eager to go along with whatever his older brothers wanted.

Now he had a tone of command in his voice, as if killing that cowboy had turned a key inside him. Nick heard it himself, and while it surprised and maybe even scared him a little, he liked it.

He liked it even more when Logan jumped to do what he was told.

The girl moaned. Nick tightened his hold on her. She lifted her head, said "What . . . ," and started to writhe in his grasp.

Nick dug the gun barrel into her side and told her, "Stop it. I don't want to hurt you."

"Let go of me." Her voice was a low, furious rasp.

"Not until we're finished here."

And maybe not even then, Nick thought. It was a wild idea, but it appealed to him. So did the feel of the girl's lithe body molded against him.

Logan had pouched his iron and gone back to collecting valuables. When he reached the back end of the car, he nodded and called, "That's it."

Nick backed toward the front of the car, taking the redhead with him. He told Logan, "Go out the other way."

Logan hesitated. "What are you doing?"

"Never you mind about that. We need to get out of here."

"But you—" Logan stopped short and looked worried, even with the mask over the bottom half of his face. But he didn't waste any more time arguing and ducked through the vestibule at the front of the car.

"Let me go," the girl said. This time, she sounded genuinely frightened.

"I don't think so," Nick said. He pulled her around the sprawled body of the man he'd knocked out a few minutes earlier. The gent was starting to stir a little.

The older woman who'd been sitting with the girl said, "Please don't do this. You can't."

"I can do whatever I want, lady," Nick told her with a sneer. "I'm the one with the gun."

He dug the barrel harder into the girl's side. She gasped, but she stopped struggling. He manhandled her through the front vestibule, onto the platform, and down the steps. When he jumped to the ground and took her with him, his grip slipped a little and she tried to break away. He grabbed her tighter and jerked her against him again.

Logan had gotten their horses from the men who'd been holding the mounts during the holdup. All along the train, outlaws were emerging from the cars with bags of loot. Up at the express car, Spalding himself jumped to the ground with the big canvas pouch that had been locked in the safe.

"Give me a hand with her," Nick said to Logan.

"This is a bad idea, Nick."

Saying his name like that was foolish, Nick thought, then realized that it didn't really matter. The girl was bound to hear their names, anyway, if he kept her with them for very long.

Despite his objection, Logan reached down from the saddle, grasped the girl's arm, and hung on to her while Nick quickly swung up on his horse. Then both of them held her and lifted her into place in front of Nick. She didn't try to fight. Nick felt her trembling. From fear or from anger? he wondered.

That didn't matter, either.

Spalding rode up and reined in beside them. Curses spilled from the boss outlaw's mouth for a moment.

"Nobody said anything about taking prisoners," he told Nick.

"A hostage, boss, just in case anybody comes after us."

Spalding glared at him. "When the time comes, she's your responsibility."

Nick didn't want to think about that. Not now. He shrugged his acceptance of what Spalding said.

Spalding muttered another curse, then swung his mount

around and waved his arm at the other men. They jabbed their heels into their horses' flanks. In a ragged line, the outlaws galloped away from the train, taking the loot and a redheaded captive with them.

This first job as a member of the Spalding gang hadn't gone exactly the way Nick had expected.

But as he held the girl's supple form in front of him on the horse, he sure as blazes couldn't complain.

Chapter 6

Andrew felt strong but gentle hands on his shoulders, lifting him and helping him rest his head on something soft. He pried his eyes open, looked up into his sister's face, and realized his head was lying in Rosanna's lap.

When he started to push himself up, she put a hand on his shoulder again and pressed down.

"Just lie there and rest," she told him. "You were knocked unconscious. We don't know yet how bad you're hurt. You could be seriously injured."

Andrew started to insist that he was fine, but before the words could emerge fully from his mouth, his head began spinning crazily. He let himself slump back and allowed Rosanna to comfort him.

After a moment, he asked, "Are we still on the train?"

"That's right. It won't be going anywhere for a while. I believe members of the crew and some of the passengers are out now, trying to clear the tracks so we can go on to Chugwater."

"Wait'll Duff finds out about those robbers," Andrew muttered. "Did they kill anyone?"

"I don't know." Rosanna paused. "But there's bad news, Andrew. They took Fiona with them."

His eyes widened. Again he tried to push himself up. This time, he made it to a sitting position. Carefully, since his head still didn't feel very stable, he turned to look at Rosanna.

"You mean they kidnapped her?"

"That's right. The man who hit you with his gun did it. After he struck you, Fiona tried to fight him, and he hit her, too, but with his fist. That stunned her enough to knock the fight out of her. While he was hanging on to her . . ." Rosanna shrugged. Her face and voice were bleak as she went on. "I suppose he decided that he wanted to take her with them. They all galloped off a few minutes ago."

Andrew sighed and tried not to let anger and despair overwhelm him. He forced his brain to work.

"Once the track is cleared, it shouldn't take us long to reach Chugwater. That means the bandits won't have a huge lead on any posse that goes after them. Duff should be able to trail them, and I'll bet that friend of his, Elmer Gleason, is a good tracker, too. We'll find them and rescue Fiona."

Rosanna raised finely arched eyebrows. "*We?*"

"I'm going with Duff and any other members of the posse, of course."

"Andrew, you're injured. There's a long, bloody welt on your head. You may have a concussion or even worse."

"Nonsense. I'm sure that by the time we get to Chugwater, I'll be fine."

"But—"

"It was my job to protect you ladies," Andrew interrupted her. "I failed that in every respect. Not only did those men steal from us, they carried off an innocent young woman as well. They can't be allowed to get away with that."

"And I'll wager they won't," Rosanna said, then added bluntly, "But you're not Duff or Falcon, Andrew."

"I'm still a MacCallister."

She regarded him for a few seconds, then nodded slowly.

"You are, at that," she admitted. "But right now, you're an injured MacCallister. Why don't you lie back down and rest until we reach Chugwater, and then we'll see what needs to be done."

Andrew knew what needed to be done. Those owlhoots needed some justice delivered to them, in the form of hot lead. But he had missed his opportunity for that—and to be honest, at the moment, he felt about as weak as a kitten. He didn't have the energy to argue with Rosanna, so he laid his head back in her lap instead.

Then he lifted it and said, "I'll get blood on your dress."

"Don't worry about it." She smiled. "You already have. But I don't care, as long as you're all right." She laid gloved fingers lightly against his cheek. "You may not have defeated that outlaw, Andrew, but you're still the most valiant man I know."

"You're a wonderful actress," he murmured. "I almost believed you."

Then he closed his eyes and drifted off into oblivion again.

Chugwater

Duff was in town again today because he knew a train was due and it was getting to be time for his cousins to arrive. Christmas was only a couple of weeks away.

Besides, Duff wasn't going to pass up an opportunity to see Meagan. That would be easier if she lived at the ranch, as she would if, say, they were married.

But she had her dress shop here in town, with her living quarters handy right above it. Asking her to marry him and move to Sky Meadow was the same as asking her to give that up, unless *she* made the ride into town every day. Duff knew how much the shop meant to her. This whole line of thinking was one reason he'd been hesitant to make any big changes.

He put the matter aside for the moment. He was a thinking man, not a brooding one.

He sat in Fiddler's Green with Elmer and nursed a beer. Wang Chow, the young Chinese man who served as cook at Sky Meadow, was with them today. Wang, who had trained as a priest at a Shaolin temple in China, had turned his back on the peaceful tenets of that religion in order to avenge his murdered family.

This led to him becoming a fugitive, so he had traveled to America and found a new home, thanks to a fortunate encounter with Duff. The meeting had been lucky for both of them, since Wang, a deadly hand-to-hand fighter, had saved Duff's life more than once. He was more friend than employee, although Duff paid him generously.

A few times, men drinking in Fiddler's Green had objected to having a "Chinaman" invade their sanctum. Some bruises, sore heads, and the occasional broken limb later, nobody other than strangers to the area ever took exception to Wang coming into the saloon with Duff and Elmer.

Biff Johnson, the owner and a veteran of the Seventh Cavalry, who had named the place after an old cavalry legend, carried fresh mugs of beer from the bar and set them in front of Duff and Elmer. Biff employed attractive young women to work as hostesses and serving girls, but he was an unpretentious man who didn't mind delivering drinks himself, especially to his friends.

In fact, he skillfully carried a third mug for himself and pulled out an empty chair so he could sit down with the three men.

"To your health, gentlemen," he said as he lifted his beer, "and best wishes for the season."

"I'll drink to that," Elmer said, and proceeded to do so.

"Ye'll drink to a great many things, I'm for thinkin'," Duff commented with a smile.

"Well, a fella always likes to be sociable." Elmer looked at

Wang. "I got to wonderin' . . . do Chinese folks celebrate Christmas? I was never there around that time of year."

Wang shook his head. "Very few people in my homeland share that faith. Most have never even heard of Christmas. I find it a very interesting tradition, however. Inspiring, in fact."

"Well, if'n they was to celebrate it, I reckon they'd shoot off a bunch of fireworks to do it."

Wang smiled and said, "It is most interesting, is it not, that my people invented gunpowder for festivities rather than killing?"

"And 'tis too bad that more people don't use it that way," Duff put in. "Sometimes, though, burnin' powder is the only choice a fella has."

The men sipped their drinks—with the exception of Wang, who never imbibed—and chatted amiably, until Duff dug his watch out of his pocket and flipped it open.

"The train should be comin' in soon," he said. "I'll be strollin' down to th' station. You boys can stay here if ye like. If Andrew and Rosanna arrive, I plan to bring them here to meet Biff."

"And I look forward to meeting them," Biff said. "Having a couple of famous thespians in Fiddler's Green will be a mark of distinction for the place."

"They may be famous," Elmer said, "but accordin' to Duff, they ain't uppity and all full o' themselves."

Duff chuckled and said, "Aye, 'tis the salt o' the earth, my cousins are. Like all the MacCallisters."

He drank the last of his beer, snapped his watch shut, and stood up. Elmer and Wang got to their feet, too.

"We'll amble on down there with you," Elmer said.

The depot building was a sturdy brick structure on the edge of town and fairly new, like the railroad itself. The platform next to the tracks was made of brick as well, instead of being floored with the usual thick, heavy planks. Duff, Elmer, and

Wang climbed the steps at the end of the platform and looked along the tracks to the east. The train was nowhere in sight.

"What time's it supposed to get here?" Elmer asked.

Duff nodded toward a blackboard mounted on the wall. "Two twenty-five, accordin' to the schedule. And 'tis only two-fifteen. We're a wee bit early."

"You are eager to see your relatives again," Wang said. "That is understandable."

Elmer said, "You must miss all your kinfolks back in China."

"Our separation is regrettable"—Wang shrugged philosophically—"but that is how things must be. One may rage against fate, but it is like raging against a mountain. There it stands, immovable despite any complaints."

"I dinna ken if I agree wi' that," Duff said. "Sometimes a man has to battle fate, whether he stands any chance o' winnin' or not. 'Tis a noble thing 'to take arms against a sea o' troubles.'"

"You're quotin' that Shakespeare fella, ain't you?" Elmer asked.

"Only in a glancing fashion."

Duff took out his watch, checked the time again, then strolled over to the ticket window, where an agent for the C&FL waited on the other side, sitting on a stool.

"What can I do for you, Mr. MacCallister?" the man asked.

"The two twenty-five, 'tis on time?"

"As far as I know. It should be pulling in soon."

"Ye've had no word of any delays?"

"No, not at all." The ticket agent frowned. "Why? Is there a problem?"

"Nae, not that I'm aware of." Duff didn't explain that he had started to get a funny feeling while he was in Fiddler's Green, an instinctive prickling on the back of his neck that seemed to be telling him not all was right with the world. He couldn't explain it himself, so he knew it wouldn't make sense to anyone else.

The ticket agent said, "The engineer on this run is Eugene Clancy, and the conductor is Lawrence Keating. They're good men, and they believe in keeping to the schedule. I'm sure the train will be coming in sight at any minute."

Duff nodded and rejoined Elmer and Wang at the edge of the platform. His keen-eyed gaze followed the tracks eastward, until they seemed to dwindle down into a single line and then disappeared.

Nothing. The minutes ticked past, and the next time Duff looked at his watch, the hands told him it was two-thirty.

Elmer must have sensed his friend's unease. "Train should'a been here by now, huh? Lotsa things can happen to delay a train. Doesn't have to be anything bad."

"Oh, I ken that," Duff said. "We'll wait a bit longer." His eyes narrowed. "But if too much time goes by, I'll be for mountin' up and ridin' along the tracks to have a look."

"And Wang an' me will be right with you if you do," Elmer said.

Duff waited a half hour, knowing that all sorts of mechanical problems could plague a train and slow it down. He checked with the ticket agent, who checked with the telegrapher and reported that they'd had no news from stations down the line about any delays.

When it was straight up three o'clock, Duff knew that was long enough. He said, "I'll be takin' a look along the tracks," and started to stride off the platform.

"Wait," Wang said. Duff turned and saw his Chinese friend pointing along the tracks to the east.

"Wait for what?" Elmer asked. "What're you pointin' at, anyway? I don't see a blasted thing except steel rails, telegraph poles, and wires."

Duff peered along the tracks, too, and after a moment, he smiled.

" 'Tis an eye like the proverbial eagle ye have, Wang," he said. "But you're right. Tha' be the train comin'."

"I think you're both seein' things," Elmer groused, but no sooner were the words out of his mouth than the faint sound of a train's whistle drifted to their ears. Elmer muttered, "Yeah, yeah, I reckon you were right, Wang."

The train was moving at a fast clip. It grew larger in the distance. The men waiting on the platform saw smoke curling thickly from the stack of the big Baldwin locomotive. The shrill wail of the whistle sounded again. Duff heard the low, almost-inaudible hum of the rails vibrating.

People who had tickets or who were there to meet someone came from the station lobby and congregated on the platform. The train seemed to grow larger as it approached. The massive engine, billowing smoke, was an impressive sight.

Brakes squealed, and the train slowly rolled and shuddered to a halt with the engine beyond the station, lined up with the elevated water tank, and the passenger cars next to the depot platform. A blue-uniformed conductor swung down from one of them and started across the platform, looking agitated about something.

Duff remembered what the ticket agent had told him and moved to intercept the conductor, lifting a hand to stop him as he did so.

"Mr. Keating," Duff said, "is there bein' a problem? Why was the train late?"

"A *problem*?" the conductor snapped impatiently. "I'd say that being held up by outlaws is a *problem*! Now get out of my way, sir. I have to notify headquarters of what's happened."

Duff's strong grip on the man's arm stopped him. "Was anyone hurt?"

"A passenger were killed. Now step aside and let me do my job, please."

Duff let go of the conductor and took a step back. His heart slugged heavily in his chest. One passenger dead . . . He had no reason to think one of those unfortunate souls was Andrew or Rosanna. He didn't even know for certain that they were on this train. But he would go through every car if he had to, in order to be sure.

As he turned toward the train, though, he heard a familiar female voice call his name.

"Duff! Over here!"

There they were, both of them, coming along the platform toward him. Relief flooded through Duff, to be replaced an instant later by a new feeling of concern, because Andrew was leaning on Rosanna as if unsteady on his feet, and he was hatless, with a makeshift bandage bound around his head.

Duff hurried toward his cousins. Elmer and Wang followed closely behind him. "Andrew, you're hurt," Duff said as he came up to them.

Andrew gestured vaguely toward his head. "It's nothing," he said. With a thin smile, he added, "This old noggin of mine is too hard for a mere gun barrel to do much damage."

"Ye were hit with a pistol? Those scoundrels! We'll take ye to Dr. Urban's office. He's a fine medico."

"I can see to that, if you'll tell me where it is," Rosanna said.

Duff put a hand on her shoulder. "You're not hurt?"

"Not a bit," she assured him. "Andrew's the one who needs medical attention. But *you* need to talk to the local law, Duff, and raise a posse to get after those outlaws. They took a young woman who was traveling with us and carried her off as a prisoner. You have to find them and help her." Rosanna paused and then added, "Her name is Fiona Gillespie."

The name didn't mean a thing to Duff, but the fact that a young woman was helpless in the hands of desperadoes was more than enough to rouse his ire. He said, "Where did this happen?"

"About five miles east of here, I'd estimate," Andrew said. "Near a large, wooded knoll. The outlaws rolled some boulders down from it to block the tracks and force the train to stop."

"Sounds like Buster's Hump," Elmer said. "We can find the place without any trouble." He added, "I'm Elmer Gleason, if you don't recollect."

"Aye, my good friend Elmer, an' this is Wang Chow," Duff said. "But there'll be time for everyone t' get t' know each other later. I'll raise that posse, as ye said, and get after those thievin' wolves." He gripped the shoulders of both Andrew and Rosanna this time and added, "We'll bring your friend back safely, never ye doubt that."

He hurried away, with Elmer and Wang following him. None of them noticed the puzzled frowns that Andrew and Rosanna directed after them and then turned toward each other.

Chapter 7

Utah

The sudden rattle and crack of gunfire in the distance made Falcon MacCallister sit up straighter in the saddle. He reined his horse to a stop and leaned forward, listening intently. His ruggedly handsome face was reminiscent of a bird of prey, as befitted his name.

Then he forced himself to relax, shook his head, and said, "Nope. No, sir, not any of my business, whatever it is. I'm just riding through these parts."

No one was there to hear him except his horse. This was an area of semiarid valleys between mountain ranges that thrust up abruptly from the hard-packed ground. He'd passed through a Mormon settlement a day's ride back and knew other communities like that were scattered around, but overall this country was mighty sparsely settled.

Falcon was on his way to Wyoming to spend Christmas with his cousin Duff on Duff's ranch. Falcon had been there for the founding of Sky Meadow and had seen Duff on occasion since then, but it had been a while. When Duff's letter had caught up to him, Falcon found the idea of spending the holidays with family appealing. He was getting older, upward of forty now, and for a man in his profession, this meant he had already pushed the odds past the break-even point and was living on borrowed time—more than likely.

Youngest son of the legendary mountain man Jamie Ian MacCallister, Falcon had inherited his father's skill with a gun and fighting ability. Actually, he had probably surpassed Jamie when it came to speed and accuracy with a gun. That ability, along with a thirst for adventure, had sent him into a lot of dangerous places and situations over the years. He had scouted for the army, worked as a lawman, been a stagecoach guard and a troubleshooter for the railroads. He would lend a hand to just about anybody, if it promised excitement and was the right thing to do.

Because of that, there were bad hombres roaming around who would like nothing better than to get him in their gunsights. Falcon had gotten in the habit of riding wary.

He never had to go looking for trouble. It usually found him, anyway.

So as he heeled his horse into motion again, he told himself sternly to just ride around whatever that ruckus was. A long line of red sandstone bluffs rose about half a mile to his left. The shots seemed to be coming from a canyon cut back into those bluffs.

"Not my business," Falcon said again as he drew even with the canyon mouth. He rode on for about ten yards, feeling proud of himself for his resolve.

Then he hauled back on the reins, grimaced, and muttered a curse. He pulled the horse around, bumped his heels against the animal's flanks, and sent it charging toward the canyon.

Sometimes it just didn't make any sense for a man to fight against his destiny.

He weaved through some big slabs of rock that had split off from the canyon walls in ages past and slammed to the ground. About a hundred yards in, the canyon curved sharply to the left. The shots were louder back here and the sound bounced off the canyon walls, setting up echoes that were almost as deafening. Falcon slowed his horse as he neared the bend, not wanting to charge headlong into trouble without knowing what it was about.

As he rounded that curve, he immediately spotted two covered wagons. He doubted if this canyon led anywhere, and he sure hadn't seen any signs of a trail running through it. The pilgrims who belonged to those wagons must have driven in here for some other reason. It was pretty obvious what that reason was.

At least a dozen Indians were riding in a big circle around the wagons, uttering shrill war whoops and firing rifles and arrows toward the vehicles.

Falcon reined in sharply and pulled his horse over into some rocks along the base of the canyon wall. With their attention focused on the wagons, none of the Indians seemed to have noticed his arrival. He hauled his Winchester out of its saddle sheath and dropped to the ground.

He knelt behind a rock and studied the scene in front of him. His mouth tightened into a grim line as he counted four bodies sprawled motionless near the wagons. A couple of them had so many arrows stuck in them that they looked like pincushions. All the mules hitched to the wagons were down, also skewered by arrows.

Powder smoke spurted from the wagons as the defenders who were left tried to put up a fight. As Falcon watched, one youngster climbed out of a wagon bed and over the driver's seat to try to get a better shot at the Indians. He brought an old single-shot rifle to his shoulder, but before he could draw a bead and pull the trigger, an arrow struck him in the throat. The boy lurched up, dropped the rifle, and pawed at the shaft for a second before pitching to the ground. He landed in a limp heap.

It was hard to tell at this distance, but Falcon didn't figure the boy had been more than twelve years old.

He would never get any older.

Biting back another curse, Falcon nestled his cheek against the smooth wood of the Winchester's stock and aimed. He squeezed the trigger. The Indians might not have noticed the rifle's sharp crack amidst their own whooping and howling and the gun thunder that already filled the canyon.

One of them sure knew something had happened. He jerked, arched his back, and toppled off his pony, drilled perfectly through the heart. Falcon worked the Winchester's lever, shifted his aim, and fired again, scarcely in more time than it would take a man to draw a breath. Another Indian yelled, threw his hands in the air, and went backward off his racing pony.

The Indians might have believed that the first man to fall had been hit by a lucky shot from the wagons. With the second one shot off his pony, it was more obvious that something else was going on. Several of the attackers stopped circling and whirled their ponies to look back along the canyon.

Falcon cranked off two more shots as swiftly as he could work the rifle's lever. An Indian sagged over his mount's neck after Falcon's slug struck him in the chest; one had opened his mouth to howl in anger when a bullet shattered his teeth, pulped his tongue, and bored on through to sever his spinal cord. He fell like a puppet with its strings cut.

In a handful of seconds, Falcon had killed four of the Indians and whittled down the odds. He was still outnumbered, though. They had spotted him in the rocks, and four of them broke off the attack and charged toward him, hollering and shooting as they came.

Arrows whipped through the air around him. Slugs spattered against the rocks. Falcon had decent cover, but not enough time. He could bring down probably two of them, but the other two would overrun his position.

Usually, it was better to face trouble head-on. Falcon left the Winchester lying on the rock and sprinted back to where he had left his horse. He vaulted into the saddle, hauled the horse around, and put the reins between his teeth as he drew both of the revolvers he carried under his coat, one in a regular holster on his right hip, the other in a cross-draw rig on his left.

"Hyaaahhh!" he shouted at the horse as he sent the animal lunging out of the rocks and straight at the four Indians.

Obviously surprised by his attack, they skidded their ponies to a stop and tried to take better aim, instead of just firing wildly. They were well within range of the heavy revolvers, though. Falcon veered back and forth, guiding the horse with his knees, as he fired each gun in turn, left, right, left, right.

His .45-caliber slugs blasted two of the Indians from their mounts. Another twisted, but remained mounted, as he clawed at his midsection where one of Falcon's bullets had punched into his guts. The fourth Indian loosed an arrow, which came close enough to clip some fringe off the buckskin coat Falcon wore. The next instant, Falcon shot him through the throat.

The whirlwind attack carried Falcon right through the now-riderless ponies as they scattered in panic. He looked up the canyon and saw that the remaining Indians had closed in around the wagons. One warrior, whooping triumphantly, fired his rifle into the back of a wagon. Another leaped from his pony and landed on the seat of the same wagon, howling ferociously and brandishing a knife as he ducked under the canvas cover.

The closest of the warriors whirled his pony to raise his rifle as Falcon pounded toward him. The man squeezed the trigger, but nothing happened. The rifle was empty.

Even in the thick of battle, Falcon had instinctively kept up with how many shots he'd fire. He had two rounds left in one gun, a single cartridge in the other. He fired one of the pair in the left-hand gun and saw the Indian with the empty rifle jolted backward as the slug smashed through his forehead and on into his brain.

Another man charged at him, whooping and trying to get close enough to slash at Falcon's head with a tomahawk. Falcon

ducked underneath the blow and fired his right-hand gun upward at an angle. The bullet went in under the Indian's chin and
cored through his brain.

That left two enemies and one bullet. The Indian at the back
of the wagon jerked his pony around. The animal reared, slashing at the air with its hooves, as the Indian thrust his rifle past
the pony's neck and fired it one-handed. Falcon felt the heat of
the slug against his cheek. At the same time, the gun in his left
hand roared and bucked as he fired his last round. The Indian
flipped backward and thudded to the ground.

Falcon pouched both irons as his horse wheeled toward the
back of the wagon. He barely had time to yank his knife from
its sheath attached to his belt before a yelling shape leaped from
the tailgate, flew through the air, slammed into him, and knocked
him out of the saddle.

Both men crashed to the ground, landing so hard that the
impact broke them apart. Falcon rolled to get some room. As
he surged to his feet, he had to suck in his belly to avoid a slashing swipe of the Indian's blade. With the same blinding speed
that made him deadly with a gun, he thrust with his knife. The
keen edge raked along the Indian's upper arm. The man yelled
and swung a backhand that Falcon avoided, with two or three
inches to spare.

For a moment, each of them parried and thrust, steel ringing
against steel, and sparks flying as the blades clashed. It was like
a duel with sabers, only at closer range—so close, Falcon could
hear the Indian panting and smell the bear grease on his hair.

Then the Indian stuck a foot behind Falcon's knee and jerked
his leg out from under him. Falcon went down, but with his
free hand, he grabbed the front of the Indian's buckskin shirt
and dragged the man down with him. Locked together, each
using his left hand to hold off the other's knife hand, they
rolled over and over on the hard, rocky ground.

When they came to a stop, Falcon was on the bottom. The
blood-smeared point of the Indian's blade hovered near his left

eye, held off only by the strength of Falcon's arm. Falcon's knife was almost touching the Indian's throat. Only the warrior's strength kept the blade from going home. It was a classic standoff, fueled by hate and desperation.

The Indian was wiry and powerful, but Falcon's body was overlaid with thick slabs of muscle. He was a MacCallister, a born fighting man, and slowly but surely the blood of the clans that went back generations gave him the advantage. The Indian's knife arm buckled slightly. Instantly Falcon seized on that and hauled him to the side. At the same time, he bucked up from the ground. The Indian toppled off him, Falcon rolled to bring his greater weight into play, and the Indian's strength gave out. Falcon's knife ripped into his throat, cutting so deeply that the blade grated on bone. The Indian spasmed as blood sprayed across his chest and into Falcon's face.

Death followed quickly. Falcon saw the glassy-eyed stare and pushed himself up. He turned, let himself fall into a sitting position next to the warrior's body, and stayed there for a long moment, breathing hard. That had been quite a battle.

Is it over? Falcon looked around. None of the Indians were moving. He had been trying to kill with every shot and it looked like he had succeeded. An eerie silence hung over the canyon, broken only by the sighing of a cold wind.

No sounds came from the wagons, either, and that didn't bode well.

After a few minutes, Falcon pushed himself wearily to his feet. He reloaded his revolvers and slid them back into their holsters. Then he walked to the back of the nearest wagon and looked over the tailgate.

Three bodies lay inside: an old man, an old woman, and a younger woman. The old man had an arrow lodged in his shoulder, but it was a bullet to the head that had killed him. Falcon saw the red-rimmed hole above the right eye.

The women had been knifed to death, probably by the warrior Falcon had just killed. The blade had ripped them up horribly before a swipe across their throats ended their lives. From the looks of it, the Indian had enjoyed inflicting such carnage.

Since he couldn't do anything for these unfortunate pilgrims, he turned away from the wagon and checked the bodies lying on the ground. Two were men, one a middle-aged woman, the other a boy in his teens. Falcon figured the two men were the heads of these families and thought as well that they had driven the wagons into this canyon hoping to take shelter when the Indians jumped them. That hadn't worked out. Indian ponies were a lot faster than mules and wagons.

He walked over to the other wagon. The youngster who had caught an arrow in the throat lay crumpled beside one of the front wheels. Falcon shook his head sadly and turned away. He was going to have a heap of burying to do. He wouldn't ride away without seeing to it that these folks were laid to rest decently, though.

The Indians could lay where they had fallen. Buzzards had to eat, too.

He still needed to look inside this second wagon. He parted the canvas cover that hung over the back, rested a hand on the tailgate, and peered into the gloomy interior. He didn't see any corpses, which came as a slight surprise. The boy shouldn't have been in this wagon alone. But the middle-aged woman was probably his ma, and one of the men his pa. Maybe the older boy was his big brother.

What Falcon needed to do, distasteful a chore though it might be, was to go through these folks' belongings and try to find out who they were. Maybe he could make some markers for them, even though it was inevitable that the elements would claim whatever he did . . .

He was just turning away from the wagon when he heard the pitiful wail from inside it.

Chapter 8

Falcon froze right where he was. At first, he thought crazily that there was an animal of some sort inside the wagon. Then he realized the cry *did* come from an animal—a human animal.

That was a baby hollering in there.

Falcon wheeled back around and rested both hands on the tailgate this time as he peered over it. It was late enough in the day by now that the shadows were thick under the canvas cover. He didn't see anything moving.

"Kid?" Falcon asked tentatively. Then he cursed himself for being dumb. A child as young as this one sounded couldn't answer him.

The wailing stopped short. Falcon tensed with worry. The baby was just reloading with air, though. The angry sobbing rolled out again, stronger than ever. Falcon spotted a sudden jerking movement under what he had taken to be a pile of blankets on one side of the wagon bed, as if a fist or foot had just poked against it.

The next second, he hauled himself up and over the tailgate and knelt next to the blankets.

This close, he could tell that the crying definitely came from under the blankets. He took hold of the heavy wool and lifted it carefully. There was more than one blanket, so he removed them in layers until he revealed two shapes lying there: a young woman, maybe nineteen or twenty, and the baby lying in her arms. The child waved its arms and kicked its feet, and more wails came from its tear-wet, scrunched-up face.

The woman wasn't moving. From the pale, stricken face and the dark stain on the front of her dress, Falcon figured she was dead. Mortally wounded by the Indians, she could have crawled in here with the baby and pulled the blankets over them, hoping that the savages wouldn't find the infant.

Of course, if Falcon hadn't come along when he did, the baby would have been luckier if it *had* been found. The Indians would have either taken it with them and adopted it into the tribe, or else they would have dashed its brains out on a rock. Either of those would have been better than lying here helplessly and dying of thirst and starvation.

Falcon reached out and gently took hold of the baby's hand. "Hush now, little fella," he said quietly. "Or is it little gal? Doesn't matter. You're all right now."

His touch and voice instantly soothed the infant. The crying trailed away in a bubbling sound.

His words had another effect. He caught his breath as the young woman suddenly let out a gasping sigh and rolled her head toward him.

"You . . . ," she whispered. "You're . . . a white man?"

Falcon was too cool-nerved to let a surprise like this throw him. He said, "Yes, ma'am, I am. You're all right now."

That was a lie. With such a large bloodstain on her dress, she was far from all right. Falcon had been convinced she was dead, and now she couldn't be more than mere moments away from it.

"The . . . Indians?" she breathed.

"All gone. They'll never hurt anybody again."

"G-good . . . We tried to . . . get away from them . . . couldn't . . ."

"You should rest now, ma'am."

"The . . . baby . . ."

"Right here," Falcon assured her. "And doing just fine." He had already looked over the long garment the infant wore and hadn't seen any blood except some that had smeared off the woman's dress. "Not hurt at all."

"Take . . . take care . . ."

"Of the baby? I give you my word that I will." What else could he say at a time like this? He thought of something and quickly lifted the nightshirt-like garment to check. "What's his name?"

The woman hadn't opened her eyes while she was talking. Now she did, but in the fading light, Falcon couldn't tell what color they were. He could see how big and filled with pain they were, though.

"Oh!" the woman gasped. "Oh, it hurts . . ." She panted for a second; then all her muscles appeared to loosen. "That's . . . better . . . Ma . . . Oh, Ma, you're . . ."

The air went out of her in another long sigh. After a moment, Falcon grimaced and used two fingers to close her unseeing eyes.

He took hold of the baby and gingerly worked the boy out of her embrace. The infant squirmed and kicked and started crying again. Falcon cuddled him against his shoulder. He had no children of his own, but he had held nieces and nephews on occasion. Anyway, human beings had *some* instincts about such things, even rough old hellions such as himself.

"There now," he said. "Don't cry. It's going to be all right."

He hoped that wasn't another lie.

It was well past nightfall by the time Falcon got all the burying done. He wished he could have taken the time to dig indi-

vidual graves for all the slain pilgrims, but he wanted to get away from this canyon of death. He dug two large graves and split the bodies between them. Based on the names he found in a family Bible in each wagon, he arranged them, in the best way he could, so that they lay together. If he hadn't gotten it right about who went with whom, he hoped they would forgive him from wherever they were in the afterlife.

While Falcon was doing that, the baby lay in an empty crate he had found in one of the wagons and had turned into a bed by making a nest of blankets in it. He thought the baby was too young to walk, but he didn't want the little fella crawling off.

When he was finished, Falcon took off his hat and stood beside the two large mounds of earth, which were barely visible in the darkness. He wasn't the praying sort, but he said, "God rest your souls, folks. I'll look out for the little one the best I can."

From what he'd been able to guess, one wagon had belonged to a family named Stephens, the other to the Lawdermilks. No telling which bunch the baby belonged to. He hadn't found an entry in either Bible that seemed to correspond with the infant's age and sex.

Some questions in life had no answer. This child would be getting about as fresh a start as was possible, so Falcon told himself the past didn't matter, only the future.

And that future could be dangerous if he and the youngster didn't get a move on. He had taken a closer look at the dead Indians and pegged them as members of a Ute war party. He had no way of knowing if they were just part of a larger bunch. If that was the case, their friends might come looking for them at any time. Falcon didn't want to be found here with all these Ute corpses scattered around.

The fact that he had killed twelve men in such a short period of time barely entered his thoughts. He had just done what needed to be done, that was all. Once the battle started, all he'd been thinking about was survival.

The weather was cold enough that flies weren't buzzing

around the bodies. They wouldn't start to stink for a while. By the time they did, Falcon intended to be well away from here.

He put his hat back on and walked over to the crate that sat on the lowered tailgate of one of the wagons. The baby gurgled. Falcon said, "What am I going to call you, anyway? I couldn't find your name anywhere in those Bibles. Are you a Stephens or a Lawdermilk?"

The baby cried a little, tentatively.

"Yeah, you're right, what difference does it make?"

He turned, went to his horse, and swung up in the saddle. He rode over to the wagon and reached down to pick up the crate. Balancing it on the horse's back in front of him, he held on to it with his left hand and used the right to tuck the blankets in more securely around the baby. When he was satisfied, he turned the horse and rode slowly along the canyon, back the way he had come in.

The wagons and the two mass graves lay still and silent behind them.

"I've got to figure out a better way to tote you around," Falcon said. "This isn't going to work for the long haul. Indian women carry their papooses on their backs. Maybe I'll rig something like that for you. Not that you're *my* papoose, you understand. I'm just taking care of you for the time being."

In addition to how to avoid more hostile Indians, the infant question was uppermost in his mind: *What am I going to do with a baby?* He couldn't take care of it forever, not the way he lived. He wasn't sure how far it was to the nearest settlement. Would there be somebody there who would take the baby in? Somebody responsible who would love it and take care of it?

Falcon frowned as the horse plodded along and he balanced the crate in front of him. He'd been on his way to Chugwater to spend the holidays with Duff, and it occurred to him that the town was a good-sized one. Duff seemed to like it there and thought that most of the inhabitants were decent folks. They

had taken in a wild Scotsman and made him one of their own, after all.

Even though it would mean he'd have to be responsible for the infant longer, instead of leaving him in the first place he came to, that might be his best bet, he decided. He nodded.

"I'm going to take you to Chugwater, old son," he said. "My cousin Duff can figure out what to do with you."

Chapter 9

Chugwater

Raising a posse to go after the train robbers and kidnappers didn't take long. Even though the crime had been committed outside his jurisdiction, town marshal Bill Ferrell took charge of things. Having a legally appointed lawman along made it better if any questions were ever raised about what the towns-men had done.

Duff, Elmer, and Wang were riding with the posse, of course. So were Biff Johnson and a number of the other businessmen in town who were Duff's friends. All total, twenty men were armed and mounted and ready to take up the pursuit within a half hour after the train rolled into the station.

While the preparations were under way, Duff had stopped by the dress shop and asked Meagan to go to the depot and take charge of Andrew and Rosanna.

"Ye need to have Dr. Urban take a look at Andrew's head," Duff told the lovely blonde. "And then, maybe if they could wait here until I get back . . ."

"Of course," Meagan said. "I'll take them upstairs to my rooms and make them comfortable. You just be careful, Duff.

From what you told me about the robbery, those outlaws are vicious."

"I dinna intend t' be reckless," he assured her. "But they canna be allowed t' get away wi' killin' folks and carryin' off women, t' say nothing of all the loot they stole."

They were standing on the front porch of the dress shop as they talked. Duff took her in his arms to kiss her before he rode out with the posse, clearly not caring that they were in public view.

Neither did Meagan. She put enough passion in the kiss to make sure Duff wouldn't forget he had a very good reason to be careful.

Then she hurried to the train station to find Duff's cousins. Andrew and Rosanna were sitting on one of the benches in the lobby, Meagan discovered. To her surprise, Dr. Urban was already there, sitting beside Andrew and putting the finishing touches on a bandage he had fastened around Andrew's head.

"Keep that dressing on there tonight and I'll check on you again tomorrow," the doctor said. "You'll be staying here in town, I hope?"

"We'd planned to go on out to Sky Meadow, our cousin's ranch," Andrew explained.

"I'm familiar with Mr. MacCallister's ranch, but I'd advise that you remain here, at least for tonight. Head injuries are nothing to take lightly, and I'd like to examine you again after some time has passed."

"Thank you, Doctor," Rosanna said. "We can get rooms at the hotel, I'm sure."

"Or you can stay with me," Meagan spoke up to offer.

Smiles lit up the faces of the twins. They hadn't noticed her until now.

"Meagan!" Andrew said. "How wonderful to see you again." He winced slightly, probably from the pain in his head. "Even under less than auspicious circumstances."

Rosanna got to her feet and hugged Meagan. "We've been

looking forward to spending time with you again," she said with a smile, even though the day had clearly taken its toll on her.

Meagan had met the MacCallister twins earlier in the year, while she and Duff were in New York. They had even taken in a play in which Andrew and Rosanna were performing. Not surprisingly, considering how Duff felt about her, his cousins had been quite taken with her right away.

Dr. Urban snapped his medical bag shut and said, "I'll leave our visitors in your capable hands, Miss Parker."

Meagan said to Andrew and Rosanna, "Duff stopped by my shop a few minutes ago and asked me to make sure the two of you were all right. Why don't we go back to my place and wait there for the posse to return? I have quite comfortable living quarters above the shop."

"That's very kind of you, dear, and we'll take you up on it for now, although with all of our bags, we really should stay at the hotel," Rosanna said. "Otherwise you'd be crowded out of your own place. But this *has* been a very trying day, and we appreciate your consideration."

She took hold of Andrew's arm and helped him to his feet, despite his protest that he didn't need any assistance. He seemed fairly steady on his feet, but got a little shaky as they left the depot and walked along Clay Avenue. The weather was still warm for December, but the downright hot temperatures of a few days previously had retreated.

There were stairs inside the dress shop, but Meagan took them up the outside staircase to that entrance and led them into her parlor. She got them settled on a comfortable divan and then went to the kitchen to start a pot of tea brewing.

Once that was going, she came back into the parlor and sat down in an armchair across from Andrew and Rosanna.

"Duff told me a little about what happened," she said, "and I heard other people in town talking about it on my way to the station. A gang of outlaws stopped the train and killed a passenger?"

"That's right," Andrew said. "One poor fellow was gunned down right in front of us. The same man who shot him is the one who lambasted me with his pistol and then carried off poor Miss Gillespie."

"That's the young woman who was kidnapped?"

"Fiona Gillespie," Rosanna said. "The name doesn't mean anything to you, Meagan?"

A frown creased Meagan's forehead. "No, I don't think so. Should it?"

"Duff never mentioned her?" Andrew asked.

"No."

This was getting more puzzling all the time.

"She's from the same village in Scotland where Duff grew up," Rosanna explained.

"Oh. Dunoon, you mean." Meagan nodded. "He's talked about some of the people who live there, but I don't recall him ever mentioning Miss Gillespie. I hope she's all right."

"So do I," Rosanna said. "Andrew and I met her in Glasgow and befriended her. She works for us now."

"And you brought her to America to see an old friend of hers from back home. That was very kind of you."

Something was stirring inside Meagan now. She didn't want to call it *jealousy*—but she couldn't help but wonder why Duff had never mentioned Fiona Gillespie. Of course, it was possible she was just an old family friend, or even a mere acquaintance, and Duff simply hadn't thought about her since coming to America himself.

Meagan put those feelings aside. She wasn't a petty person by nature, and she wasn't going to start being one now. Besides, the most important thing was that Miss Gillespie needed rescuing from those desperadoes who had carried her off.

With Duff MacCallister in the posse, there was a very good chance of that. Duff wasn't alone, either.

"I'm not sure how kind it was, bringing her here," Andrew said. "So far, all we've really managed to do is put her in danger."

Meagan summoned up a smile and said, "Duff and his friends Elmer and Wang are with that posse. Those outlaws won't stand a chance."

Buster's Hump

Elmer pointed at the tracks on the ground and said, "They headed off to the north, all right, the whole sorry lot of 'em."

Wang threw a leg over the back of his horse and dropped lithely to the ground. He moved alongside the hoofprints, crouching low to study them. After several minutes, he straightened and looked up at Duff, Elmer, and Marshal Ferrell, who sat their horses at the front of the posse.

"Sixteen men on horseback, I make it," he said. "And one horse was carrying double, no doubt the one with the prisoner."

"You can't be that sure about such a muddle of prints," Elmer scoffed. "Too many o' them hoofprints look alike, and they're all on top of each other."

"I wouldna bet against him," Duff said. "Wang has a mighty keen eye."

"So do I, for my age. And I been trackin', man and boy, for nigh on to forty years."

"Sixteen men," Wang said calmly.

Marshal Ferrell said, "I reckon we'll find out when we catch up to them. At least we can be pretty sure that they don't outnumber us."

"Nae, I believe we'll be evenly matched, for the most part," Duff said.

Elmer muttered, "In numbers, anyway."

Duff knew what his friend and foreman meant. Most of the posse members were courageous enough, and as frontiersmen, they had faced trouble from time to time in the past. However, when it came to sheer fighting ability, they didn't really compare to hardened owlhoots.

Still, Duff trusted his own abilities, and those of Elmer and Wang, and Ferrell was a tough, competent lawman. If they could take their quarry by surprise, that, along with the weight of numbers, might be enough to swing the advantage their way.

"They're a couple of hours ahead of us," Ferrell said. "We won't be able to catch up to them by nightfall."

"Then we'll whittle down their lead as much as we can," Duff said, "and maybe one or two of us can scout on ahead after dark and locate them."

By that, he meant that he and Wang would do the scouting. If anyone could follow a trail at night, it was Wang Chow, and he also had an almost-supernatural ability to move smoothly and quietly, almost invisibly. Duff had considerable experience at reconnaissance, too, from his time serving in Egypt with the Black Watch, the 42nd Regiment of Foot in the British Army.

The posse rode north, with Wang taking the lead and following the trail. The others followed him.

At first, it seemed the outlaws were taking no pains to conceal their trail. That made sense to Duff. When they rode away from the railroad tracks, all they were interested in was putting as much distance as they could between them and the scene of their crime.

Later, they had started to be more careful, going out of their way to cross rocky stretches of ground, where their horses wouldn't leave as many prints. They rode into creeks and followed the streams for a mile or more before emerging. Those tactics would have thrown a lot of pursuers off their trail—but not Duff and Wang. Their experience, canny instincts, and sheer doggedness enabled them to pick up the trail each time. But each of those instances *cost* them time.

The posse tried to make up for it by pushing their horses hard whenever the trail was easy to follow. But the sun kept sinking in the west, and eventually it dipped behind the mountains and dusk fell like a thick curtain, followed quickly by night.

They had just picked up the trail again after another detour through a creek. Ferrell called a halt and said, "We might as well make camp here. It's a level spot, and we'll have good water for us and the horses. Still, some graze along the bank, too."

"Aye," Duff agreed. "'Tis a suitable location. Elmer, can you see to rustlin' up some coffee and victuals?"

"Sure, as long as you're not expectin' me to fix any o' that neeps an' haggis you're so fond of." Elmer's shudder could be seen even in the rapidly fading light. "That ain't food."

"Coffee, biscuits, and bacon will be fine."

"How come the Chinaman ain't in charge o' the grub? He's a pretty fair cook, though it pains me to admit it."

"Wang and I will be leaving shortly to take up the trail again," Duff said.

"I'm not sure how you figure on tracking those varmints in the dark," the marshal said.

"Their passage disturbs both the land and the air," Wang said. "The essence of such disturbances takes time to fade. With luck, I will be able to sense that essence."

Ferrell shook his head and said, "I don't know any more than I did when I asked the question. But if you can follow them, more power to you, Wang."

Wang just inclined his head in acknowledgment of the sentiment.

Although the delay chafed at Duff, it was necessary to let the horses rest and also to give Elmer a chance to prepare the meal. The coffee was ready first. Duff swallowed a cup of the strong black brew. Wang drank clear, cold water from the creek. Then they took the sandwiches Elmer had made for them from biscuits and bacon and set out on the outlaws' trail again.

Chapter 10

Badwater Canyon

The firelight painted flickering red shadows on the stone walls of the old abandoned ranch house. Nick Jessup walked toward it, carrying a lantern in one hand and a plate of food in the other.

He stepped through a doorway, where the door itself had rotted away, leaving just the opening. A muffled sound came from his right. When he turned in that direction, the lantern light revealed a figure bound hand and foot, sitting with her back propped up against the wall. The girl had a gag in her mouth. Her red hair had come loose and spilled thickly around her shoulders.

"I brought you something to eat," Nick said.

More muffled noises came from the girl. She was probably cussing him. For a young woman who'd looked rather genteel at first, she had quite a vocabulary—although some of what she'd said had been expressed in such a thick Scottish burr that Nick hadn't really understood all of it. He could tell she was mad at him, though.

Kent Spalding hadn't been happy with him, either. Carrying off prisoners from the train hadn't been part of the plan. Spalding had gotten over his annoyance during the long ride back here to the hideout. Having a hostage wasn't a bad idea, just in general. Having such a young, pretty hostage was even better.

Nick knew what some of the other members of the gang were thinking: They would be taking turns with her sooner or later. Nick didn't intend to let that happen. He might be a killer, a train robber, and a bank robber, but he didn't mistreat women. Hank had taught his brothers that: No matter how much of a badman you were, you never hurt a respectable woman.

Some of Spalding's men probably felt the same way. Nick hoped so. Together they would keep this young woman from being molested.

That was his plan, anyway.

"Just settle down," he went on. "I know you can't eat with that gag. The only reason I put it on you in the first place was because my ears were getting tired from all your yelling. If you promise not to do that anymore, I'll take the gag off and you can have some supper. Is that a deal?"

She glared at him. Her eyes blazed with fury in the lantern light.

He sighed and said, "I'm only gonna give you so many chances at this, miss. Now, I'll say it again. If you promise not to yell and cuss at me, I'll take the gag off and you can eat. Do you promise?"

For a second more, she looked daggers at him, but then she jerked her head in a curt nod.

"Good," Nick said. He set the lantern on the ground, out of reach of her legs so she couldn't kick it over. He stepped closer to her and said, "Bend forward a little so I can get to the knot at the back of your head."

She did so. She was still muttering something, but it wasn't as loud as what she'd been trying to say earlier. Nick found the knot in the bandanna that was serving as a gag and untied it. The task wasn't easy one-handed, but he managed.

"There," he said as he pulled the gag away from her mouth. "That's better, isn't it?"

She gagged and spat and made smacking noises. When her mouth worked, she said, "What did ye do wi' that thing, wrap a dead rat in it? Och, the taste! The awful, awful taste!"

"I'm sorry," Nick said sincerely. "Maybe I shouldn't have done that. You were giving my nerves a lot of wear and tear, though."

She looked up at him. Her lips drew back in a snarl.

"What did ye expect me t' do? Give ye me warmest thanks for manhandlin' me like a *hoor* and carryin' me off from tha' train?"

"Settle down. You need to eat something. It's just stew, but it's not bad." He hunkered on his heels beside her and dipped up a spoonful of the stuff. "Open your mouth and I'll feed you."

With a sullen expression on her face, she opened her mouth and waited for him to put the spoon in it. He hesitated and added, "Don't try to bite me, or you'll be sorry."

"If ever I decide t' bite ye, 'tis ye who'll be sorry."

Nick spooned the stew into her mouth. She chewed and swallowed and said grudgingly, "'Tis not bad."

"An old-timer that we call Doc made it. He seems to be a pretty good cook." Nick fed her more of the stew. "I'm glad we're getting along better now."

"What makes ye think we are?"

"You're cooperating and not cussing me."

She gave him a narrow-eyed stare. "Aye, but cut me loose and let me get me hands on a gun, and then ye'll see how well I cooperate. Better yet, 'tis a claymore I'd rather be wieldin'."

"What's a *claymore*? Some kind of revolver?"

"Nae, 'tis a sword used by the Highland warriors."

"You're not a warrior," Nick said. "You're a girl."

"Put a fine blade in me hands, and then we'll see."

He laughed and said, "You're starting to scare me a little. What's your name, anyway? I'm Nick."

He didn't give her his full name. He could admit to himself that he was taken with her, at least a little, but he figured it wouldn't hurt to be cautious.

Anyway, she had already heard Logan call him by his first name, back there on the train.

She didn't respond to his question about her name, so he tried something else as he hunkered there, feeding her.

"You sound more Scottish now than you did back on the train. Of course, we didn't really talk all that much. And when you got wound up and started cussing me, you *really* sounded Scottish."

"Rousin' my ire brings out the Highland blood in me, I reckon."

He gave her another spoonful of stew.

"I like the way it sounds. It's really pretty . . . and so are you."

"Save yer flattery, Mister Outlaw. I canna stop ye from doin' whate'er ye want to me, but ye'll not win me over."

"I'm just trying to be nice—"

"Ye lost yer chance at that when ye struck poor Mr. MacCallister with your gun and kidnapped me."

Nick frowned and said, "Wait a minute. That gent you were traveling with, his name is MacCallister?"

"Aye. Andrew MacCallister. The lady is his sister Rosanna."

"Do they happen to be related to an hombre named Duff MacCallister?"

The girl looked genuinely surprised. "Duff is their cousin. Do ye ken him?"

"We haven't actually met," Nick replied grimly, "but I sure as blazes know who he is. I've got a mighty big score to settle with him, too."

She was silent for a long moment after that. Finally she said, "Dinna forget about the rest o' tha' stew."

"Oh. Yeah, sure, here you go." He fed her another spoonful. "Sorry. Talking about Duff MacCallister stirred up some bad memories."

"'Tis all right." She paused, then said, "If ye still want to ken me name . . . 'tis Fiona. Fiona Gillespie."

The moon hadn't risen yet, so all Duff and Wang had to track by was starlight. Duff hoped that Wang really could sense those "disturbances" he'd talked about. During the time Duff had known him, Wang had been able to back up every claim he had made.

Mountains loomed darkly ahead of them. Duff studied the dimly seen peaks and said, "I believe yonder heights are known as the Grabhorns."

"You are familiar with them?" Wang asked.

"Nae. I've seen them from a distance and on maps, but 'tis only the name I ken about them."

"It is difficult to tell, but they appear to be rather rugged."

"Aye. Plenty of hiding places for skunks like the ones we're after, I'd say."

They rode on until they had entered the foothills at the edge of the mountains. Duff looked up at the sky with narrowed eyes. The stars were disappearing, swallowed up by clouds moving in from the north. He glanced to the east, saw a faint silver glow at the horizon.

"The moon will be up soon," he said, "but by the time it rises enough to help us any, the clouds will cover it up. 'Twill be no good to us then. We might as well stop and make a cold camp, then try to pick up the trail in th' morning."

Wang said, "Wait. Look there."

He pointed at the sky above the Grabhorns. Duff spotted a dim orange glow among the low, rapidly moving clouds.

"Is tha' firelight reflected on the clouds?"

"I believe it is the light from a rather large campfire. If not for the clouds, we would not have noticed it."

An icy breeze touched Duff's face. That was what was bringing the clouds in. Behind them would be a stiff, frigid wind heralding a winter storm.

"I canna think of anyone who would have a campfire up in here except those outlaws we're after. Do ye reckon we can follow the light on the clouds and find their camp?"

"We can try," Wang said simply.

"Aye, 'tis worth a shot. Come on."

The reflection of the fire on the clouds came and went as the scudding masses shifted, but Duff and Wang were both keen-eyed enough to spot it again. The terrain became more rugged, full of towering bluffs and deep canyons, all under the looming black mass of the Grabhorns.

Finally Duff and Wang reined in at the mouth of a canyon, barely able to make out the opening because the clouds completely covered the sky now and a thick gloom had settled over the landscape.

"Somewhere in there," Wang whispered. Voices traveled at night. They didn't know if the outlaws had posted guards this far out from their camp, but it was possible.

"Aye," Duff agreed. "But hard to say how far."

Wang tilted his head back and looked up at the bluff above them.

"I can climb that, follow the canyon along the rim, and find out more," he said.

"Ye would need t' be a mountain goat to climb that, Wang."

"There are mountains in China. I climbed some of them that were much taller and steeper than this."

Duff considered the suggestion for a moment, then said, "Ye can give it a try if ye'd like. If ye fall, sing out and I'll catch ye."

Wang chuckled. "I believe you would try, my friend."

"Aye, that I would." Duff paused. "Be careful."

Wang dismounted, walked over to the rock face, and felt around on it for a few seconds. Then, apparently satisfied, he gripped a couple of tiny projections, found another one for his feet, and began to climb.

In his dark clothes, Wang was practically invisible against the bluff. Duff followed his friend's progress as best he could as Wang climbed higher and higher. Finally Duff couldn't see him at all anymore.

The next hour seemed eight or nine times as long as it actually was, as Duff waited for Wang to return. He had dismounted, too. He paced around while the horses cropped idly at a few tufts of grass that remained among the rocks.

When Wang dropped down to the ground without any warning, Duff stiffened and reached for his gun. Then he realized that Wang had returned and breathed out. "Och! Ye took a year off me life there."

"My apologies," Wang murmured. "I located the miscreants' hideout. It is about a mile from here, although the canyon twists back and forth so much that reaching it may require a trip that is actually twice that long. There is an old stone dwelling that appears to be abandoned, as well as the ruins of a few other structures and some tents. I believe the prisoner, Miss Gillespie, is being held in the old house. One of the outlaws went in and out of there with food and water."

"Sounds like you're right," Duff said. He had been thinking about how they should proceed if Wang found the hideout. "Could a couple of men climb down into the canyon?"

"I believe they could, if they exercised enough caution."

"Then that's our job. Elmer and the rest o' the posse will come in through the canyon and occupy the attention of the outlaws, while you and I get into the house and free that girl. Then we'll have the bunch of them trapped between our forces."

Wang considered that, then said, "A worthy strategy, one

that offers a good chance of defeating the enemy, while at the same time assuring the young woman's safety. But one of us will have to return to the posse and bring them to this spot."

"You're well-suited to the job. I'll wait here, just in case anything happens while you're gone."

"Without being able to see the stars, it is difficult to estimate the time, but I believe it will be close to dawn before I can make it back with the others."

"Dawn," Duff said. " 'Tis a good time for an attack."

Chapter 11

Again, to Duff, the wait seemed longer than it really was. He sat alone on a rock near the canyon entrance. If he had been able to see the stars wheeling through the sky above, he would have been able to keep track of the time better, but the clouds were solid.

The wind that had brought them in dropped the temperature lower. Duff was glad he had brought along his sheepskin coat. He turned its collar up and tugged his hat down. He was tired, but his service in the Black Watch had taught him how to stay awake and alert even when weariness threatened to overwhelm him.

As the blackness took on a slightly lighter tinge of grayness in the east, telling him that dawn was approaching, he heard the soft *clip-clop* of horses approaching at a quiet, careful pace. A moment later, the tall shapes of mounted men loomed out of the darkness.

The group reined in. Three men swung down from the saddles and led their horses over to Duff, who had stood up from the rock where he'd been sitting for the past few hours. His muscles were stiff from the cold and inactivity. He rolled his shoulders to loosen them.

"'Tis been quiet in there," Duff reported to Wang, Elmer, and Marshal Ferrell, who had joined him, leading their horses. "All the scoundrels must be asleep, save perhaps for a couple on guard."

"They must think they're safe, up here in the middle of nowhere like this," Elmer said. "But we'll disabuse 'em o' that notion here pretty quicklike."

"I'm sure Wang has explained the plan to you."

"He has," Ferrell said. "How much time do you want us to give you before we move in?"

Duff looked at Wang and said, "You're the one who's been in there. What say ye?"

"Half an hour," Wang replied. "By then, we should be in position."

"You got it," Elmer said. "Good luck."

"Aye, we can always use fortune on our shoulders," Duff said.

He and Wang left their horses there and started climbing the bluff. Wang went first, since he had been up there earlier and knew the best route. Duff tried to duplicate his friend's movements, although the poor light made that difficult.

The only really important thing, of course, was that he not fall off. He didn't, and a fairly short time later, he and Wang reached the top.

Once they were up there, he found that following the canyon rim wasn't too hard. They just had to be careful not to approach too closely, so that they wouldn't kick any rocks into the canyon and cause a racket that might alert the outlaws.

After they had gone quite a distance, Wang touched Duff on the arm to stop him, then led him over to the edge. They knelt there and peered down into the canyon. The campfire that had guided them here had burned down to a pile of glowing orange embers. Every so often, a branch popped and a little tongue of fresh flame licked up for a few seconds before dying down again. Horses blew and shuffled around in a pole corral. A few snores were even faintly audible. Those were the only sounds in the canyon.

Wang pointed and said, "There is the old house."

Duff could make out the structure, but just barely. Wang had had a better view of it earlier when the campfire was still a good-sized blaze.

Duff's eyes had adjusted to the darkness well enough that he saw several tents as well. He knew some of the outlaws would be sleeping inside them.

"Is there a guard inside the house?" he asked.

"I do not know."

"I suppose we'll find out. Come on."

The eastern sky had lightened more, but they still had to work mostly by feel as they began climbing down into the canyon. The rock wall was steep, but passable. A few times, Duff wound up hanging by his hands while he searched for footholds. Sometimes they were small, but he always found them.

The wind began blowing harder. It whistled and howled through the canyon. Duff glanced up and saw that it was shredding the clouds. A few late stars were visible. The sunrise, when it got here, would be fairly bright.

He and Wang needed to be on level ground again by then. If the outlaws started stirring around and one of them were to glance up and spot them on the canyon wall, they would be easy targets, Duff thought grimly.

Yet they couldn't afford to hurry too much, either, because that risked a bad fall, possibly a fatal one.

Like so many other things in life, Duff reflected, *the path to success is a narrow one, with deep pitfalls on both sides...*

In this case, however, he and Wang reached their destination safely, dropping the last foot or so to the ground and landing lightly. They paused there at the base of the canyon wall, hunkered among some boulders, to catch their breath and recover from the strain of the climb.

While they were doing that, Duff took a look around the outlaw camp to see if anyone was moving around yet. While he was doing that, a man crawled out of one of the tents and stumbled off a few yards to relieve himself. Duff hoped that when he was finished with that, he would go back into the tent to sleep some more. Instead the man turned toward the fire and knelt beside it to stir up the embers. He fed in a few twigs and soon had a small blaze going again.

"We'd best make our move while his back is still to us," Duff whispered. Wang nodded agreement. They rose from their crouches and cat-footed swiftly toward the old stone dwelling. The house had no windows on the rear, probably because the only view in that direction was the canyon wall. Duff considered that another stroke of good fortune.

Luck had smiled on them so far, but it was a fickle thing. Proof of that came a moment later when one of the train robbers stepped around the corner of the building and came toward them. His head was down and he wasn't really paying attention to anything except what was right in front of his feet. Duff and Wang froze.

It would have been too much to hope that he wouldn't notice them. His head came up and his eyes widened in surprise. He grabbed at the gun on his hip.

By that time, Wang had already launched a spinning kick. His foot caught the outlaw on the jaw and knocked him senseless to the ground. The blow made a little noise, and so did the man's gun as it slipped from the holster and struck a rock on the ground. Duff and Wang stood tense and motionless as they waited to see if the slight racket had caught anyone's attention.

Nothing else happened. The wind continued blowing, muffling the crackle of flames from the campfire and any other sounds. Duff could see Wang fairly clearly now. He looked up, saw that the clouds were mostly gone, and a thin strip of pale rose and gold had appeared low in the eastern sky, just above the rimrock.

Duff had been keeping a rough count in his head. He knew it was time for Elmer, Ferrell, and the rest of the posse to be making their move.

No sooner had that thought gone through his head than shots suddenly sounded from the direction of the canyon mouth.

"Here they come," Duff said quietly.

Around on the other side of the old house, men shouted curses and questions. Running footsteps slapped the ground. Duff heard men calling to each other inside the house as well. Some of them had spent the night in there with the prisoner.

Duff hoped they hadn't abused the young woman. If they had, he would see to it that all of them faced justice for it. Of course, they would hang, anyway, for the man they had killed during the train robbery. That is, if they survived the ruckus that was about to break out.

Gunfire increased, and the yelling diminished. It was time for him and Wang to make their move, Duff decided. He indicated with hand signals that Wang should go to the left around the house, while he went around the right. Duff drew his gun and slipped along the wall in that direction.

When he rounded the corner, he spotted several men carrying rifles and running in the opposite direction, toward the canyon mouth where the fighting was taking place. None of them glanced back at the house.

It was possible, even likely, that the outlaws had left a guard inside the old house. Duff knew he and Wang probably wouldn't be able to just waltz in there and free the prisoner. He looked along the front of the house, saw Wang checking around the other corner, and motioned that he would go in first. Wang nodded to show that he understood.

Duff took a deep breath and headed for the doorway. It was

just an open space now, the door itself having rotted away. He could see a small remnant of a leather hinge, that was all.

With the Colt thrust out in front of him, Duff wheeled through the doorway and dropped into a low crouch as he swung the gun from side to side. In the gloom, he spied a faint movement to his right. He couldn't just blaze away at the dimly seen shape because he didn't know where the prisoner was.

Then his eyes adjusted enough for him to realize that the figure wore a tall, steeple-crowned sombrero. He didn't think that was likely to be the young woman from the train. A harsh curse in Spanish, followed instantly by the crash of a rifle shot and a spurt of muzzle flame confirmed it.

Duff was already diving to the ground. The bullet whistled through the air above him.

His gun roared and bucked against his palm as he triggered it. The slug punched into the outlaw's guts, low on his body, and doubled him over. He had managed to work the rifle's lever and throw another round into the firing chamber before he was hit. In his agony, his finger jerked the trigger again, but he had already fallen forward and rammed the muzzle into the hard-packed dirt floor. The back blast blew the barrel apart and sent hot shards of metal slashing into the train robber's face, adding to his pain. He screamed as he fell to the ground.

Duff scrambled to his feet and drilled a bullet through the writhing man's brain, putting him out of his misery—and eliminating him as a possible threat.

"Miss Gillespie! Are ye in here? Miss Gillespie! 'Tis a friend!"

"Oh!" That startled, frightened exclamation came from a woman. "In here!"

Duff thought she was in the next room. He darted into the door between the chambers, with his gun still held ready, not knowing what waited for him.

The sky had lightened enough outside for him to see more and more in here. He saw a slender figure cowering against the far wall.

"Miss Gillespie? My name is Duff MacCallister. I've come to take ye out o' here."

"Thank heavens!" She came toward him, and as she did, he realized she wasn't tied up. In fact, she had a knife in her hand. She threw it down as Duff heard a slight noise behind him and looked over his shoulder to see that Wang had come into the room.

Fiona Gillespie explained, "I . . . I stole that knife from one of them. He never knew. I was going to use it to . . . to kill meself . . . before I'd let them have their way wi' me."

"Well, ye dinna have to worry about that now. This is my friend Wang Chow, and a bunch more of our friends are out there doin' battle wi' those bank robbers and killers. Do ye ken if there are any more o' the varmints here in the house?"

"I don't think so. They . . . they left Bedoya to keep an eye on me. Is he . . . ?"

"Aye. He willna bother any innocent lass ever again."

"Thank you. I . . . I was so scared . . ."

Her voice trailed off. Her eyes rolled up in their sockets. Duff knew what was about to happen and would have sprung forward to catch her as she collapsed, but Wang was quicker. He caught her and lowered her gently to the ground.

"Stay here wi' her, Wang," Duff said. "I'll be for seein' how the rest of our bunch is faring against those animals."

Kent Spalding cursed bitterly as he knelt behind a rock and fired his gun toward the posse members who had taken cover farther down the canyon.

"This is your fault," he said to Nick Jessup. "They might not have been able to raise such a big posse if you hadn't carried off that girl."

Nick was worried about the posse, but he was also nervous that Spalding, who was known to have a bad temper, might turn and blast him just out of sheer venom. He told himself to keep an eye on the boss outlaw. He wouldn't hesitate to defend himself if Spalding tried to gun him.

Logan, who was also firing from behind a nearby rock, started reloading his pistol and said, "Don't be so hard on the kid, Spalding. With a dead man and a nice pile of loot, don't you think they would have come after us, anyway?"

"And your brother was responsible for that dead man," Spalding said. His lip curled in a snarl as he triggered again. "No point in worrying about any of it now, though. They've got us bottled up here. We'll fall back to the old house. They can't root us out of there, unless they brought some dynamite with them."

"Maybe they did," Nick said worriedly.

Spalding just snarled at *him*.

Then the boss outlaw waved his gun and shouted to the other men, "Fall back! Fall back to the house!"

Still firing as they ran, the men darted out from cover and raced up the canyon. Bullets from the posse whacked through the air around them.

One man stumbled and arched his back as a slug drilled between his shoulder blades. Momentum carried him several more steps before he pitched forward on his face.

Another man clutched his leg. Crimson welled between his fingers. He kept moving, desperation making his nerves and muscles work despite the wound. He even twisted around and threw a couple of wild shots back at the posse as he hobbled along.

The fleeing outlaws rounded the last bend and came in sight of the abandoned ranch headquarters. The old stone house was about fifty yards away. The corral lay a hundred yards off to the right. The horses were milling around, spooked by the gunfire. The wind was carrying the powder smoke away from them. If they had been able to smell it, they might have panicked.

A shot blasted from behind the stone wall around the old well. The outlaw running in the lead twirled around from the slug's impact. His legs tangled and he went down in a limp sprawl that signified death. A second shot sounded and another man fell heavily.

"They've gotten in back here!" Spalding yelled. "Head for the corral!"

An open pole corral doesn't seem like a very good place to make a stand, Nick thought. But maybe Spalding intended for them to get their horses and try to fight their way back through the canyon and out the front door. They would lose a lot of men in the process, but some of them might make it.

The man behind the stone wall stood up to get a better shot. Something about the tall, broad-shouldered figure was familiar, Nick realized. Then he knew where he had seen the man before, and the shock of recognition was like a punch in the gut.

That's Duff MacCallister. The last time Nick had seen him, he had killed Hank and Sherm.

Nick yelled incoherently and emptied his revolver in MacCallister's direction. He would have charged the man out of pure hate if Logan hadn't clamped a hand around his arm and pulled him toward the corral with the others.

"Come on!" Logan said.

"Why? We're trapped! And that's MacCallister!"

"I don't care, we're gonna do what Spalding says."

Spalding barked orders to the dozen men who were still with him. "Some of you keep that man down. Half a dozen hold off that posse. The rest of you get the horses saddled."

"Why?" a man asked. "Where can we go?"

Spalding shoved his gun in the man's face. "Just do as you're told!"

That got all of them hopping to follow Spalding's commands. Nick thumbed fresh cartridges into his gun and blasted away at MacCallister. The barrage from Nick and a few other outlaws forced MacCallister to take cover behind the wall again.

Spalding continued shouting, directing his men here and there like a general in a battle, which, in a way, was exactly what he was. When several members of the posse from Chugwater tried to come around the bend in the canyon, a fierce volley from the outlaws forced them back. Some of them leaned out to snipe at the gang, but their fire wasn't effective.

Men threw saddles on horses and hastily tightened cinches. When enough of the animals were ready to ride, Spalding bellowed, "Mount up! Mount up!"

So we're going to make a final charge, Nick thought. There was nothing else they could do. The men who hadn't already ducked between the corral rails or scrambled over them did so now and vaulted into the saddles.

"Follow me!"

A man swung the corral gate open. Spalding galloped out, but instead of heading down the canyon toward the entrance, he turned the other way. Nothing lay in that direction except the blind end of the big gash in the mountains.

A few of Spalding's men hesitated, then followed him. The others trailed after them, because to charge straight into the posse's guns was suicide, especially since they would be badly outnumbered now. MacCallister fired several shots at the fleeing outlaws and knocked one man off his horse, but the others were moving too fast. They thundered around another bend and were out of sight of MacCallister and the rest of the posse.

The canyon's end loomed ahead of them. Thick brush grew along its base. Spalding, in the lead, looked like he planned to ride at full speed into the stone wall. *That is loco,* Nick thought as he grimaced, but like the others, he followed.

At the last moment, Spalding hauled back on his reins. He was out of the saddle in a flash, grabbing some of the brush and pulling on it. To Nick's amazement, the thick brush moved as if it had been tied together.

Which it had, he realized as a section of brush large enough to conceal a narrow crack in the wall swung clear of the opening. This was a back door, unknown to Nick and Logan as new members of the gang. But if Nick judged by the shocked expressions on the faces of the other men, they hadn't been aware of it, either.

Clearly, Kent Spalding had prepared for the day when he and his men might be trapped in here.

"Go!" he called as he waved them forward. "One rider at a time! You'll come out in another canyon. Follow it out of the foothills."

"The loot's back there in that old house," one man complained.

"And so's that sharpshooter behind the well," Spalding snapped. "There'll be other trains."

Fiona is back there, too, Nick thought as he bit back a groan of despair. He didn't want to leave her, but there didn't seem to be any choice.

Just as there would be other trains to rob, maybe he would see Fiona Gillespie again, too.

In fact, he thought as he followed his brother into the narrow crevice that was going to lead them to safety, he was counting on it.

Chapter 12

Duff watched Elmer and the rest of the posse sweep past the old house in pursuit of the outlaws. They vanished around the next bend in the canyon. Duff expected to hear the sounds of battle erupt again.

They did, but following the flurry of gunshots, he was surprised to see the men from Chugwater reappear, falling back around the bend. They dismounted and took cover behind the bulging rock wall, then began returning the fire.

Duff glanced at the house as he automatically shoved fresh rounds into his gun's cylinder. He was concerned about the young woman, but he was sure she had just fainted from the strain of the ordeal she had gone through. Anyway, Wang was in there to protect and care for her.

Duff snapped his revolver shut and trotted toward the bend where the rest of the posse had gathered to continue the battle with the train robbers.

Elmer spotted him coming and raised his voice over the roar of gunfire. "Duff, is the girl all right?"

"Aye, I believe so. From what I could see, she was. Just very frightened. Wang is looking after her." Duff nodded up-canyon. "The miscreants ha' gone to ground again?"

"Yeah, they've holed up in a bunch of rocks and brush against the blind end of the canyon. Ain't nowhere they can go, so we've got 'em trapped." Elmer shrugged. "I figured we oughta go ahead and charge the varmints, but the marshal said we'd lose too many men. So he ordered everybody to fall back here. I reckon he's probably right, but I still don't like it. Never did care for layin' siege to a place."

"We dinna want to get men killed for no good reason, though," Duff pointed out. He frowned in thought. "Something bothers me. If the outlaws knew they were going to be boxed in, why did they take their horses?"

Elmer frowned, too, and said, "Yeah, that's a mighty good question. Why go to that much trouble . . ."

"Unless they were sure they could get away," Duff finished for his foreman. He looked around until he spotted Marshal Ferrell and hurried over to the lawman, who was thumbing cartridges through a Winchester's loading gate.

"You all right, Duff?" Ferrell asked as he glanced up.

"Aye, but something is wrong here, Marshal. Those desperadoes must have a way to escape, or else they wouldna have taken their horses when they fled."

Ferrell looked confused. "Maybe they just didn't want to give up the horses. Or they planned to try charging out through us."

"They gave no sign o' that," Duff pointed out.

"Noooo." Ferrell rubbed his chin. "Blast it, Duff, you think there's another way out of this box canyon?"

"Tell the men to stop shootin' for a minute."

The posse members were keeping up a fairly steady fire, which made it difficult to tell if the outlaws were returning those shots. Ferrell turned and yelled, "Hold your fire! Hold your fire!"

The shooting gradually died away. As the echoes subsided,

too, Duff listened closely for a moment, then said, "No one is firin' from the end of the canyon."

Ferrell cursed. "Now what do we do?"

"Someone has to check and see if they're still there."

"Make theirselves a big ol' target, you mean," Elmer objected. "Blast it, anybody who steps around that bend is gonna be easy pickin's."

"I'll go," Duff said.

"Doggone it, I knew you was about to say that!"

Duff smiled. "Dinna worry, Elmer. I wouldna risk my life if I dinna think there's a good chance they're gone."

"Tell that to the bullets flyin' at you," Elmer groused.

Ferrell passed the word to the other men not to get trigger-happy while Duff was checking out the situation. They didn't want to get spooked and shoot him. He'd have enough to contend with if the outlaws opened fire on him.

With the gun still in his hand, Duff nodded to Elmer and then stepped around the bend. He was in the open, in full view of anyone hidden in the brush and rocks along the base of the wall at canyon's end. His muscles tensed. He didn't really expect the shock of a bullet, but the possibility was enough to make him wary.

Holding the gun level and ready to fire, he strode forward.

With each step, his confidence grew. Maybe the outlaws were just letting him get closer, but he didn't think so. By the time he had covered half the distance, he was convinced they were gone, had escaped somehow.

No shots rang out. Duff reached the rocks, moved around them in a cautious crouch, and began exploring the thick brush. He saw empty cartridge cases on the ground, where the outlaws had put up their fight, but no other sign of the fugitives.

Then he spotted a section of brush that looked odd somehow. When he looked closer, he saw immediately that it was a makeshift gate, camouflaged to look like natural growth. He grabbed hold of a thick branch with his free hand and pulled.

The whole section of brush swung out. Behind it was a narrow crevice, just wide enough for one man to ride through. As soon as Duff saw it, he knew what had happened.

He leaned forward and listened intently. He didn't hear any hoofbeats coming through the crack, no voices of men. The outlaws were well and truly gone.

Shaking his head in disgust, he walked back out, where Elmer, Ferrell, and the others could see him, and pouched his iron. As he walked toward them, they came out from behind the bend and gazed at him curiously.

"Gone?" Elmer called.

"Aye. They had themselves an escape route back there. A crevice hidden in that brush."

"We'd better get after them," Ferrell said.

Duff shook his head. "Nae, the path is so narrow tha' one man wi' a rifle can close it off to pursuit. Most o' them are probably long gone already and putting more distance betwixt us and them wi' every moment tha' passes. I'm afraid 'tis gotten away they are."

Ferrell cursed again. "They killed a man, kidnapped a woman, and stole who knows how much loot from that train."

"Aye, and while there's nothing we can do about the poor murdered fellow, the girl is safe, and there's at least a chance the loot is still in their camp. We should go and see."

"Well, there's that," Ferrell admitted. "A couple of you boys keep an eye on that end of the canyon, just in case they try to double back and surprise us."

"That ain't likely to happen," Elmer said.

"Nae," Duff agreed, "but 'twill not hurt anything to have a care."

The men Ferrell assigned to the task stayed there, while the rest of the posse led their horses back toward the old abandoned ranch house, where Wang and Fiona Gillespie waited.

Wang saw them coming, of course. It was virtually impossible to surprise him. He came out of the old house to greet them and said, "The young woman is resting inside."

"Did she wake up from her faint?" Duff asked.

"Yes. I was able to talk more to her and confirm that she is not injured and was not mistreated by her captors."

Ferrell said, "Well, we can be thankful for that, anyway, even if the varmints did get away."

Wang raised his eyebrows. "The outlaws escaped?"

"Aye," Duff said. "This canyon has a back door tha' was well hidden."

"A shame." Wang inclined his head toward the house. "There are also numerous canvas bags in there containing wallets, rings, watches, and other valuables, plus several boxes taken from the safe in the express car on the train. The locks are broken, but the contents, mostly cash, appear to be safe."

"Well, glory hallelujah, that's good news, too," the marshal said. "We got the girl and the loot back." He shook his head. "I sure would've liked to see those skunks hang for gunning down the man on the train, though."

A voice said tentatively, "Excuse me?"

The men swung around quickly to see Fiona standing in the doorway. She was pale and clearly shaken, and she rested a hand on the jamb to steady herself as she spoke. "I want to thank all of you. I owe ye a huge debt I'll never be able t' repay."

Duff, Elmer, and Marshal Ferrell all took off their hats politely as they faced her. "'Tis no need o' ye repayin' us," Duff assured her. "We were happy to help you, and just sorry ye had t' go through such an ordeal."

"That's the truth," Elmer added. "Mighty glad to hear that you're all right, ma'am."

A weak smile appeared on her face for a second, but a worried look quickly replaced it. "Did I hear ye say . . . that the men who did those terrible things got away?"

"Aye, tha' they did," Duff said.

"Were . . . were any of them killed?"

"A few."

A shudder went through Fiona. She leaned harder against the doorjamb, as if Duff's answer had weakened her even more.

"I know you'll think it's . . . it's insane . . . but could I . . . see them? The ones who were killed? I dinna believe I'll ken it's true unless I . . . I lay eyes on them for meself."

"Sorry, ma'am," Ferrell said gruffly, "but I don't think that's a good idea. Duff, why don't you and Elmer and Wang take charge of the young lady and get her back to Chugwater as quickly as you can? The rest of us will clean up here and bring along the carcasses and the loot."

"Tha' sounds like a fine idea to me," Duff said. "Come along, Miss Gillespie. Ye can ride wi' me. That horse o' mine willna have any trouble carryin' double."

For a moment, Fiona looked like she might argue, but then she summoned up another weary smile and nodded. The posse had brought along Duff's and Wang's horses. Duff swung up into the saddle and extended a hand for Fiona to grasp. Effortlessly because of his great strength, he lifted her and settled her on the horse's back in front of him, being very careful and gentle as he did so.

Elmer and Wang mounted up as well. Leaving Ferrell and the rest of the posse to attend to the grim details here in the canyon, they rode out.

"How long will it take us to reach Chugwater?" Fiona asked.

"We should get there sometime this afternoon," Duff told her. "We can go a mite faster now than when we were in pursuit, because we dinna have to worry about followin' a trail. At the same time, our horses are tired and we canna push them too hard."

"No, there's no need for that," Fiona agreed. "I'm safe now."

"Aye, that ye are," Duff said, "and 'tis mighty sorry I am that ye got such a rude introduction t' Wyoming!"

Chapter 13

Since he and Fiona obviously shared a Scottish heritage, Duff intended to ask her where she was from and who her people were, but before he could get around to that, she leaned back more heavily against him, her head lolled onto his shoulder, and her breathing became deep and regular.

She was sound asleep, obviously worn out from everything that had happened, and he didn't have the heart to disturb her.

Elmer looked over at them, grinned, and waggled his bushy eyebrows. Duff just glared at him. He hoped Elmer wouldn't try to make any more of this than it really was. He was quite happy with the way things were going with Meagan, and he didn't want anything to interfere with them. That was why neither of them had tried to nudge their relationship to the marrying stage.

Meagan wouldn't be jealous, though, even if Elmer started wagging his tongue. She was too levelheaded for that.

And strictly speaking, having Fiona's warm, shapely form pressed against him like this certainly didn't feel *bad* . . .

Wang was his usual impassive self during the ride. Duff was grateful for that.

Fiona didn't stir until they paused at a creek to rest the horses and let them drink. Then she looked around in apparent confusion and said, "Oh . . . Where . . . What . . ."

"You're all right, Miss Gillespie," Duff assured her. "We're just stoppin' for a few minutes, and then we'll be on our way to Chugwater again."

"I'm sorry. I didn't mean to fall asleep. It must have been uncomfortable for ye—"

Elmer said, "Ol' Duff didn't look like he was too uncomfortable, missy. I don't reckon you have to worry about that."

Fiona blushed. Duff wrapped his arm around her again and lowered her to the ground so she could stretch her legs. Duff swung down after her and said, "Dinna pay any attention to this old rapscallion. He's right that ye dinna have to worry, though. Takin' you back to Chugwater is no trouble."

"I owe ye a great deal, though, Mr. MacCallister," she said shyly, with her eyes downcast. "There's no tellin' what might ha' happened to me if ye hadn't rescued me from those outlaws."

"If it hadn't been me, 'twould'a been Wang or Elmer or one of the other fellows. One thing ye'll find about Westerners, we dinna allow womenfolk to be mistreated."

Duff, Elmer, and Wang all refilled their canteens from the cold, clear creek. Fiona took a long drink from Duff's canteen and smiled as she handed it back to him. A short time later, they mounted up again and resumed their journey to Chugwater.

Fiona chattered incessantly now, asking questions about the flora and fauna and the physical landmarks they passed. She was so curious about everything that Duff didn't have a chance to ask the questions he had wanted to bring up with her earlier. He supposed there would be plenty of time for that, once they got back to town. He had gotten the feeling that his cousins Andrew and Rosanna had befriended the young woman on the train, so he was certain he'd be seeing more of Fiona in the future.

When they came in sight of the settlement, Fiona asked excitedly, "Is that Chugwater?"

"Aye."

"'Tis larger than I thought 'twould be, from hearing Mr. MacCallister and Miss MacCallister talk about it."

"Well, it ain't a big town like San Francisco or Boston," Elmer drawled. "Folks around here like it, though."

Fiona shivered. "I hope there's a good fire in the hotel. The air has a definite chill to it."

"Och," Duff said, "ye should've told me ye were cold. 'Tis givin' ye my coat I would'a been doin'."

"I couldn't take the coat off the back of the man who saved me life," she insisted. "Anyway, we're almost there."

"Aye, 'tis true."

She moved a little inside the circle of his arm. Her back rested against his broad chest.

"And ye've been sharin' yer warmth wi' me already," she commented as she looked back over her shoulder with a smile.

Duff cleared his throat and glared at Elmer, who was grinning again.

It was the middle of the afternoon, so quite a few people were on the street. A curious crowd gathered around Duff and the others as they rode in. Shouted questions filled the air. Most folks in town had heard about the train robbery and Fiona's kidnapping. The young woman's presence meant the posse had succeeded in rescuing her, but the curious townspeople wanted to know the details. They wanted to know if the posse had recovered the loot, too.

"Marshal Ferrell and the rest o' the lads will be back later," Duff told them. "They can explain everything. Right now, I want to get this young lady someplace where she can rest."

He reined his horse to a stop in front of the Dunn Hotel, Chugwater's best hostelry, where Andrew and Rosanna would be staying. Someone must have run inside to alert them to

Duff's arrival, because both of his cousins emerged from the hotel, coming out onto the front porch in a hurry. Andrew had a neat bandage fastened around his head.

"Fiona!" Rosanna said. "Thank heavens you're safe."

"You *are* unharmed, aren't you?" Andrew asked as he stepped forward to help her down from the horse. Duff had a good grip on her arm, too, so Andrew didn't have to support too much weight.

"I'm fine," Fiona replied. She sobbed a little in what sounded like relief as she threw her arms around Rosanna's neck and hugged the older woman. "I'm so glad that the two of you are all right." She turned to Andrew and hugged him as well. "You're not hurt too bad, are you?"

"This?" Andrew gestured toward the bandage on his head and gave her a cocky grin. "It'll take more than that to dent this thick old skull of mine. Don't worry about me, Fiona."

"Oh, that's such a relief, Mr. MacCallister."

"You should call me . . . No, never mind. Call me anything you like." Andrew turned to Duff, who had also dismounted, along with Elmer and Wang, and extended his hand. "I knew that if anyone could bring this girl back safe and sound, it was you, Duff."

" 'Twas not me alone," Duff said as he clasped his cousin's hand. "I had plenty o' help from these two"—he pointed with a thumb at Elmer and Wang—"and the rest o' the posse."

Fiona stepped up to him and laid a hand on his forearm as she said, "But 'twas ye who came charging in there like a Highland warrior and killed that terrible outlaw. 'Twas ye who saved me from whate'er dreadful fate those men had in store for me. And I can ne'er thank ye enow for that."

She took him by surprise, moving her hand up to the back of his neck and pulling his head down as she came up on her toes. Before he knew what was happening, she had pressed her mouth to his and gave him a long, intense kiss. He wanted to draw away, but the warm, insistent sweetness of her lips seemed to freeze his muscles for several seconds.

He might be a MacCallister, but he was only human, after all.

The crowd in the street in front of the hotel porch demonstrated their approval with a loud, lusty cheer. That noise seemed to break the spell Duff was under. He lifted his head and blinked around at the grinning onlookers.

And one who wasn't grinning, he realized with a shock. Meagan stood there among the citizens of Chugwater. She didn't appear to be upset, but she definitely seemed surprised by the sight of a beautiful, redheaded young woman kissing Duff.

"Meagan!" Duff said as he turned away from Fiona. He stepped down from the porch and tried to go to Meagan, but the crowd was thick and slow to get out of his way. By the time he was able to clear a path, the blonde who meant so much to him was gone.

There weren't many places she could have gone, he told himself. Back to her shop was the most likely. Fiddler's Green, perhaps. He was sure he could find her.

He looked back over his shoulder at Elmer and Wang and said, "I'll be for seein' you fellows later."

"Go on," Elmer said, waving him into motion. "Go find the gal." He chuckled. "Appears to me you got some 'splainin' to do."

Andrew watched with an intent frown on his face as his cousin walked off. He wasn't watching Duff, though. He was looking at Fiona, who stood there with anger and disappointment warring on her face.

That reaction lasted only a second, though, before she controlled it and forced it off her features. As an actor with many years of experience, Andrew recognized that ability when he saw it in others.

Fiona was smiling as she turned to Rosanna, who hugged her

again. "You must be exhausted," Rosanna said. "We have a room for you, right across the hall from our suite. Why don't you come on up, and we'll get you all settled in so you can rest."

"Me bags—" Fiona began.

"They're in your room," Andrew said. "They were brought here from the station yesterday, after the train rolled in."

" 'Tis much obliged I am to ye, sir."

Andrew smiled, shook his head, and said, "Don't thank me. I wasn't much good to anybody for a while after that clout on the head. But my beautiful and efficient sister took charge of everything."

"Someone had to," Rosanna said, "but it wasn't really that much work." She linked arms with Fiona. "Come along, dear." Then, glancing over her shoulder, she added, "Are you coming, Andrew?"

"I'll be back up in a bit," he said. "A small errand to take care of first."

"All right," Rosanna said with a slight frown, "but don't overdo. You're still recuperating, you know. Dr. Urban told you not to tire yourself."

"I don't intend to," Andrew said.

Satisfying my curiosity shouldn't be that *exhausting,* he thought.

Chapter 14

Meagan was in the dress shop, the first place Duff looked for her.

With her back turned toward the door, she was adjusting a dress on a mannequin when Duff came in. She had to know he was there, because the little bell, which hung over the door, had jingled when he opened it. She took her own sweet time about turning around, though.

He was about to say something when she finally turned to face him. She was smiling. He didn't find the expression all that reassuring.

"Duff, I'm so glad you're back safely. I always worry when you ride off to go after badmen like that."

"Aye, they were a pretty bad bunch," he said. "Fewer of them now than there were, though."

"There was a fight?"

"A good one. And to my regret, most o' the varmints got away."

"But not before you rescued Miss Gillespie. The way she told it, you came charging in with guns blazing like some hero in a dime novel."

"I wouldna go so far as t' say that," Duff replied with his usual modesty, even though the description *was* pretty close to what actually had happened. "And Wang was wi' me, which the lass seems to have forgot to mention. Also, Marshal Ferrell and Elmer led the rest o' the posse in the real battle wi' the thievin', murderin' scoundrels."

"While you rescued the pretty Miss Gillespie."

"Well, ye wouldna wanted her to be hurt, would ye?"

"No," Meagan admitted. "I wouldn't have wanted that. I don't blame you for helping her."

"Good."

"And I'm sure she was very grateful to you. That was obvious, over there on the hotel porch. How many times did she express her gratitude to you on the ride back here, Duff?"

Holding back an exasperated sigh, he said, "Nothin' of the sort happened while we were on our way here, and ye can ask Elmer and Wang about that if ye'd like."

"Elmer would lie to protect you."

"Wang wouldn't," Duff pointed out.

"No," she admitted, "he probably wouldn't, even though you saved his life when the two of you first met. Honesty is very important to him."

"And to me as well, and I'm tellin' ye, ye dinna have any reason to be jealous o' Miss Gillespie."

Meagan laughed, came closer to him, and laid her hands on his shoulders.

"All right, Duff," she said. "I believe you. Actually, I believed you all along."

"Ah! Ye were just hoorawin' me, as the cowboys say. 'Tis good to know."

"Well . . . mostly I was just having some fun with you. But I have to admit, it *was* a little disconcerting to walk up and see you with your arms around another woman, kissing her, especially one as young and pretty as Miss Gillespie."

"That's no' quite what happened. *She* was kissin' *me*, and I dinna have my arms around her."

"You most certainly did," Meagan insisted. "You may not be aware of it, but you can ask anyone who was there whether you returned her embrace."

"Well . . . if I did . . . 'twas just an instinctive reaction, ye ken."

"And as for who was kissing whom, that's hard to say when my own lips weren't involved, isn't it?"

"I suppose." This discussion wasn't really an argument, he thought, but whatever it was, he wasn't going to win it, and he knew that. So he might as well not waste any time trying, he told himself as he slipped his brawny arms around Meagan's waist. "The most important thing is tha' ye dinna have any reason to worry."

He would have followed that statement with a kiss, but at that moment, the bell over the door rang again. Duff growled under his breath and glanced over his shoulder to see which of the ladies of Chugwater had picked a very inappropriate time to come dress shopping.

It wasn't a woman. Duff's cousin Andrew stood there. Duff let go of Meagan and took a step back and to the side.

"Sorry to interrupt," Andrew said.

"You're not interrupting anything," Meagan assured him. "Welcome to my shop, Mr. MacCallister."

"Call me Andrew." He smiled. "We *are* practically family, after all."

Duff was about to point out how that wasn't strictly true, at least not yet, but before he could say anything, Meagan asked, "What can I do for you, Andrew? Although I suspect it's Duff you were actually looking for."

"That's true, but I would like to talk to you sometime about making a dress for my sister. Your designs are the equal of anything I've seen in New York or London or Paris."

"It's very kind of you to say so."

"That's not flattery. I'm being honest. Right now, though, I need to talk to Duff."

It occurred to Duff that a gesture to demonstrate how much he trusted Meagan might be in order. He said, "Anything ye have to say to me, Andrew, ye can say in front o' Meagan."

"I'm not sure—"

"Anything at all," Duff insisted.

Andrew still looked dubious, but he said, "All right. I just have a question to ask you. Did you know Fiona in Scotland?"

Duff leaned back a little, almost like he'd been slapped in the face. His eyes widened as his eyebrows rose in surprise.

"Ye mean *Miss Gillespie*? Was I acquainted wi' her in Scotland, *before* I came to America?"

"That's right."

Duff glanced at Meagan and saw sparks of suspicion in her eyes again. She looked very interested in how he was going to answer Andrew's question.

Simple, direct, and honest was the best way. "As far as I ken, the first time I ever laid eyes on the lass was at dawn this morning, when we attacked that outlaw hideout up in the Grabhorns."

"You're sure about that? You didn't know her back in Dunoon?"

Duff was getting a bit irritated now himself at Andrew's insistent questioning. "I tell ye, I dinna ken the lass. Just what she's told me about herself today, and that's blessed little. She dinna seem to want t' talk much."

"Saving her lips for other things, perhaps," Meagan said dryly.

Duff almost responded angrily to that, but he controlled his temper and said, "I suppose I canna claim for absolute certain tha' I never saw her in Dunoon. I dinna ken everyone who lived there. Nor do I recall any Gillespies. But I canna swear that she didn't live there, only that I *did not* know her."

"I believe you," Andrew said, "but I'm puzzled, because according to her, the two of you were great friends back there. Perhaps . . . *more* than friends."

Duff swung toward the door, no longer bothering to conceal his anger.

"I'll get to the bottom o' this," he declared. "I'll have a talk wi' the lass right now—"

Andrew held up a hand to stop him. "If you don't mind, I'd like to speak with her first. Rosanna and I have grown close to Miss Gillespie over the past few weeks, and I want to find out why she told us those things that evidently weren't true."

"Why she lied, you mean."

Andrew shrugged. "Sometimes people have . . . a different view of the truth, let's say. But as you put it, Duff, I'll get to the bottom of it."

Duff thought about what his cousin had said and finally nodded.

"Ye go ahead and talk t' the lass, Andrew, but I want t' hear what ye find out."

"Of course. I'll see you later. Will you be staying in town tonight?"

"Aye. We can meet for dinner at the City Café."

"Agreed," Andrew said with a nod. He nodded to Meagan as well and pinched the brim of his hat. "I trust you'll be joining us for dinner, Miss Parker?"

"We'll see about that," Meagan said.

Andrew's mind was whirling as he returned to the hotel, but not because of his head injury. Other than a mild ache from time to time, that had faded into the background.

No, he was curious about the whole business involving Duff and Fiona. Or rather, *not* involving Duff, to hear him tell it. Andrew knew that his cousin was an honest man. If Duff insisted that he didn't know Fiona Gillespie, then Andrew really did believe him.

Which meant that Fiona had lied, no matter how Andrew had phrased it when he was talking to Duff and Meagan. Andrew wanted to know why. He wanted to know the truth, too.

Only one person could tell him that.

He went into the two-bedroom suite he was sharing with Rosanna and found his sister in the sitting room.

"Is Miss Gillespie resting?"

"You mean *Fiona*? No need to be formal at this point, Andrew. Yes, I suppose she is. She said she was going to lie down. I told her we'd have supper with her later."

"I'm going to eat with Duff and Miss Parker at some place called the City Café."

Rosanna looked a little irritated. "Did you tell them I'd be there, too? You really should consult with me before you commit us to anything."

He could have pointed out that she had promised Fiona they would dine with her without asking him about it, but he didn't. Instead he said, "Something's come up."

"Not something bad, I hope?"

"That depends. I'm sure you recall how puzzled we were when Duff didn't react at all to Fiona's name yesterday when we told him she'd been carried off by train robbers."

"That *was* strange," Rosanna admitted. "I was the one who commented on it to you, you'll recall, after Duff left."

"And a short time ago, downstairs on the porch, did Duff look like a man with an old flame in his arms while she was kissing him?"

Rosanna frowned. "Not really. In fact, I'd say that he looked surprised."

"There's a good reason for that," Andrew said. "He doesn't know Miss Gillespie. He claims he never laid eyes on her before today. Although he did qualify that a little by saying that she might have lived in Dunoon, but he never met her."

Rosanna stared at him for a long moment, then said, "That's impossible. Fiona said they were old friends. *More than old friends.* She spoke as if they might have gotten married if Duff hadn't met Skye McGregor."

"That's the impression I had as well. But according to Duff, it's not true."

Rosanna stood up from the armchair, where she'd been sitting, and straightened her skirt with a jerk.

"One of them has to be mistaken. Perhaps she's just slipped Duff's mind."

"If they were as close as she made it seem? That doesn't sound likely."

"No," Rosanna said. "It doesn't. But if that's the case . . ."

"She lied to us," Andrew finished.

Rosanna started toward the hallway door. "We need to get to the bottom of this."

Her brother chuckled. There wasn't much genuine humor in the sound.

"Duff said the *exact* same thing. Getting to the bottom of things must be a MacCallister quality."

Rosanna ignored that, opened the door, and stepped across the hall to rap softly on the door of Fiona's room.

"Fiona, dear, are you awake?" She knocked again. "We need to talk to you. Fiona?"

The doorknob rattled quietly, then turned. The door swung back a few inches. Fiona peered out at them. Her eyes were a little puffy, and her red hair was slightly disheveled from the pillow.

"What is it?" she asked. "Is it time to have supper already?"

"No, we just need to ask you a few questions," Andrew said.

"Questions?" she repeated. "I don't understand."

"About Duff," Rosanna said, "and the way the two of you knew each other back in Scotland."

Fiona's face turned pink. "I assure ye, ma'am, there wasna ever anything improper—"

"I suppose not," Andrew said, "since Duff claims that he

never knew you at all. That he never met you until today, in fact."

Fiona's gaze went back and forth between brother and sister. Her jaw tightened, and her eyes glittered angrily.

"And ye believe him, don't ye?"

"He's our cousin," Andrew said.

"And he's never lied to us," Rosanna added.

Fiona drew in a deep breath, then stepped back and said, "Come in. I'll not have this conversation standin' in the hall like low-class knaves."

Andrew and Rosanna followed her into the room, which was simply but comfortably furnished. The bedspread was rumpled where she had been lying on it, but the covers hadn't been turned back. She sat on the edge of the bed and nodded toward the room's one armchair and the ladderback chair at the dressing table.

"Sit down, the both o' ye," she said sharply.

"I don't appreciate being given orders," Rosanna said.

"Why don't ye finish that, mum? Ye don't appreciate bein' given orders by the likes o' me, ain't tha' what ye meant?" Fiona covered her face with her hands, but she didn't cry. Her voice was muffled as she went on, " 'Tis sorry I am for snappin' at ye. Ye dinna deserve it, either o' ye. 'Tis nothin' but kind to me ye've been, ever since we met."

"I hope so," Andrew said. "Because of that, I believe we have a right to hear the truth from you."

Fiona lowered her hands and nodded. She was pale but still dry-eyed.

"Aye, ye do have that right. And here's the Lord's honest truth. I've been in love wi' Duff MacCallister since I was naught but a lassie twelve years of age. But Duff ne'er knew I even existed. If he claims now never to ha' laid eyes on me, 'tis likely true, as far as he kens. Because any time his blessed gaze swept o'er me, 'twas like I wasna there. He had no interest, ye see, in a scrawny, scabby-kneed urchin like me."

"You're hardly that now," Rosanna said.

"Perhaps not, but I was in those days. Duff has been in America for several years now, ye ken."

Andrew nodded and said, "That's true. So you were telling us the truth when you said you came from Dunoon, but you didn't actually know Duff while he lived there."

"Nae," she said in a hushed voice. "But that didna keep me from lovin' him, as I just told ye."

Rosanna said, "So you wanted to come to America and find him to . . . what? Tell him how you feel about him?"

"Aye! He's famous back home, ye ken. Everyone in Dunoon has heard o' Duff MacCallister, the glorious native son who went to America and became a rancher and Indian fighter and slayer of outlaws! Why, every time Ian McGregor receives a letter from him, the White Horse Pub is packed to the rafters because everyone wants to hear about Duff's latest adventures."

Andrew nodded slowly. What they were dealing with here, he realized, was a girlish crush combined with a bad case of hero worship. Fiona had inflated Duff in her mind until he was some sort of mythic figure, and she might even sincerely believe at times that the two of them had been sweethearts in the past. The human mind was capable to talking itself into wild dreams that had no connection with reality.

Similar thoughts must have been going through Rosanna's mind, because she said gently, "I think I understand, dear, but just because you wish something were so, that doesn't make it true."

"Is there no truth in the plays ye perform?" Fiona responded. "No truth in the great works of drama?"

"Well, of course, there are some universal truths—" Andrew began.

"And those are all make-believe!" Fiona flung her hands out. "Stories made up by degenerate fellows only interested in their next coin or drink or willin' lass! So, why canna my hopes and dreams have some truth to them, too? Duff MacCallister and I are meant to be together."

Andrew and Rosanna just looked at each other, unable to come up with any response to that.

Fiona sat back and smiled, evidently satisfied with herself.

"Besides," she said, "there be a way I can *make* it come true."

"What do you mean by that?" Andrew asked warily.

"Me old gran had the power," Fiona said. She lifted a finger and held it next to her eye. "The power o' second sight, and the power to make things come true. She was a witch, ye see, and she passed the power on to me. Before I e'er left Scotland, I cast a spell to ensure Duff MacCallister will love me forever!"

Chapter 15

Duff and Meagan were sitting at a table in the City Café, a rather plain name for the nicest eatery in Chugwater. Norman Lambert, the owner, and Quinton Collier, the headwaiter, made sure that anyone dining at the City Café had a fine, satisfying experience.

Duff had no complaints about the surroundings. The table was covered with a snowy cloth of Irish linen, and the silver and crystal of the place setting shone in the soft light. The company was certainly pleasant. He could think of no prettier sight at which to gaze across a table than the sensuous blond beauty of Meagan Parker.

But despite that, his mind was whirling and he felt at a loss as to what he should do next, a very unusual and disconcerting feeling for Duff MacCallister.

"I dinna ken what else to tell ye," he said.

"You've said enough," Meagan assured him. "You've explained the situation over and over, Duff, and made it very plain that you don't know Miss Gillespie and had no . . . romantic reasons . . . for rescuing her."

"Nary a one," Duff declared.

"So what it comes down to is that I either believe you . . . or I don't." Meagan smiled warmly. "And have you ever given me any reason to think that you'd lie to me about something as important as this?"

Duff shook his head. "I hope not."

She reached across the table and rested her hand on his. "You haven't," she assured him. "You've always been very truthful—"

Whatever else she was going to say was a mystery; at that moment, her hand tightened on Duff's and she fell silent. He looked at her and saw that she was gazing past him at the café's entrance. He looked around in that direction himself as Rosanna and Andrew came in, along with the beautiful, red-headed young woman Duff had rescued from the train robbers.

"Did you invite that woman to have dinner with us?" Meagan asked.

"I did not. But there must be a good reason Andrew and Rosanna ha' brought her along."

Duff's natural politeness prompted him to signal Quinton Collier and ask for another chair to be placed at the table, which was round and would accommodate another person. It would be more crowded with five instead of four, though.

Fiona looked nervous and uncomfortable as she came up to the table and stood between Andrew and Rosanna. Andrew took off his hat and said, "Good evening, Meagan. I apologize in advance for any awkwardness, and I realize that it was quite forward of me to ask Miss Gillespie to join us. However, I believe that it might be best to clear the air, and the best way to do that is to bring everything out in the open."

Meagan coolly said, "You're welcome, of course, Miss Gillespie. After everything you've been through, I'm sure you could use a good meal."

"Aye, 'tis true," Fiona agreed. "I'll be thankin' ye for your hospitality, ma'am."

"You don't have to call me *ma'am*," Meagan said with a shake of her head. "I'm not that much older than you."

"I dinna mean to imply—"

"Why don't we all sit down?" Rosanna suggested.

Duff had gotten to his feet when Andrew and the ladies joined them. He sat down now. Andrew held Rosanna's chair and then Fiona's. Collier brought cups of coffee for the newcomers. Duff told him, "We'll be orderin' in a bit, Quinton."

"Of course, Mr. MacCallister," the headwaiter replied.

The table was in a corner, off a bit by itself, so there was at least a semblance of privacy, although diners at nearby tables probably could hear what was going on if they tried.

Duff leaned forward, clasped his hands together in front of him, and frowned. "Miss Gillespie," he began, "I hear that ye've been sayin' some odd things—"

Fiona's chin lifted defiantly. Her earlier air of discomfort and deference vanished.

"Not that odd," she said. "Nothing I said was completely untrue."

"You and I were never friends back in Scotland."

"I considered ye a friend, Mr. MacCallister. Duff. I would ha' done anything for you."

"But that doesna mean that *I* knew *you*."

"No," she replied grudgingly. "I suppose it doesn't."

"Then we're in agreement," Rosanna said, "that you and Duff were never . . . sweethearts."

Fiona still wore a defiant expression, but she shrugged and said, "We were not."

"Good. That's settled, then—"

Fiona interrupted Andrew by saying, "But we *will* be." She leaned forward, stared intently at Duff, and went on: "You and I are meant to be together, Duff MacCallister. I have the second sight, inherited from me ol' gran, and 'tis the future I've seen, a future in which the two of us are in love and growin' old together surrounded by our bairns. 'Twill happen, and there be nothin' ye can do to stop it!"

"Nae!" Duff's hand slapped down on the table. The sharp crack made other diners look around at them—the ones who weren't unobtrusively observing the scene already. "Nae, I tell ye. It willna happen."

A confident smirk appeared on Fiona's face. "The powers tha' I've called upon to do me bidding say that it will."

"Powers?" Duff repeated, looking confused now. "What are ye talkin' about?"

Andrew sighed and said, "Miss Gillespie believes that she has . . . well, occult powers."

"She thinks she's a witch?" Meagan exclaimed.

"Ye've all seen the Scottish play," Fiona said. "Ye ken such things as witches exist in Scotland."

"*Macbeth* is just a play," Andrew said. "Shakespeare made it up."

Fiona crossed her arms and sat back. "Did he now?"

Meagan said, "Let me guess. You have a cauldron, and you stirred up some potion in it and drank it and now you're convinced that magic will make Duff fall in love with you."

"Mock me all ye want. And for your information, me methods are me own, and I've no wish to share them wi' ye."

"Oh, I don't want to know," Meagan said. "You can keep your madness to yourself."

Duff held out both hands and made a conciliatory gesture.

"Let's just all settle down," he said. "We've established that there was nothin' between meself and Miss Gillespie in the past, and since I dinna believe in witchcraft, 'tis no' likely there'll be anything in the future. So there's really nothin' for any of us to squabble about—"

"Ye said *no' likely*," Fiona broke in. "Ye dinna say *'twas impossible*."

"Well, I'll be for sayin' it now, then. You're a comely lass, an' brave enow to come to a new land, but me heart is already spoken for."

"We'll see."

Meagan let out an exasperated "Oh!" and pushed her chair back. "I seem to have lost my appetite," she said. "Andrew, Rosanna, I'm sorry, but I believe I'll have to excuse myself."

"Ye dinna have to go—" Duff began.

"I think it best that I do." Meagan relented enough to smile briefly at him as she stood up. "We'll talk later. Good night."

Duff and Andrew got to their feet as well. Duff wanted to ask her to stay, but he knew she was right. Fiona's stubborn insistence that she and Duff were linked had cast a pall on the evening that wasn't likely to lift.

"I can at least walk ye back to your shop," Duff offered.

"That's not necessary. I'll be fine." Meagan smiled and nodded at Andrew and Rosanna. "Good night."

"Good night, dear," Rosanna said.

"Good night," Andrew added.

Duff didn't know what to say. He stood there feeling foolish as Meagan left the restaurant, and he didn't like it.

When he looked at Fiona, who was sitting there evidently very satisfied with herself, anger welled up inside him. The lass had a right to feel whatever it was she felt, he supposed, but that didn't give her the right to complicate everyone else's life.

" 'Tis an apology I owe ye, Andrew, and ye, Rosanna, since I asked the two o' ye to have supper wi' me, but I must be going."

Fiona said, "You don't have to go anywhere, Duff."

"Aye, I do." He reached for his hat, which he had placed on the floor beside his chair. He settled it on his head and started toward the door. "I'll bid ye all a good evenin'."

From the corner of his eye, he saw Fiona frowning darkly. If she really *was* a witch, whatever was going through her head right now probably included Shakespeare's "eye of newt" and other mystical ingredients.

"Good night, Duff," Andrew called after him.

By the time he reached the street, Meagan was at the end of the block, heading for her dress shop and the living quarters above it. Duff's long legs allowed him to catch up to her before she reached her destination.

"Meagan," he said, "wait up. I told ye I'd walk wi' ye."

"And I told *you* that's not necessary," she said without slowing down or looking at him.

Duff wasn't going to give up. He adjusted his pace to hers and said, "Miss Gillespie admitted flat-out tha' there was never anything between us back in Scotland."

"That doesn't mean there couldn't be something here."

"No, there can't, because I've nae interest in the lass. I canna make it any plainer than that."

Meagan slowed and then stopped, turning to regard Duff solemnly with her arms crossed over her chest.

"And she couldn't have made it any plainer that she intends to win your affections, anyway. She's going to try to take you away from me, Duff." She drew in a deep breath. "Technically, I don't have any real claim on you, you know."

"But ye do. Ye've won my heart, and no one can take it away from you."

Meagan smiled and shook her head. "Things like that are easy to say."

"'Tis the truth!"

"And I know you believe that. But Miss Gillespie is very attractive and, more to the point, very determined." Meagan paused. "Then there's also the matter of her being a witch to consider."

Duff stared at her for a long moment and managed not to burst out laughing. He didn't think she would appreciate it if he did that.

"Ye dinna put any stock in such a ridiculous claim, surely."

"Do I believe in witchcraft?" Meagan shrugged. "Not really.

But since she brought up Shakespeare, remember . . . 'there are more things in heaven and earth,' Duff Tavish MacCallister, 'than are dreamt of in your philosophy.' "

He shook his head. "She can cast all the spells she likes, but 'twill do her no good. She canna change my heart."

"I hope you're right, Duff," Meagan said. She sounded almost sad now. "I really do."

"I am," he replied without hesitation. "Now, will ye be for lettin' me walk ye the rest o' the way home?"

"I suppose so." A little shiver went through her. "Actually, it's a chilly night, and I wouldn't mind having an arm around me."

"And I wouldna mind providin' the arm."

He did so, and they strolled on toward Meagan's shop. Duff hoped they had put this little unpleasantness behind them. He didn't have any idea what Fiona would do, now that he had let her know in no uncertain terms that her trip to America to find him wasn't going to bear the fruit she had hoped it would.

Fiona had been working for Andrew and Rosanna. The best solution was probably if she left with them when Christmas was over and they resumed their acting tour. Duff bore her no ill will, but he didn't want her hanging around Chugwater and annoying Meagan, either.

Nobody wanted a witch for Christmas, even one as pretty as Fiona Gillespie.

Chapter 16

Utah

Falcon MacCallister had faced many determined foes in his life, but he wasn't sure if he'd ever had to deal with one as stubborn and immovable as the one confronting him now.

"Come on," he said with a note of desperation in his voice. "It's simple. All you've got to do is open your mouth and *eat*."

The baby boy he had rescued from the ambushed wagons a couple of days earlier just stared at Falcon for a moment, then screwed up his face and started to cry.

"Dadblast—" Falcon bit back the curses that wanted to spill out of his mouth and set aside the small piece of biscuit he'd been trying to get the baby to eat. He picked up the blanket-wrapped youngster and cuddled him against his chest. The baby's wails so close to his ear made him wince more than the blast of a gun ever had.

"What is it you want?" Falcon had faced all sorts of odds without panicking. He was renowned for his coolness under fire. But his nerves were on the verge of cracking after struggling with this infant for two days. "Can't you just *tell* me what it is you want?"

Well, no, he chided himself. *Of course, the baby can't tell me.*

The boy couldn't talk yet. He probably couldn't walk, either, although Falcon hadn't actually tested that. As best he could guess, the kid was about a year old. Walking and talking weren't that far off, but the boy wasn't there yet.

He patted the baby on the back and tried to calm him. "You shouldn't be too awful cold. I've got that blanket around you, and there's a good fire." A bigger fire than he liked building when he was out on the trail, in fact. A man with enemies tried not to call too much attention to himself. "I reckon it must be that you're hungry, as little as I've gotten you to eat. But I don't figure we're gonna stumble over a wet nurse here in the middle of *nowhere,* Utah!"

When it came to feeding the baby, Falcon had pondered long and hard about what to do, casting his memory back over things he had seen and heard tell of. He had a can of condensed milk in his pack of supplies, so he had opened it, soaked a rag in it, and let the kid suck on that. It had seemed to work for a while, but a child this old needed solid food, too, Falcon decided. He had tried putting one bean at a time in the baby's mouth, but the boy always spit them out.

Tiny pieces of bacon hadn't gone over any better. The baby just made faces at them. Finally Falcon had gotten the idea of soaking little chunks of biscuit in the milk, and that had worked at first, too.

But then the baby started spitting them out. All Falcon could figure was that he was already sick and tired of them.

He sat there beside the fire, jogging the baby up and down a little with one arm, making sounds like a cowboy riding nighthawk and trying to keep a spooky herd from stampeding. A thought came to him, and with a frown, he picked up the piece of biscuit he'd failed with a few minutes earlier, scooped up a couple of beans with his finger, and used his thumb to work them around in the palm of his hand until he had turned them into a sort of mush. He got a glob of it on his thumbnail and slipped it into the baby's open mouth.

The crying stopped. The baby frowned at him, reminding Falcon of an old man pondering the mysteries of a misspent life, then smacked his lips.

Falcon stuck some more of the mush in his mouth. "Well, all right," he said as the baby ate that, too.

He set the baby on the ground, propping him up between some rocks, where he'd been earlier, and quickly mixed up some more of the mush. He added a little milk and bacon grease to it. It reminded him of gravy and didn't look that appetizing, but if the kid would eat it, Falcon didn't care what it looked like.

"There you go," he said. "You just like all your food mixed up together, don't you?"

The baby's only answer was to make a face and let out a long, loud grunt, which made Falcon roll his eyes.

"Lord," he said, "can't I just go back to fighting renegades and badmen?"

The baby's solemn, intent expression turned into a smile. He gurgled. Falcon would have sworn that the little varmint was laughing at him.

The first day on the trail with the infant, Falcon had rigged a sling with a blanket to carry the boy. He could use it either in front or behind him, so he was able to move the baby around and keep from getting worn out by carrying him in one place.

Today he had the kid in front of him, resting on his chest. The baby was awake and staring up into Falcon's face, apparently with great fascination. From time to time, he opened his mouth and let a spit bubble swell out until it got too big and popped. Falcon laughed at the surprised expression on the baby's face every time that happened.

"For somebody who can't talk or do much of anything else,

you're pretty entertaining at times," he told the kid. "I'm gonna have to think of something to call you—"

He stopped short and raised his head, frowning as the sound of gunfire drifted to his ears. The pops and cracks were still a mile or so ahead, he judged. Still frowning, he said, "You reckon we ought to turn around and ride the other way?"

The baby chortled, worked a chubby hand out of the blankets wrapped around him, and waved it around.

"Yeah, you're right, if I'd done that the last time I heard shooting, you'd likely be dead by now. I wouldn't have wanted that. There's no reason to think this is the same sort of deal, though. This could be something that'll just get us in more trouble than we'd want."

The baby belched.

"All right, all right, don't go spitting up your breakfast. We'll have a look-see. But I'm not promising we'll stick our nose in."

This morning, they were riding through a broad, shallow canyon. The steep, rocky walls were about two miles apart. In between were flats with some grass here and there, but mostly rock and sand. A twisting line of thicker vegetation marked the course of a small stream. Country like this wasn't good for much ranching or farming. Indians could live on it—precariously—by hunting. Falcon knew that some prospectors had been lucky enough to find gold, silver, and copper deposits scattered through the region. Mostly, though, it was just empty and ugly.

Falcon tightened his left arm around the baby and kneed his horse to a faster pace. He could still hear the shooting over the hoofbeats. He didn't slow until he was close enough to see a haze of powder smoke floating in the air near the left-hand wall of the canyon.

Falcon reined in, dismounted, and looked around for a place to put the infant. He wasn't going to carry a baby into a gunfight. He found a small, sandy basin in the middle of some rocks and laid the kid there, where he couldn't crawl away. As cold as it was, Falcon knew he didn't need to worry about snakes, spiders, or lizards. They were all either dead or denned up at this time of year.

Satisfied that the baby couldn't go anywhere, Falcon pulled his Winchester from its saddle sheath and stalked on foot toward the gunfire. From the sound of the shots, quite a battle was going on. He figured the combatants would be concentrating on each other, and not likely to notice him sneaking up on them. Still, he took advantage of what cover he could find, mostly rocks and scrubby greasewood bushes, anyway, as he closed in.

He wasn't the only one hunkering behind rocks, he saw as he drew nearer and studied the scene before him. He saw five men who had taken cover behind boulders and were throwing lead toward the dark mouth of a tunnel in the canyon wall. That opening had to be a mine entrance, Falcon thought. It looked too regular to be a natural cave.

Somebody was holed up in there. The five men wanted to root out whoever it was. Falcon had no way of knowing which side was in the right. He didn't like to horn in when he wasn't sure of the game.

During a slight lull in the barrage of shots from the men outside the mine, someone stepped into the open, thrust a rifle at the attackers, and fired. The weapon's heavy boom told Falcon it was a Sharps. The man wielding it ducked back out of sight to reload.

That glimpse had been enough to tell Falcon something about the defender, though. He was tall, whip-lean, and had gray hair and a gray moustache. Clearly an old-timer, but not a feeble one. Not the way he handled that Sharps.

Unfortunately for him, his shot didn't find any of his enemies. It seemed to annoy them, though. They started shooting again, blasting away with even more fervor this time. The echoing gun thunder rebounded from the stone walls and filled the shallow canyon.

At the rate they were shooting, it didn't take long for their guns to empty. The reports died away as they started reloading again.

That gave the defenders inside the mine—there were at least two—an opportunity to strike back. The scrawny, gray old-timer Falcon had seen earlier reappeared and fired that old Sharps again. At the same time, a second man stepped into the tunnel mouth and opened up with a Winchester, spraying lead around the rocks where the attackers had taken cover. Unlike the Sharps, which admittedly packed more of a punch, the Winchester held fifteen or sixteen rounds, and the man using the rifle triggered most of them as fast as he could work the Winchester's lever.

He didn't just fire blindly, either. As Falcon heard the high-pitched scream of bullets ricocheting, he realized that the man with the Winchester had placed his shots where they would wreak the most havoc among the attackers—and maybe, with some luck, hit one or two of the men.

This second defender was a head shorter and a lot rounder than the first man Falcon had seen. He was clean-shaven and his hair was darker, but he carried himself with an air that said he was no spring chicken himself.

One of the slugs he'd sent bouncing around the rocks must have found a target. A man let out a pained howl, followed by a torrent of colorful cursing. The pudgy old fellow with the Winchester howled, too, in triumph, and pumped the rifle over his head like an Indian war chief taunting his foes. He dived back inside the tunnel as a fresh volley from the attackers sought him. Falcon saw bullets splattering on the rock wall next to the tunnel mouth and kicking up dirt and gravel in the opening itself.

Things were different the next time the shooting slacked off.

One of the attackers called to his companions, "We're never gonna get those two old pelicans outta that mine! As long as they've got ammunition, they can hold off an army from in there!"

"What about dynamiting 'em, Craddock?" one of the other men asked. "I got a good arm. I reckon I could toss a stick of dynamite in there from where I am."

The man called Craddock rested on one knee and mulled over the suggestion. Even from where Falcon watched, still unnoticed, he could tell how deeply in thought Craddock was.

"All right," he finally said. "I don't like it. Too big a chance of caving in that tunnel. But I don't see how else we're gonna be able to deal with them. Go get your dynamite, Horley."

Falcon still hadn't made up his mind what he was going to do. The conversation he'd overheard had confirmed that only two men were inside the mine tunnel, and five-to-two odds rankled him, just on general principles.

The fact that the attackers were willing to use dynamite on the two old men in the mine rubbed him the wrong way, too. He still didn't know who any of these men were, or who was in the right in this conflict, but he was starting not to care. His instincts told him that the five men in the rocks were the ones he should oppose.

And if there was anything Falcon MacCallister had learned over the years, it was to trust his gut.

So when one of the men sprinted over to a group of horses picketed about fifty yards away, where the men in the mine couldn't get an angle to shoot at them, Falcon knew what he was going to do. He watched as the man rummaged around in a saddlebag and took several items out of it. He dashed back to the rocks to rejoin his friends, who'd been peppering the mine entrance and making sure the pair of old-timers kept their heads down.

The man who had run to the horses and back fiddled with

the things he had retrieved. Falcon had a pretty good idea that he was attaching a blasting cap and fuse to a stick of dynamite.

That guess was confirmed as the man held the red-wrapped cylinder of explosive out as far away from him as his arm would reach. Falcon saw the length of fuse dangling from the dynamite and estimated that it would burn for at least a minute before setting off the blast. The man used his other hand to snap a match to life and held the flame to the end of the fuse.

As he did, Falcon raised his Winchester to his shoulder and drew a bead. The man holding the dynamite flung his hand in the air, ready to throw the cylinder with its sputtering fuse.

Falcon squeezed the rifle's trigger.

Chapter 17

The Winchester cracked and kicked against Falcon's shoulder. The man about to throw the dynamite yelped as his arm jerked. Falcon's expertly aimed bullet had creased him.

The dynamite, with its fuse still burning, slipped from the man's suddenly nerveless fingers and dropped to the ground, bouncing a little as it landed.

The man wasted a second staring down at it in horror. Then he bent over and tried to pick it up with his other hand. He must have thought he still had time to grab it and fling it toward the mine entrance.

But he fumbled it, and the dynamite skittered away from him. Now he realized he didn't have any more time to spare. He dived after the cylinder and started stomping at the fuse in an attempt to put it out.

While that was going on, the other four men reacted to Falcon's shot. They whirled around, lifting handguns and rifles to return his fire.

From his vantage point, though, they were out in the open, and he had no trouble putting a bullet at the feet of one of the men, close enough to kick dust on his boots and make him hop wildly.

"Drop the guns," Falcon shouted, "or the next shot drills somebody!"

By this time, the would-be dynamiter had succeeded in putting out the fuse before the blast went off. He slumped to a sitting position on the ground with his back propped against the rock he'd been using for cover. He clutched his wounded arm with his other hand. Falcon saw that from the corner of his eye and figured the man was no longer an immediate threat.

The same couldn't be said of his four companions. They hesitated after Falcon's warning shot, but not for long. Then they opened up on him, doubtless figuring they had him outnumbered and outgunned.

They'd called the tune and opened the ball, he told himself. He fired again, and this time one of the men yelled and went down as the slug drilled through his thigh. Falcon shifted his aim as he worked the rifle's lever. Bullets whistled around him and smacked into the rock behind which he knelt, but he remained cool as he squeezed the trigger again. This bullet broke another man's arm.

The other two attackers scattered to hunt for better cover. In doing so, they accidentally gave the men in the mine clear shots at them. The Sharps boomed again. One of the attackers stumbled, flung his arms out at the sides, and arched his back as the heavy slug punched into his body and tore all the way through to create a fist-sized hole as it blew out the front. The man dropped his gun and pitched forward. He caught himself on hands and knees and, somehow still alive, tried to push back to his feet.

That was enough for the lone man who hadn't been hit yet. He yelled, "Let's get out of here!"

The first man Falcon had shot and the other one with a wounded arm flanked the man with the bullet-ripped thigh and hauled him upright. They kept supporting him as they all hustled toward the horses. The uninjured man helped the one who'd been shot through the body with the Sharps. Falcon had stopped firing when it was obvious the threat was over, but the man in the mine with the Winchester hurried the attackers on their way by peppering the air and ground around them with slugs.

Falcon didn't stand up until all the men were mounted and galloping off down the canyon. The most seriously injured of the bunch was slumped forward in his saddle, over his horse's neck. Falcon didn't think the man would last long, ventilated the way he was.

He hadn't been shooting to kill, since he still didn't know exactly what was going on here. Clearly, the men in the mine didn't feel the same way. Because they'd been the ones under attack, he couldn't blame them for that. But he hoped he hadn't gotten himself neck-deep in more trouble than he'd bargained for.

He still had that baby to look after.

With that thought in his mind, he hurried back to the little basin in the rocks, where he'd left the boy. He blew out a relieved breath when he saw that the baby was lying there sleeping peacefully.

"Hey, mister!" somebody yelled. "You still out there?"

That would be one of the men from the mine. Falcon hunkered on his heels for a moment beside the baby, studying him just to make sure everything was all right. He watched long enough to see the blanket steadily rising and falling in time with the baby's breathing.

Then, satisfied, he straightened, turned, and strode back toward the tunnel.

"Hello, the mine!" he called. Even though he had helped the two men holed up there, he was careful about approaching. He still didn't know who they were or what had led to the fight.

"Come on in, mister." That was a different voice, belonging to the second man. "We're mighty obliged to you."

"And I'd be obliged to you fellas if you'd step out where I

can get a look at you," Falcon said as he came to a stop beside one of the boulders the attackers had used for cover. He saw a splash of blood on the ground nearby.

A laugh came from the mine. "I don't blame you for being cautious, friend," the first man said. "Out here in the middle of nowhere, if a man doesn't keep his wits about him, he sometimes doesn't live very long. Come on, Twister."

The two of them walked out of the tunnel mouth. Seeing them in the open like that, Falcon was struck by how tall and scrawny one of them was, and how short and roly-poly the other one was. He was close enough to see that his guess about their ages was correct. They were in their late fifties or early sixties, he estimated. Both had deep brown, weathered faces that testified to many years spent out in the elements.

Their rough canvas work clothes, along with everything else about them, told Falcon that they were prospectors. Desert rats—although this wasn't completely desert country up here.

The slender one had the Sharps tucked under his arm. The fat one carried the Winchester, but with the barrel pointing toward the ground. Falcon didn't sense any threat from them. He moved farther out into the open himself. They all came to a stop with twenty feet separating Falcon from the two men.

"I hope you're not another claim jumper who helped us run off those varmints just so you can steal our mine for yourself," the scrawny man said. He wore what seemed to be a habitually dour expression.

"Is that what they were?" Falcon asked. "Claim jumpers?"

"That's all we can figure," the fat man said. "We never saw 'em before, and as you can see, we don't have a whole heap of a lot that'd interest plain thieves."

He waved a pudgy hand to indicate their camp near the tunnel entrance. They had an old patched tent, a few supplies, a pair of swaybacked saddle horses, and a couple of pack mules that had seen better days.

"Is this claim worth jumping?" Falcon said.

The scrawny prospector narrowed his gimlet eyes even more. "That ain't the kind of question a gentleman usually asks."

"Since this fella risked taking a bullet for us," the fat one said, "I reckon we can let that pass, Hardpan." He grinned at Falcon. "The answer is kind of still open to debate, but it ain't lookin' too promising."

The one called Hardpan blew out a disgusted-sounding breath.

"I'm Twister McCoy," the fat prospector went on. "This grumbler is Hardpan Hawkins."

"Falcon MacCallister," Falcon introduced himself.

The name drew looks of surprised recognition from both men. "The famous gunfighter?" Hardpan said.

"*Notorious* might be a better word," Falcon answered with a slight smile.

"I don't know," Twister said. "From everything I've heard about you, Mr. MacCallister, you're usually on the right side of any fight you get into. You sure were here. I figure those hombres would've killed us. They could've kept us bottled up in there and starved us to death, if nothing else."

"Although that would have taken a whole heap longer for some of us," Hardpan added dryly.

Falcon said, "They didn't have the patience for that. They were about to blast you out with dynamite."

The eyes of both prospectors widened. Twister gulped and repeated, "*Dynamite?*"

"Yep. One of them was about to fling a stick of it in the tunnel when I creased his arm and made him drop it." Falcon pointed. "Fact is, it's still lying right over there, if you don't believe me."

"Oh, we believe you, we believe you," Hardpan muttered.

Twister walked over to the other rock, where the dynamite, with its fuse burned mostly away, was where the attacker had dropped it. He poked at it with the butt of his rifle.

"Stop that," Hardpan snapped. "After we came through all that shooting, you want to blow us up now?"

"I'm not gonna blow us up," Twister said. "The blasting cap's got to go off to set off the dynamite. You know that. It's not like soup."

Falcon knew that *soup* was what some men who worked with explosives called nitroglycerine, which was more unstable than dynamite. But dynamite wasn't anything to mess around with, either. He was glad when Twister left the cylinder alone and walked back over to him and Hardpan.

"You're welcome to share our fire if you want," Hardpan said. "We've got coffee and some salt pork—"

He stopped short as an eerie wailing sound came to their ears.

"What in blazes is that?" Twister exclaimed.

"Some kind of hurt animal?" Hardpan guessed.

"Not exactly," Falcon said. "More like a hungry animal, unless I miss my guess. I'll be back in a minute."

He felt relatively safe in turning his back on the two old-timers, although he was ready to spin around and bring up the Winchester if either of them made a sudden move.

Nothing of the sort happened. He found the baby awake and crying. He reloaded the rifle and slid it back into the saddle boot.

"Come on, varmint," Falcon said as he picked up the baby, cradled him in his left arm, and headed back toward the mine tunnel. Hardpan and Twister watched him with surprised stares as he approached.

"That's a baby, Mr. MacCallister!" Twister said.

"You think so?" Hardpan asked. "It's been so long since we've spent much time around civilized folks, I wasn't sure."

"Where'd you get a baby, Mr. MacCallister?" Twister asked.

"Don't go asking a man where babies come from," Hardpan told him. "You're just betraying your own ignorance."

"I know where babies come from," Twister protested. "I'm just askin' where that particular one came from, and how Mr. MacCallister wound up with it. Is he yours, Mr. MacCallister?"

"Call me *Falcon*," he stressed. "And if you mean, am I this little one's pa, the answer is *no*. We just wound up traveling together a few days ago."

Quickly Falcon explained how he had come upon the two wagons being attacked by the Ute war party, the only survivor from the settlers being the infant he now cradled against his chest.

"Then you don't even know the little tyke's name?" Twister asked.

"Nope. I thought maybe I could figure it out from the family Bibles I found, but no such luck. I reckon whichever family he belonged to, they hadn't gotten down to adding him to the book."

Hardpan said, "Well, what in the world are you gonna do with him? No offense, but I don't see how a man like you can carry a baby around with him all the time."

Falcon laughed. "None taken. You're absolutely right. This little fella needs a home and a family, and I'm going to try to find one for him. I'm on my way to Wyoming to see my cousin and spend Christmas with him. His ranch isn't far from a nice settlement, and I'm hoping somebody there will want to take the baby in."

Twister nodded and said, "That sounds like a pretty good plan. In the meantime, you said he was hungry . . . ?"

"That's what it sounded like when he was crying. He's calmed down now, but I figure he'll start up again any time. I've been feeding him mush made from biscuits and milk and bacon grease—"

"We should be able to do better than that," Hardpan said. "I'll cook some flapjacks, maybe mash up a piece of one with some molasses."

"Sounds good," Falcon said. "I'm obliged to you."

"Not as much as we are to you," Twister said. He shuddered. "Dynamite."

Chapter 18

The flapjacks that Hardpan cooked over the campfire turned out surprisingly light and fluffy. Falcon put a piece of one in a tin cup, added canned milk and molasses, and mushed up the mixture with a spoon. The baby ate the result without any hesitation, sucking it down greedily.

Twister tore off another piece of flapjack and pressed it into the baby's right hand. The kid closed his fingers around it, waved the hand in the air for a moment, and then crammed the bit of flapjack into his mouth, where he gummed it enthusiastically.

"Youngsters this age are getting to the point where they like to try feeding themselves," Twister said. "He'd probably been doing that some already, and when you started spoon-feeding him all the time, he didn't like it. That's probably one reason he was cranky. Mostly, it's his teeth coming in that had put a bur under his saddle, though."

Hardpan stared at his partner and asked, "Where in blazes did you learn so much about babies and their eating habits?"

"I wasn't always a desert rat, you know."

"Yeah, but don't try to tell me you had a wife and kids of your own, a long time ago. I know that ain't true."

Twister shrugged beefy shoulders. "Well, I never been hitched, that's right enough. But I had a sister who was married, back in West by God Virginia, and she had young'uns. I was around them some. Enough to pick up a few things."

Hardpan just snorted.

Falcon had been enjoying a cup of coffee from the prospectors' battered old pot and a tin plate of flapjacks and salt pork. He swallowed another sip of coffee and asked, "How'd you two wind up riding together?"

Questions like that were considered unwarranted prying, unless you'd already become friends with the folks you were talking to. Considering that he had fought, if not side by side, at least against the same enemy as these two old-timers, Falcon didn't think he was out of line.

"We met back in St. Louis . . . what was it, Hardpan? Nigh on to forty years ago?"

"Yeah, I guess."

Falcon had figured out already that Twister was the more garrulous of the duo. He went on, "We were working as bull-whackers for a freight line there. Made a bunch of trips back and forth on the Santa Fe Trail. We got to be friends, which'll happen if you're fightin' Indians and renegades together."

"Wild times," Hardpan said.

"Yeah, but there was a lot good about them, too. And we saw a lot of the country."

"Something to be said for that," Falcon agreed.

"The freight line went bust," Twister continued, "so we had to find new jobs. We'd already said we'd stick together for a while, so we tried our luck at some other things. I drove a stagecoach for a while"—Twister poked a thumb at his friend—"and Hardpan here rode shotgun for me. We clerked in stores for a while—"

"Hated it," Hardpan interjected with a shake of his head.

"Yeah, we never cared much for bein' shut up inside. After the war, which we stayed out of, by the way, we worked on the railroad for a while when the Union Pacific was laying track across Kansas. There was another fella in the crew whose head was full of dreams about finding gold and making a fortune, and I reckon some of that rubbed off on us, because we saved up our money until we could afford a prospectin' outfit and took off to find a gold mine."

"You ever strike it rich?" Falcon asked.

Hardpan let out another disgusted snort, but Twister said, "We found some color here and there. Never enough to make us rich, and every vein we found played out too quick, but we made enough to buy more supplies and head out again. Been doin' that for quite a while now." A smile wreathed his round face. "I reckon you could say the years sorta got away from us. It's hard work, but we enjoy it."

Falcon nodded. "A man can count himself lucky if he finds something he enjoys doing, especially if it pays him to do it."

"It could pay better," Hardpan said.

The baby started fussing a little. Falcon picked him up and jogged him up and down until a loud belch came from him. Twister laughed.

"Yep, I remember my sister's kids doin' that. Sometimes they'd spit up on your shoulder, too."

"So I've learned," Falcon said.

The baby dozed off while leaning against him. Falcon waited until he was sure the infant was good and asleep, then laid him down carefully in a nest of blankets. He reached for his cup to finish off the coffee.

"You say you're—" Hardpan began, but Twister motioned for him to lower his voice.

"Once you've got a baby asleep, you don't want to wake 'em up again," he said quietly. "That's something else I learned."

"Fine, fine," Hardpan said, then resumed his question at a lower volume. "You're headed for Wyoming, you said?"

"That's right," Falcon replied. "A ranch called Sky Meadow, near the town of Chugwater."

"Never heard of it, but you're right, you'll more likely find a home for that kid in a place like that. Nobody out here who would take him in." Hardpan downed more of his coffee. "It's early enough you could make a few more miles in that direction."

"Hardpan!" Twister said. "Are you trying to run off our guests?"

"You didn't let me finish, blast it. What I was trying to say is, you could make a few more miles, but what's the point? Won't make any difference in the long run. You're welcome to stay here tonight."

Twister nodded in approval and said, "That's being more hospitable."

"That's generous of you," Falcon began.

"Not really," Hardpan said. "As shot up as they were, I don't think it's likely that bunch of claim jumpers will double back and hit us again . . . but I can't guarantee that won't happen. If it does, we'll stand a better chance with a gent like you siding us, Falcon."

"That's true," Twister admitted. "I reckon I'll sleep better tonight if you're around."

Falcon considered, then said, "If I stick around, you'll cook up another mess of those flapjacks in the morning?"

A rare smile appeared on Hardpan's narrow face. "I don't see why not."

"Then you've got a deal. The kid and I . . . and my horse . . . could use a little extra rest, I expect."

"You're going to have to come up with something to call him besides *the kid*," Twister said.

"I'm not sure I want to give him a name if he's going to be

raised by somebody else. Seems like they'd have the right to decide what he's called."

"That's good thinking, I guess," Twister said. "How much longer do you think it'll take you to reach Chugwater?"

"Four or five days, I'd say, if the weather holds."

"I suppose that's not too long to keep calling him that. It's not like he can answer to it, either way."

Falcon, Hardpan, and Twister all agreed that it would be a good idea to take turns standing guard during the night. The old-timers had been jumped once. It could happen again.

Nothing unusual occurred, though. The night passed peacefully, and the next morning dawned cold and cloudy. Falcon studied the clouds and sniffed the air and concluded that the sky was just overcast. No rain or snow was in the cards for today.

The baby was still sound asleep in his blanket nest. Falcon went to check on his horse, and when he returned, he found Hardpan and Twister deep in an apparently earnest conversation. Coffee was boiling in the pot, but Hardpan hadn't started cooking breakfast yet.

They broke up their palaver, and Twister said, "Hardpan and I have been thinking about something, Falcon."

"What's that?"

Twister jerked a thumb toward the tunnel mouth. "You've been too polite to ask us specifically how these diggin's are turning out for us, but we don't mind telling you ... We haven't found a speck of color in there."

"It's a promising location," Hardpan put in, "but that doesn't mean there's actually any gold."

Falcon frowned and said, "If you haven't found any gold, why do you think those hombres were trying to jump your claim?"

"They don't know that we haven't found anything," Twister

said. "And like Hardpan just told you, all the signs say there *could* be gold here. Maybe they figured we'd already done the hard work of getting the tunnel started, and they could move in and extend it until they hit a vein, if that hadn't happened already."

Falcon considered that theory, then shrugged, not really committing to accepting it, one way or the other.

"Anyway," Hardpan said, "here's the point. We're just about ready to give up on this hole and try our luck somewhere else. When you've been at it as long as we have, you learn to trust your instincts when they tell you you're just wasting your time."

Falcon understood that. He trusted his instincts all the time, and they seldom, if ever, steered him wrong.

"Where are you thinking about going?" he asked.

"Actually, we've already been talking about that," Hardpan said.

"We thought we'd head for Wyoming," Twister said. "And since you're already heading in that direction . . ."

Falcon lifted his eyebrows. "You want to ride with me and the kid?"

"Seems like a good idea. A bigger group always has a better chance than a smaller one. You never can tell, there might be some more of those Ute war parties around."

Twister had a point. Falcon knew they weren't completely out of danger from the hostiles, especially if the bodies of those he had killed back at the wagons had been discovered.

"There are outlaws in these parts, too," Twister went on. "It'd just be safer to travel together."

Safer for you two old-timers, Falcon thought. They were worried that they would encounter more trouble, and they'd stand a better chance of surviving with a gun-handy hombre like Falcon MacCallister on their side.

Not that they were defenseless. Both men still had some of

the bark left on them. In fact, Hardpan had inflicted the only fatal injury to the claim jumpers the day before—assuming the man with the Sharps slug through his body had died. Falcon didn't believe any other outcome was possible with a wound like that.

The three of them together would make a formidable trio. And to tell the truth, Falcon had worried about what would happen to the baby if his luck ran out. He didn't expect that, but a man had to be prepared for it.

"There's no mining around Chugwater, as far as I know," he cautioned them. "It's ranching country."

"Is it in the south part of the territory?" Hardpan asked.

"Yeah, between Cheyenne and Fort Laramie."

Twister said, "We've heard rumors of gold strikes farther north in the mountains. We were already thinking about checking them out before you ever came along, Falcon."

Hardpan nodded. "That's true."

"Well, shoot, it's a free country," Falcon said. "I can't very well tell you that you *can't* go to Wyoming. And it'd be downright unfriendly of me to say we can't ride together." He nodded. "Partners, then, the four of us, until we get to Chugwater."

"Partners," Hardpan agreed.

"Including the kid," Twister added with a grin. "But if we have to decide anything, he doesn't get a vote."

"I don't know about that," Falcon said. "He generally votes at the top of his lungs."

They didn't get in any hurry about breaking camp. The sun had been up for an hour before they rode away from the now-abandoned mine tunnel. Somebody else might come along, a year from now or ten years from now, and try to do something with it, but it wasn't Hardpan and Twister's concern anymore.

The canyon ran generally northward. They followed it until it petered out into some flats that afternoon. They turned in a more northeasterly direction then.

The baby fussed some, ate some, slept some. Falcon had to stop and change him several times during the day. Every time they came to a creek, he washed out some of the thick pieces of cloth he had salvaged from one of the wagons to use as make-shift diapers. He had managed to stay ahead of the infant's digestive system so far, but he didn't know how long that would last.

It brought a smile to his face when he thought about how he usually kept track of how many bullets he had left, not how many clean diapers. Some of the badmen he had faced in the past would get a real horselaugh out of his current situation. But it was at least partially of his own doing, so he couldn't complain.

The mountains and foothills fell behind them as they rode across rolling plains. The highest elevation around appeared to be a line of bluffs that jutted up about four hundred yards to their right. Falcon kept an eye on the bluffs, more out of habit and not because he actually expected anyone to be lurking over there.

But late that afternoon, when he caught a glimpse of movement at the edge of the bluff, he stiffened in the saddle. An instant later, he saw a spurt of powder smoke and heard the distant report of a shot.

"Down!" he called to Hardpan and Twister, but the warning came too late. Twister grunted as his hat flew off his head. He toppled out of the saddle and crashed to the ground.

Chapter 19

Normally if he'd been bushwhacked, Falcon would have kicked his feet free of the stirrups, grabbed his Winchester, and dived off his horse to hunt for cover, unless he knew there was some shelter he could reach quickly while mounted.

With the baby resting in the sling against his chest, Falcon couldn't do that. He leaned forward, hunched protectively over the infant, and jabbed his boot heels into the horse's flanks, sending it lunging forward in a gallop.

He wished he knew how bad Twister was hit, but he didn't have time to check on the old-timer.

"Head for those trees!" he called to Hardpan.

At this time of year, the trees in a clump about a hundred yards ahead of them were bare, so they wouldn't offer much concealment. The twisted trunks wouldn't provide much actual protection, either. But they were the closest cover of any kind.

Falcon didn't hear Hardpan's horse following him. He twisted his neck to look back. Hardpan's mount had spooked and was dancing around not far from where Twister had fallen. Hardpan fought to bring the animal under control, and when he did, he jerked the Sharps to his shoulder and fired at the bluff.

Falcon didn't think Hardpan would hit anything, although the Sharps would carry that far easily. But maybe the old-timer would keep the bushwhacker distracted enough to give Falcon a chance to get to cover with the baby.

From the corner of his eye as he turned his head to face front again, Falcon caught a glimpse of Twister scrambling to his feet. If he was still that spry, maybe he wasn't wounded too bad. Falcon hoped that was the case.

He hauled back on the reins as his horse thundered up to the trees. With his left arm clamping the kid firmly to his chest, he swung down, almost before the horse stopped moving. Picking out the largest of the trees, he laid the baby on the ground at the base of the trunk, positioning the infant so the tree was between him and the ambusher on the bluff.

With his young charge as secure as Falcon could make him under the circumstances, he ran back to his horse and yanked his rifle from its scabbard. He picked out another tree—which didn't come close to shielding his tall, broad-shouldered frame—and leaned against it as he shouldered the rifle.

Out in the open, Twister was trying to catch his horse, but the animal was too spooked and Twister wasn't fast enough.

"Come on, you fool!" Hardpan shouted at him as he extended a hand.

"Your horse can't carry both of us!" Twister replied. He yelped and jumped as a bullet fired from the bluff kicked up dirt not far from his feet.

The puff of smoke from that shot gave Falcon a target. He cranked off three swift rounds and hoped that would be enough to make the son of a buck keep his head down for a minute.

Twister's most recent brush with death must have made him decide to risk riding double with Hardpan, after all. He reached up and clasped wrists with his partner. Hardpan grunted so loudly as he hauled Twister up on the horse behind him that Falcon was able to hear it from where he was. Hardpan wheeled his mount. The horse galloped valiantly toward the trees with the double load on its swayed back.

Another shot from the bluff struck the ground just behind the horse. Falcon threw more lead up there. A moment later, the horse pounded behind the trees. The two old-timers weren't safe, but at least they weren't completely exposed to the bushwhacker's fire anymore.

As far as Falcon could tell, only one rifleman was up there. The lone claim jumper who hadn't been wounded? That was possible, but he wasn't sure it made sense. Hardpan and Twister had abandoned those diggings. If stealing the claim was the goal, nobody had a reason anymore to kill them.

Such things could be hashed out later. Right now, Falcon took advantage of the lull in the shooting to thumb several fresh cartridges through his Winchester's loading gate.

The two old-timers ran up and took positions behind other trees. Hardpan was skinny enough to do that, but like Falcon, Twister stuck out quite a bit. He didn't have his rifle, either. It was still in its sheath attached to his saddle. His horse had run off a ways and then stopped to mill around aimlessly.

Hardpan had his Sharps, though, and he loaded it quickly and efficiently with the skill born of long practice.

Falcon called over to Twister, "I thought you were dead, the way you fell off that horse!"

"Did you see what that varmint did to my hat? A perfectly good hat! When I felt that bullet part my hair, I guess I jumped some. I never did sit a saddle that good."

"You weren't hit?"

"Nope." Twister rubbed his backside. "These bones of mine are too old to be taking jolts like the one I got when I landed, though. I'm gonna be mighty stiff and sore in the morning!"

"Better than being mighty dead in the morning," Hardpan growled.

"Yeah, I can't argue with that." Twister cocked his head to the side. "Hey, I don't hear any more shooting from that bluff."

Neither did Falcon, but when he listened intently, he thought he picked up a faint rataplan of hoofbeats, as if someone were riding away quickly.

"I think maybe that bushwhacker has lit a shuck," he said. "You think he was one of those claim jumpers?"

"No chance," Hardpan replied without hesitating. "I caught a glimpse of him behind the rock where he was hidin'. That was an Injun shooting at us. Maybe a friend or relative of one of those Utes you told us you killed, Falcon. He'd have a grudge against you, and he could've tracked you this far."

Falcon frowned. He supposed it was possible, but the idea seemed far-fetched to him—just like the chance of the bushwhacker being one of the claim jumpers who had attacked the old-timers' camp. Neither of those explanations totally satisfied him.

Of course, it was possible the man on the bluff had intended to shoot all of them and steal everything they owned. The answer could be that simple. Hardpan had seemed convinced that he had seen an Indian—he didn't have any reason to lie about that, as far as Falcon could see—but he could have been wrong.

And the most important thing was that they were all still alive—including the baby, who had woken up and started crying again.

"I know how you feel, little one," Twister said. "I sorta feel like bawling my own self."

They waited awhile before leaving, just in case the bushwhacker was trying to trick them and lure them back out into the open. Finally, though, Falcon whistled for his horse, mounted up, and went to fetch Twister's horse.

After that, Falcon had changed the baby's diaper and given him a piece of flapjack left over from breakfast that morning, so he'd have something to gum.

With those vital chores taken care of, they all rode northeast again. Falcon would have liked to get farther away from that bluff, but the country to their left had turned into rough, copper-colored breaks that would have slowed them down considerably and been very hard on the horses. Their best route was to follow this bench that butted up against the rise.

All three men kept a wary eye on the bluff, but didn't see any more signs of trouble. Late in the day, the slope gradually began dropping off. By the time they made camp for the night, the bluff had fallen behind them. Falcon was grateful for that. They might come across other places that would be good for an ambush—almost certainly would, in fact—but at least they didn't have to worry about this one anymore.

While Hardpan was preparing supper that night, after they had made camp, the scrawny old-timer commented, "We're getting a mite low on supplies. In another few days, we're liable to run out of flour, beans, and coffee."

"Not coffee!" Twister said, utterly aghast.

"Yep, I'm afraid so."

"That's including my supplies?" Falcon asked. They had pooled everything they had.

"Yeah. I'm sure you planned on replenishing yours along the way. Do you know of a town around here?"

Falcon thought about it, absentmindedly tickling the baby under the chin as he did so. "I've heard tell of a settlement in this area called Carlsburg. I haven't been there, though, and don't know exactly where it is. We might miss it by a few miles and ride right past it."

"Well, we'd better find it," Hardpan said, "or else we're liable to get pretty hungry. I don't want to listen to a lot of crying and blubbering." He looked at Twister. "The baby's liable to get a mite fussy, too."

"Hardy-har-har," Twister said.

"We'll find it," Falcon said confidently. "In fact, I'll ride on ahead and scout around some tomorrow."

"No, we'd better stick together," Hardpan said. "Just in case somebody jumps us again."

Falcon kept his face impassive in the firelight. He didn't care much for anybody giving him orders, which was why he never worked for the army as a scout for too long at a time.

But he just nodded in agreement with what Hardpan said, because he was curious. The old-timer's quick response to Falcon's suggestion that they split up had him curious. It was almost like Hardpan *expected* another attack.

That was what Falcon had wanted to find out in the first place, when he'd made the suggestion that he himself knew wasn't a very good idea. Something else was going on here. Hardpan—and maybe Twister, too—was keeping a secret from him. Secrets had a way of putting folks in danger. Falcon didn't like that.

But he would play along for now, he decided, because that might be the fastest way to get to the truth.

Good fortune was with them, or at least it appeared so. Around midday the next day, Falcon pointed to several columns of white smoke rising into the air ahead of them and said, "Those are coming from different chimneys. That's got to be a settlement, probably Carlsburg."

"Thank goodness for that," Twister said. "We might be able to get by without flour and beans, but not coffee."

"If there's a store," Hardpan said, "I imagine you'll want to see if they have any licorice, too."

Twister grinned. "Nothing wrong with a little treat now and then. Thought I might see if I could find something for the younker, too."

A quarter of an hour later, they rode up to a bridge that

spanned a fast-flowing creek. A sign nailed to a bridge post read: CARLSBURG POP 157 OTTO KRAMER MAYOR.

"Looks like you were right," Twister said to Falcon. "This is Carlsburg, all right."

Hardpan grunted and said, "They ought to have called it Kramerville. Look at those businesses."

Falcon had already noticed that several of the buildings in town had signs that bore the same name. He saw Kramer's Livery Stable, Kramer's Blacksmith Shop, and Kramer's Mercantile. It was no surprise that what looked like the only saloon in town was also owned and operated by the mayor, but at least the name of the place varied slightly. The sign along the awning over the boardwalk of the saloon read: KRAMER'S ACE-HIGH SALOON.

What was surprising was the sight of the young blond woman who slapped the batwings aside and burst out of the saloon, screaming in fear.

Chapter 20

Chugwater

Duff MacCallister was faced by a dilemma. Several days had passed since the train robbery and the posse's subsequent rescue of Fiona Gillespie and recovery of the stolen loot. Dr. Urban had pronounced Andrew MacCallister sufficiently recovered from his head injury—there had been no complications, thank goodness—that he could travel again.

Which meant that Andrew and Rosanna could leave the hotel and come out to Sky Meadow to stay, as had been their intention all along.

But Fiona also had a room at the hotel and, technically, was still working for Andrew and Rosanna. There was room in the ranch house for her, but Duff didn't know how Meagan would feel about him and Fiona living under the same roof, even as a temporary arrangement.

Normally, Duff was a decisive man. He didn't like feeling uncertain about anything.

So as he rode into Chugwater on this cool, clear morning, he was determined to settle things, one way or another.

When he walked into the hotel lobby, he spotted his cousin Andrew, reading a book, sitting in one of the big armchairs next to a potted plant. Andrew saw Duff as well and greeted him with a smile.

"Good morning, cousin," Andrew said. "What brings you to Chugwater today?"

"Why, I came to see ye and Rosanna, of course," Duff replied. " 'Twas the reason ye came to Wyoming in the first place, was it not, so ye could spend time wi' your old cousin Duff?"

"You're hardly old," Andrew said with a chuckle, then turned more serious. "Yes, indeed, that was the reason for the trip, which makes me feel rather bad about a new development."

"A *new development*? What is it now, Andrew?"

Andrew held up the book he'd been reading. He had a finger stuck in the slim, leather-bound volume to hold his place.

"A Christmas Carol."

Duff frowned and said, "Aye. I've read it. 'Tis a good little story. Me own tastes run more toward some o' Dickens's other works tha' have a wee bit more heft to them, but t' each his own."

"I read it numerous times over the years and started rereading it yesterday. That was when an idea occurred to me. I spent the rest of the day and a good part of the night writing a stage adaptation of the story. I was just looking over the original this morning to make sure I hadn't missed anything I need to include."

"A stage adaptation, ye say? Ye've turned it into a play?"

"That's right."

"Have'na people already done that?"

Andrew waved that away. "Of course. The book was such a success when it came out that various impresarios turned it into a stage production almost right away. But each adaptation is a bit different, of course, depending on who's writing it." He smiled. "I'm vain enough to believe that my version is one of the best, if not *the* best."

"And it may well be," Duff agreed. "Are ye going to perform it when ye go back out on tour?"

Andrew shook his head. "No, that will be after Christmas. The time to perform it is *now*."

"Wait," Duff said. "You're leavin' Chugwater? Going back to New York or somewhere right now?"

"Of course not! We came here to spend the holiday with you. Anyway, there wouldn't be anywhere near enough time to mount a professional production. That's why I intend to put on the performance right here in Chugwater."

Duff had to stare at his cousin for several seconds before saying, "You're going to put on a play . . . a production of *A Christmas Carol* . . . here in Chugwater? Where there be no real actors, save you and Rosanna?"

"But there are plenty of townspeople to serve as cast, crew, and audience," Andrew said. "I do intend to mount a production back East for next Christmas season, but performing it here will be valuable experience and let me know how well the adaptation works. It may be that I need to make some changes to what I've written, and the only real way to find that out is to see how it plays."

"Cousin, I think you're mad."

Andrew smiled. "It's often said of performers that they're born with the gift of madness."

"Well, ye got it, that's for certain." Duff's shoulders rose and fell. "But if tha' be wha' ye want to do, then ye should go ahead wi' it. I'll no' stand in your way."

"I appreciate that," Andrew said. "I'll admit, my biggest concern was that your feelings would be hurt. You see, if I'm going to do this, it'll be necessary for Rosanna and me to remain here at the hotel, instead of staying at Sky Meadow. It simply wouldn't be practical for us to ride back and forth to town from the ranch every day, in order to do the work that needs to be done."

"Aye, I can understand that."

The wheels of Duff's brain turned rapidly. He could see how this unexpected turn of events could be to his benefit. If Andrew and Rosanna were staying here at the hotel, then Fiona would be, too. The question of whether or not he should invite her to stay at the ranch had been settled without him having to make the decision.

"Ye dinna have to worry," he went on. "'Tis sure I am tha' I'll still be seein' quite a bit o' ye and Rosanna."

"Oh, I'm sure you will," Andrew said with a smile that suddenly worried Duff slightly, as if his cousin had something else up his sleeve.

He wasn't sure what Andrew could come up with that would be more surprising than this, however.

"I think it's wonderful," Meagan said. "To be able to watch a stage production with two such fine actors as Andrew and Rosanna, right here in Chugwater, and a performance of such a beloved story as well . . . It's just a remarkable thing, Duff."

"Aye," Duff agreed. "And just wha' the town needed to make it really seem like Christmas around here."

"'God bless us every one,'" Meagan said with an impish smile as she lifted her coffee cup.

"I'm not for thinkin' ye remind me o' Tiny Tim. More of a Christmas angel, mayhap."

They were having lunch at Vi's Pies, an excellent restaurant owned and operated by attractive, middle-aged Violet Winslow, who was Elmer Gleason's special friend. Duff had teased Elmer in the past about making an honest woman out of Violet, but neither of them wanted that right now, any more than Duff and Meagan did. There was something to be said for not fixing what wasn't broken.

In addition to the delicious pies for which the place was known far and wide, Vi's establishment offered a top-notch breakfast and lunch as well. Duff and Meagan were enjoying bountiful plates of pot roast with all the trimmings. Duff's explanation of Andrew's plans had met with an enthusiastic reception from Meagan.

"Is the town hall big enough for such a production?" she asked.

"Andrew seems to think it is, and seein' as how he's the producer and director and star, I'm for thinkin' his opinion is the only one tha' matters."

"He's going to play Ebenezer Scrooge?"

"Aye."

"I can't wait to watch it."

"Ye ken he's gonna need folks from town to play all the other parts," Duff said. "'Tis very likely he'll ask ye to take on one of them, especially since he's already well-acquainted wi' ye."

Meagan's eyes widened. "*Me?* Act in a play?"

"And why not, I ask ye? Like I said, 'twould be a verra fine Christmas angel ye'd make."

"I'm not sure there are any Christmas angels in the story, unless you count the Ghosts of Christmas Past, Present, and Future."

"Well, then, one o' them," Duff said.

"Oh, I don't know. I never even thought of such a thing."

"Ye'd better be considerin' it, because I'm promisin' ye that Andrew will be."

They finished their lunch, and then Meagan returned to the dress shop to get her work done for the afternoon. She seemed distracted when she parted company with Duff. He knew she was thinking about what he'd said.

He planned to stop back by the hotel and visit with Andrew and Rosanna, but instead he spotted the two of them walking along Clay Avenue toward the town hall. Fiona was with them, and a smile lit up her face as she saw him.

Andrew raised a hand and hailed him, saying, "Come along

with us, Duff, if you can. I'm going to have a look at the town hall and start making plans for the production."

"Are ye sure the town council will permit ye to use it?"

"I spoke to the mayor, and he assured me it would be fine. This will actually be quite a feather in Chugwater's cap, if I do say so myself."

Duff nodded. Then, being polite, he pinched the brim of his hat, nodded to Fiona, and said, "Good day to ye, Miss Gillespie."

"Hello, Duff," she said, still smiling at him. " 'Tis wonderful to see ye again. But ye really should call me *Fiona*, considerin' what's between us."

"There be naught but friendship, as far as I'm aware," he said. Actually, even that was stretching the truth. After deceiving Andrew and Rosanna into believing there was more history between her and Duff than actually existed, he didn't feel any real fondness toward her. He was too polite to act that way, though.

"Oh, now, ye ken tha' there be more than that," she insisted. " 'Tis more than friends we're destined to be, Duff MacCallister."

"I'll no' argue wi' ye, lass."

" 'Twould be a waste o' time if ye did," she said sweetly.

"Perhaps we'd better get on with what we were doing," Andrew said. "Duff, come with us."

Duff had a bad feeling about it, but he nodded and fell in step alongside Andrew. Rosanna and Fiona followed them along the street.

The town hall was unlocked. They went inside and looked around the cavernous room, where dances were held, as well as town meetings. There was a raised stage at the far end of the room, where the musicians stood when they played for the dances. It wasn't elevated quite as much as Andrew would have liked for his production, but as he commented, they would have to make do.

"It's still the only place in town big enough," he said. "I expect a good turnout."

"I'll be there, ye can count on that," Duff said.

"Of course, you will," Andrew said, "but you won't be in the audience."

Duff looked puzzled. "Wha' do ye mean by that, Andrew?"

"I mean I want you to have a part in the play."

Duff leaned back and said, "Now I ken ye truly *are* mad! I'm no actor. True, I worked for a time as stage manager o' that theater in New York, but 'tis no' the same as troddin' the boards me own self."

"You'll do just fine, Duff," Rosanna told him. "As big and handsome as you are, you're a natural actor."

"'Tis truc," Fiona said. "All of it."

Duff gave a stubborn shake of his head. "I canna do it. I . . . I would be terrified."

That drew a guffaw from Andrew. "As long as I've known you, Duff, I've never known you to be scared of anything. Cautious, perhaps, but not frightened."

"But . . . but what part would ye want me to play?"

"Bob Cratchit," Andrew answered without hesitation. "Bob is a fine, upstanding man, and you certainly fit that description."

"But he's a bookkeeper," Duff objected. "The poor lad sits at a desk all day, hunched over his ledger books. I dinna ken if I could pretend to do that."

"That's why they call it *acting*," Rosanna said with a smile. "It's true, you're not really the Cratchit type, but I'm sure you can play the part, Duff. Andrew and I will give you plenty of coaching."

"Well . . ." To his own surprise, Duff realized he was tempted by the offer. He had always enjoyed a challenge, and standing up on a stage and acting in front of an audience would be one of the biggest challenges he had ever tackled. "I suppose I could gi' it a try and see how it goes."

"Excellent!" Andrew stuck out his hand, and Duff shook it.

"Tha' really is wonderful news," Fiona said with a triumphant smile on her face. "Now ye and I will get t' spend e'en more time together, Duff."

He turned a confused frown toward her. "I dinna understand—"

"I'm going t' be playin' Mrs. Cratchit," she said. "Ye and I will be husband an' wife, just as fate intends for us t' be in real life. Andrew and Rosanna ha' promised me the part, and I intend to hold 'em to it!"

Chapter 21

"I was wonderin', Mr. Scrooge, if 'twould be possible for me to have Christmas Day free from work," Duff said. His eyes kept cutting down to the words printed on the paper he held in his hand. The cast had just started rehearsals, and he was a long way from having his lines memorized. Just being able to remember so much seemed like a daunting task.

"No work on Christmas Day?" Andrew rasped. No one was in costume yet, of course, but he had adopted a stooped posture for his role as Ebenezer Scrooge. "Bah! What is this world coming to?"

" 'Tis just tha' I'd like t' be home wi' me family, ye ken, sir."

When they had started rehearsing earlier this morning, Andrew had tried to get Duff to speak without such a thick Scottish accent. Duff's burr wasn't as strong as it had been when he had come to America, of course, but it was still easy to tell where he came from. As Andrew had explained, "Scrooge and Bob are Englishmen, you see."

Duff's eyes had narrowed. "So 'tis wantin' me to talk like an Englisher, ye are."

Andrew had frowned and said, "And being a good High-lander, you're not that fond of the English, are you?"

"Ye could say that."

"But talking like them doesn't really mean anything. It's just acting, like Rosanna said."

Duff's glower had made it plain how he felt about that.

In the end, Andrew had said, "I don't see why I can't add a line about Bob Cratchit immigrating to London from, say, Glasgow. It doesn't really change anything in the plot, and it will explain your accent."

Fiona had spoken up then, saying, "'Twill explain why he has a good Scottish wife, too."

"Yes, I, uh, suppose so."

Only a day had passed since Andrew had told Duff about the idea of putting on a production of *A Christmas Carol*. Andrew, full of energy now that he had a new project, had bustled around town and done a good job of recruiting a cast and crew.

Biff Johnson, true to type, would be playing an innkeeper. R.W. Guthrie had agreed to take on the role of the Ghost of Christmas Past. As a politician and the former mayor of Chug-water, he was accustomed to speaking in public. Rosanna would be the woman Scrooge had loved and lost in that bitter-sweet past. The burly deputy Thurman Burns, showing an un-expected desire to be a thespian, had volunteered for the role of the Ghost of Christmas Present and read selected lines well enough in an audition for Andrew to award him the role.

That left Bob Cratchit's wife, their child Tiny Tim, and the Ghost of Christmas Future as the main roles to fill. As Fiona had pointed out, Andrew and Rosanna had agreed that she could play Mrs. Cratchit, and they didn't want to go back on their word. Fiona had been the first actual member of the cast.

And since Duff had shaken hands on it, he couldn't go back on his agreement to play Bob Cratchit, either. It was an uncom-fortable situation and became even more so when Andrew said that he wanted to ask Meagan to play the Ghost of Christmas Future.

"She's perfect," he had assured Duff as they were on their way to the dress shop to ask her. Duff had insisted on coming along. He wanted Meagan to go into this with her eyes open, if she didn't just throw the two of them out of the shop. "The character is beautiful and angelic, and I don't know of anyone in Chugwater who better fits that description."

"Nae, there is no one else more suited for the role," Duff agreed reluctantly. "Tha' still doesna mean that askin' her is a good idea."

"The worst she can do is say no."

" 'Tis right I'm for hopin' ye are," Duff had muttered under his breath.

Meagan listened with obvious interest to Andrew's proposition. Her eyes lit up with excitement. Before she could respond, though, Duff had said, "There's one more thing ye need to ken before ye say *yea* or *nae*. Fiona Gillespie will be in the production, too."

"She will? Who's she playing?"

Andrew cleared his throat. "Mrs. Cratchit."

Meagan looked at Duff. "Bob Cratchit's wife? And *you're* playing Bob?"

"Aye," Duff said.

"Well, that's . . . interesting," Meagan said slowly. "How did this come about?"

Andrew was quick to say, "It's not Duff's fault. Fiona was there when I told Rosanna about my idea for the production, and she immediately asked if she could be in it. Rosanna is still quite fond of her, so she said yes. She thought that would be all right. Mrs. Cratchit was the first part that came to mind. I didn't think she was right for either of the other two main female roles, and I still don't."

"But you didn't know then that Duff was going to be playing Bob Cratchit?"

"It didn't occur to me until later that he's perfect for the part." Andrew spread his hands. "So you see, there was nothing, um, nefarious about the casting . . ."

Meagan's intense gaze moved back over to Duff. "Did you know who would be playing your wife when you took the part?"

"I dinna have any idea. Tha' be the truth."

"So what we have here is just a matter of unusual circumstances, with no ulterior motives on anyone's part . . . except maybe one."

Duff knew she meant Fiona Gillespie. "I dinna have to play Bob—" he began.

"Of course, you do," she interrupted him. "You gave your word." Meagan smiled. "And Andrew is right. You have such an air of good-heartedness about you, you're perfect for the part. Besides, it's just a play. She's not really your wife, just like I'm not really a ghost."

"Then you'll take the part?" Andrew asked.

"Yes, I believe I will, and I'm honored that you're asking me. It should be fun."

"I hope it will be."

So far, Duff wouldn't say that rehearsals had been fun. More like a lot of hard work, and slightly uncomfortable, too, because the rest of the cast and crew were gathered around watching. That meant Meagan and Fiona were both on hand, standing on opposite sides of the stage, not glaring at each other, exactly, but every time their gazes met, the air in the town hall took on a definite chill that didn't have anything to do with the December weather outside.

After working with Duff for a while, Andrew told him to take a break and called R.W. Guthrie and Rosanna up so they could go over the scenes involving the Ghost of Christmas Past and Scrooge's lost love. Duff walked over to Meagan and asked, "How do ye think 'tis going?"

"You seem to be a natural actor, Duff, just like I thought you would be." Meagan smiled ruefully. "I'm getting a little scared, myself. *Stage fright*, I think they call it."

"Ye've nothin' to be afraid of. All will be well."

While Duff was saying that, Fiona came up on the other side of him and, before he realized what she was doing, had slipped her arm through his and leaned familiarly against him.

"Ye were so wonderful, husband," she said.

"He's not *really* your husband," Meagan reminded her. "It's just a play."

"An' the play's the thing, as the old sayin' goes." Fiona smiled, but the expression didn't soften the sting in her words. "'Tis only a matter o' time before the real world and the fiction catch up to each other."

"That won't ever happen," Meagan snapped.

"Ladies," Duff said, feeling a little like he was back in Egypt with the Black Watch, caught between enemy forces. "'Tis workin' closely together we'll be doin' for the next week or so, and that bein' the case, we might as well all be on good terms."

"Fine," Meagan said. "Just as long as she remembers that she's *not* really your wife."

"And you're not really a ghost," Fiona said. "*Yet.*"

Meagan leaned forward to look past Duff at the redhead. "What does *that* mean?"

"Nothin', dear, except what I said. You're not a ghost. Ye don't *want* t' be one, do ye?"

"That sounds like a threat to me. What are you going to do, cast some sort of spell on me?"

Fiona's smile disappeared. "Dinna make light o' me powers," she snapped. "'Twill be to your eternal regret if ye do."

"That's enow," Duff said firmly. As gently as he could, he

disengaged his arm from Fiona's. "Let's all remember we're here to put on a fine play written by me cousin based on Mr. Dickens's novel. We want to entertain the folks who come to see it, do we not?"

"Of course." Meagan took a deep breath. "I'm willing to call a truce if Miss Gillespie is."

"No need for a truce," Fiona said. "No one is at war."

"All right," Meagan said, but she didn't sound convinced.

The next week is going to be interesting, Duff thought. He just hoped there wasn't more drama behind the scenes than there would be on the night of the performance.

Andrew was well-versed in all aspects of the theater, not just acting. He knew stagecraft as well, and in his youth had worked as a stage manager, prop manager, and carpenter. Since the town hall had no curtain and every proper play needed a curtain, he rigged one from pulleys, ropes, a sandbag, and several large pieces of cloth he obtained from the general store. Meagan was kind enough to sew them together to make a stage curtain. Duff, Elmer, and Wang nailed up the apparatus.

A strong man was needed to pull on the ropes and open and close the curtain. Duff could have done it easily, but he was going to be busy on stage, playing Bob Cratchit. Andrew asked the local blacksmith, Jeremiah Farnsworth, to handle the job. Farnsworth's arms and shoulders were covered with thick slabs of muscle from swinging the heavy hammer in his shop, so he would be able to haul the sandbag up and down on the ropes.

When everything was in place, it was time to test the curtain. Andrew, Rosanna, Duff, Meagan, Fiona, and several other townspeople were on hand to observe. The sandbag rested on the stage and the curtain was closed. Andrew nodded to Farnsworth, who wore a pair of gauntlets on his hands. He took hold of the rope, pulled down on it to give it a little slack, and unhooked it from where it was attached to the wall. Gripping the rope with first one hand and then the other, the blacksmith hauled down on it and raised the sandbag. As it went up, the arrangement of ropes and pulleys opened the curtain smoothly.

Andrew gave a little clap of his hands and said, "Perfect! Good job, Jeremiah."

"You fellas who built this contraption did all the real work," Farnsworth said. "I'm just the donkey who pulls on it."

"Well, that takes skill, too," Andrew assured him. "Let it back down and let's see how that part works."

Farnsworth lowered the sandbag and closed the curtain, then raised it again. Andrew told him to leave it open and said, "All right, we'll rehearse some now. Meagan, let's try your scene with Scrooge . . ."

Duff stood behind the curtain watching while Meagan ran her lines with Andrew. Someone came up beside him. He tensed when he looked over and saw Fiona.

"She's really quite good, isn't she?" the redhead commented. Fiona complimenting Meagan took Duff by surprise.

"Aye, that she is," he agreed. "And I canna wait to see her in the beautiful white gown she's making for the part. Andrew couldna found a better wardrobe mistress, as well as the Ghost of Christmas Future."

Meagan was making all the costumes that had to be specially made and not provided by the haberdasher, general store, or her own shop.

Caught up in watching the woman he cared for, Duff didn't even notice when Fiona drifted away. When Andrew and Meagan finished the scene, he applauded lightly and called, "Bravo!"

Meagan smiled as she came toward him. "Was it actually good?" she asked. "Or are you just saying that?"

"Nae. I mean, aye, I'm not just sayin' it, 'twas actually good. Really good. I'll count meself lucky if ye don't decide to leave Chugwater and go on tour wi' Andrew and Rosanna."

Meagan laughed. "I don't think that's going to hap—"

A sudden whispering sound above her made her pause and look up. Duff looked, too, and saw that Meagan had been passing underneath the heavy sandbag rigged to open and close the curtain. The rope had come loose, and the whispering sound came from it passing swiftly through the pulleys. The sandbag was plummeting straight at her.

Duff didn't stop to think. He acted purely out of instinct, throwing himself forward in a long, diving tackle. He wrapped his arms around Meagan's waist. The impact drove her backward. Duff felt something brush his leg as he and Meagan fell to the stage. She cried, "Oh!"; but the exclamation was overpowered by the heavy thud of the sandbag striking the stage next to Duff's right calf.

Duff's pulse was hammering pretty loudly inside his head, too. He heard shouts as he became aware that he was lying half on top of Meagan. Under other circumstances, their position might have been rather pleasant, but right now, Duff just wanted to make sure she wasn't hurt. He had hit her pretty hard.

But not as hard as the sandbag would have if it had landed on her head. In all likelihood, that would have been fatal. At the very least, Meagan would have been badly injured.

He pushed himself up to get his weight off her and said, "Meagan! Are ye all right?"

"I . . . I think so," she said. She looked shaken and surprised, but she was able to sit up. "Duff, what happened?"

Andrew dropped to a knee beside her with a worried, angry look on his face.

"I'll tell you what happened," he said. "That fellow Farnsworth failed to secure the sandbag and almost killed you!"

"That's a lie," Farnsworth said. He was close enough to have heard what Andrew said. "I hooked that rope good and solid!"

"If you had, it wouldn't have come loose," Andrew replied coldly. "We'll have to find somebody else to handle the curtain."

"Fine! I don't want the job, anyway." Farnsworth turned and stomped away.

"Somebody needs to run an' fetch Doc Urban," Duff said. "Just to make certain Meagan is no' injured."

"I'm pretty sure I'm not hurt," she said. "I can move my arms and legs just fine. I didn't even hit my head very hard on the stage." She looked back and forth between Duff and Andrew. "If you two gentlemen will just help me up . . ."

They got on either side of her and took hold of her arms. Carefully they lifted her to her feet. She was a little unsteady, but only for a second.

"See?" she said. "I told you I was all right."

"Even so, we're going to have to fix some more safety measures for that curtain," Andrew said. "We can't take a chance on anything like this happening again."

"Aye," Duff said as he rested a hand on Meagan's shoulder. "We canna take any chances . . ."

As he spoke, he glanced around. He didn't see Fiona anywhere. He suddenly found himself wondering where she had been when the nearly fatal accident had occurred and wishing that he knew the answer to that.

He recalled what she had said about not needing a truce between herself and Meagan. One reason a truce wasn't necessary, he realized, was if you still planned to kill your opponent . . .

Chapter 22

Carlsburg, Utah

The screaming blonde wore a short, spangled dress that had been ripped, so she had to clutch it to her in a mostly vain attempt to conceal her curved figure. Having so much skin exposed on a day like today had to be pretty chilly.

Getting cold seemed to be the least of her worries, though. A bald hombre built like a grizzly bear lunged out of the saloon after her. The girl tried to dart away from him. A long arm shot out. Thick, sausage-like fingers clamped on her bare shoulder and jerked her back. The way those fingers dug into her flesh, they had to hurt.

"Come back here, you no-good calico cat," the big man rumbled. "I'll teach you to steal from me."

"I . . . I never stole from you, Otto! I don't know how that money got in my dress. I swear!"

"Shut up," the man called Otto growled. "You think I'd believe a tramp like you, Trixie?"

He jerked her around to face him and drew back his other arm. It was clear that he was about to slap her, and given the difference in their sizes, even an openhanded blow might inflict serious injury on her.

A few yards away on the street, Falcon, Hardpan, and Twister had reined in as soon as the commotion broke out. The two old prospectors might have ridden on by, but Falcon couldn't ignore a young woman in danger, even a saloon girl who was probably no better than she had to be.

When he saw that the big, bald gent was about to hit her, he drew his gun and eared back the hammer. His voice cut through the cold air as he said, "I wouldn't do that, mister."

Otto stopped with his hand still pulled back and poised to strike. He wore a brown tweed suit. His massive shoulders strained the coat's fabric. He also wore a gray vest and a white shirt, but no tie, because the shirt's collar was open. It probably wouldn't fasten around his thick neck.

He spat out a few curses, then asked Falcon, "Who in blazes are you?"

"A man who doesn't like to see women mistreated. I reckon that's all you need to know right now. And all you need to do is let go of that girl and step back."

Otto sneered. "What is that you are carrying?" he asked. He had a definite German accent, although not so thick that it hindered understanding him. "A baby in a sling, like a redskin papoose?" He laughed harshly. "I should fear a man who carries around a baby?"

Falcon shifted the Colt's barrel slightly and squeezed the trigger. The blast of the shot was loud in the street. The bullet chewed splinters from one of the posts holding up the awning over the boardwalk, less than two feet from Otto's shoulder.

"Maybe you should be a mite worried," Falcon said dryly as he thumbed back the hammer again.

Otto had jumped at the shot, and that caused his grip to slip on the blonde's shoulder. With a soft cry of effort, she twisted free and stumbled several steps away. She came to a stop and adjusted her torn dress again, for what little good that did her.

"Otto, you've got to believe me," she said. "I didn't steal your money. I *wouldn't* steal from you. You know that."

"All you tramps are the same, Trixie. Not to be trusted."

"I've never double-dealt you," she insisted. "I've always done everything you asked."

"*Ja* . . . and hated me for it."

Keeping the gun level in his hand, Falcon said, "You don't have to grovel for this varmint anymore, miss. He's not going to hurt you. Not while I'm here."

She surprised Falcon by shooting an angry glance in his direction.

"That's the problem, mister," she snapped. "You won't always be here. You'll make yourself feel good, like some knight in shining armor, and then you'll ride away and leave me to deal with the rest of my life, including Otto here."

She was well-spoken for a soiled dove, as if she'd had some education. That didn't change what she was, but Falcon knew that life sometimes led folks down paths they never would have taken if it were up to them.

Before Falcon could respond to the blonde's bitter words, Twister suddenly said, "Falcon! On the balcony!"

Falcon's eyes and gun came up at the same time. He spotted the man standing on the balcony pointing a rifle at him. He fired a tiny fraction of a second later, letting instinct guide his aim.

The rifle cracked, too, the shot coming so close after Falcon's that the reports blended together. By the time the bushwhacker's finger contracted on the trigger, though, the slug from Falcon's gun had ripped along his forearm and then shattered the bone in his arm, just above the elbow. That threw off his aim. The bullet from the Winchester harmlessly plowed up dirt in the middle of the street.

The man dropped the rifle over the railing, along the edge of the balcony, and staggered back, howling as he clapped his good hand to his wounded arm. He lost his balance and sat down hard, then toppled over on his side and whimpered in pain.

The rifle had fallen in the street. Otto looked at it, obviously gauging his chances of leaping off the boardwalk and grabbing it.

Falcon saw that and said, "Why don't you just go ahead and give it a try? I won't mind a bit."

The muzzle of his gun was staring at Otto again. The burly man couldn't have missed that. His lips pulled back from his teeth in a savage grimace. He said, "You're in a lot of trouble, mister." A look of satisfaction appeared on his beefy face. "You just shot Carlsburg's town marshal."

Falcon drew in a sharp breath. He hadn't noticed a badge on the rifleman's shirt, but there hadn't been a lot of time to look for such things. He had acted instinctively to protect himself, the baby, and the two old-timers.

Hardpan spoke up, saying, "That fella never told us he was a lawman, and he didn't call on Falcon to put his gun away, either. You can't hold Falcon responsible for what happened."

Otto turned his glare on the old prospector. "What are you, a lawyer? You don't look like one."

"No, just a fella with common sense," Hardpan snapped. "And I'm not gonna let you or anybody else railroad my friend." He moved a little in the saddle, shifting the Sharps he held across his lap so that it pointed at Otto.

The big man was facing two guns now, and a second later, it was three as Twister swung his Winchester toward the boardwalk as well.

"Bah!" Otto said, clearly realizing that the odds were too much against him to try anything else right now.

Falcon pointed with his chin at the balcony and said, "You'd better go help your so-called *marshal* up there. I don't think he's in any real danger of dying, but he *might* bleed to death. In the meantime, Miss . . . Trixie, was it? Why don't you come with us?"

He wasn't sure where the suggestion came from. He wasn't

looking for another traveling companion. But he hadn't been looking to temporarily adopt a baby, either, or two old desert rats. Mostly, it was a matter of Trixie having a point. She *wouldn't* be safe if she stayed here with Otto.

If Falcon hadn't taken a hand in the game, Otto might have beaten her up, but then allowed her to continue working at the Ace-High. Not now, though. Not after Otto had been forced to back down. Trixie would be a reminder of that humiliation. Sooner or later, Otto would kill her to salve his wounded pride. Falcon was certain of that.

"You . . . you want me to come with you?" Trixie sounded like she couldn't believe it.

In a low voice, Hardpan said, "Falcon, are you sure this is a good idea?"

"Nope," Falcon said, "but I don't see any other alternative." He smiled at the blonde and went on, "Yes, ma'am, I do. Unless you'd rather stay here."

The glance she gave Otto was like she was looking at something vile on her shoe.

"No, I don't reckon I do," she said.

"You have any belongings inside?"

Trixie shook her head. "No, I don't live here. I've got a house . . . well, a shack . . . down the street. My things are there, what little they amount to."

"Hardpan, Twister, go with the lady while she gets her belongings. You can, ah, change clothes while you're there, ma'am."

Trixie looked down at her ruined saloon girl dress and smiled wryly as she said, "Yeah, this wouldn't be a very good outfit for riding, would it?"

"You have a horse?"

"No, but he has plenty, and gear, to boot," she said, nodding toward Otto. "I'm sure you passed Kramer's Livery when you rode into town."

Otto sneered and said, "So now you turn horse thief. I might have known there is no limit to the depths a trull like you will descend."

"Didn't I tell you to go help your friend?" Falcon said.

Trixie edged around Otto and backed toward the steps. "I'm not stealing anything," she said, raising her voice so that the townspeople, who were watching the commotion elsewhere on the boardwalks and in doorways, could hear her. "You haven't paid me what you owe me in more than a month. I figure it's worth a horse and rig."

"That's for me to decide," Otto said. "You are a thief!"

"And you're a miserable whoremonger!" She turned and hurried down the street, away from the saloon. Hardpan and Twister rode after her, both men looking dubious about the whole thing.

"You will not get away with this," Otto told Falcon in a low, fury-filled voice.

"Folks have told me that before, but I'm still here. Now, you'd better go tend to that fella. He's not making any noise up there anymore, so that might not be a good sign."

Glowering, Otto swung around and stomped into the saloon. Falcon didn't holster his gun. He kept the iron ready as he backed his horse away from the saloon. From the corner of his eye, he had seen Trixie enter an alley down the street a few moments earlier. Hardpan and Twister had followed her. Falcon headed in the same direction.

Trixie came out of a tiny shack at the far end of the alley. Somebody had nailed it together hastily from irregularly shaped planks, which meant the walls had a lot of gaps in them. Falcon figured the cold wind whistled through there like icy fingers during the winter—like now. The roof was tar paper tacked onto pieces of tin that showed through ragged holes in the covering.

Hardpan and Twister sat on their swaybacked saddle horses near the shack. Hardpan had the Sharps ready for trouble, and Twister, likewise, with the Winchester.

Trixie had pulled on a gray dress and had a shawl around her shoulders. The outfit wasn't much protection from the cold, but it was better than the ripped-up honky-tonk dress. She clutched a well-worn carpetbag.

"Ready to go?" Falcon asked her.

"Yeah, if you're sure you still want to take me along."

"Seems like the thing to do," he said. "Hardpan, Twister, you go on along to the store and get those supplies we need. Trixie and I will fetch a horse for her from the livery stable."

"Eleanor," she said.

"What?"

"My name. It's Eleanor Marshall." Her mouth twisted. "Trixie's just my whore name. Otto liked it."

"Well, then, Miss Marshall, to complete the introductions, I'm Falcon MacCallister, and these two fine gentlemen are Hardpan Hawkins and Twister McCoy. I don't figure those are their given names, but that's what I know them by."

Twister grinned. "If you want to know, the moniker Hardpan's ma stuck on him, I can tell you—"

"No, you can't," Hardpan snapped. "Let's go and do what Falcon told us to do. The sooner we get out of this ugly little town, the better."

"Yeah, I can't argue with that sentiment," Twister said. The two of them rode out of the alley, leading the pack mules.

"You didn't tell me you needed to buy supplies," Eleanor said.

"Any reason we shouldn't?" Falcon asked.

"There may be a reason you *can't*. Didn't you see the sign on the store? Otto Kramer owns it, too, just like he does nearly every business in town."

"Why didn't they just call the place Kramerville?" Falcon asked, repeating the question Hardpan had asked earlier. He had dismounted, and he led his horse as he walked out of the alley with the blonde.

"Carlsburg is the place Otto grew up, back in Germany," Eleanor explained. "I guess he wanted to sort of re-create it here, after he came to America. When he's drunk enough, he talks about being a boy there. Makes it sound like the best place there ever was." She shook her head. "Then he'd get a little drunker and start knocking one of the girls around, so I reckon if it *was* a good place, none of it rubbed off on him."

"I'm sorry. Nobody should have to live like that."

She shrugged. "Wasn't much other way I *could* live after my husband died."

"You were married?"

"Yeah. He wasn't much good, either. Bounced around from job to job and finally wound up bartending for Otto. He made enough that we were able to rent a room and I didn't have to, well, earn any money for us. Then some drunk cowhand decided to shoot up the place one night and Phil caught a stray bullet between the eyes before Otto blew the cowboy in half with a shotgun. I didn't see any of it, thank goodness, but I heard about it later. I told Otto I'd take Phil's place and work as a bartender for him. He agreed, but . . ." She laughed humorlessly. "It wasn't long before he had me doing other things, too, and I didn't fight him on it. Didn't seem worth the trouble."

"You didn't have any family you could have gone back to?"

She frowned and said, "Don't judge me, Mr. MacCallister."

"I'm not trying to. Sorry if I poked my nose into something that's none of my business."

She sighed. "If you hadn't poked your nose into something that was none of your business, *I'd* have a broken nose by now, more than likely, or worse. Once Otto was convinced I'd stolen from him, that was it. He never would have forgiven me."

"*Did* you steal from him?"

"Well, of course, I did. I told you, he hadn't paid me in more than a month. I think he'd gotten tired of having me around, and that was his way of trying to run me off."

"Sounds like a real pleasant fella," Falcon said.

"You met him. What you see is what you get with Otto Kramer."

They had almost reached the livery stable. A man stepped through the open double doors and pointed an old single-shot rifle at them.

"Hold it right there," he said. "I know what you're after, and you ain't comin' in here to get it."

Falcon and Eleanor stopped short. Falcon could tell that the lanky, lantern-jawed liveryman didn't want to be doing this. The barrel of the rifle wobbled a little. The man holding the weapon was nervous, and that could be good or bad—often bad.

"Take it easy, Thad," Eleanor said. "I guess Otto sent somebody over here to warn you that I wanted a horse, didn't he?"

The man's head bobbed up and down. "That's right. He said you and this feller were horse thieves, and I was to run you off."

Eleanor smiled and shook her head. "You know me better than that, Thad. You know I wouldn't take anything unless I had it coming to me. Why, all the times that you visited me, I made sure you were good and happy before I let you pay me, didn't I?"

The liveryman's face turned bright red. He swallowed hard and said, "We don't need to be talkin' about that."

"But it's true. We've always been friends. At least that's the way I thought of it."

Falcon's eyes narrowed as he watched Eleanor sidle closer and closer to the man. She didn't seem to be afraid of him or the rifle he held.

Or maybe she just didn't care anymore. Maybe she figured that if she caught a bullet, she would be just as well off. Either way, Falcon knew she was up to something . . .

So he was ready when she made her move, darting forward and to the side, grabbing the rifle by the barrel and shoving it skyward. The liveryman jerked the trigger and the rifle boomed, but the bullet sailed harmlessly into the air.

The next instant, Falcon's fist crashed into Thad's jaw. The punch made the liveryman let go of the rifle and backpedal swiftly with his arms windmilling as he tried to catch his balance.

He failed and collapsed into a stunned heap.

"Thanks for not killing him," Eleanor said. "Thad's not a bad sort. He's just scared of Otto, like everybody else around here." She tossed the now-empty rifle into a pile of straw as she walked into the livery barn. "I'll go pick out a horse."

Falcon grunted and tried not to grin. Eleanor might be a soiled dove and a thief—but she had sand, he had to give her that.

Angry yelling from down the street made him jerk his head around, followed closely by the boom of Hardpan's Sharps.

Chapter 23

Falcon looked along the street. He saw Hardpan and Twister's horses, along with the pack mules, tied at the hitch rail in front of the general store. Quickly he stepped into the barn, bent over, grabbed the front of the liveryman's shirt with both hands, and hauled Thad to his feet.

With his face only inches from Thad's, he told the groggy liveryman, "If you bother that lady again, I'll come back down here and kick you up one way and down the other. You got that?"

"Uh . . . uh-huh," Thad managed to say as he bobbed his head again.

Falcon gave him a shove that sent him staggering back against one of the pillars along the barn's center aisle.

"Eleanor, there's something going on down at the store," he called.

She turned from the gate, where she was looking into one of the stalls. "I was afraid of that. You'd better go see about your friends. I'll be all right here."

He wasn't sure about that. Otto Kramer struck him as a

pretty treacherous sort. But he wanted to see if Hardpan and Twister were all right, so he turned and left the livery barn in a hurry. As he trotted toward the mercantile, he held the baby against his chest with his left arm, while his right hand hovered near the butt of his gun.

"I've got to start carrying you on my back," he muttered to the kid. "Seems like you'd be safer there."

Unless somebody tries to backshoot me, he thought. Honestly, for a gunfighter, there really wasn't any good place to tote around a baby.

Maybe he should have left the youngster with Eleanor. But that wasn't a good idea, either. He had just met her and didn't know how trustworthy she was. She had admitted that she stole from Kramer—although he probably deserved that.

Five steps led up to the high porch in front of the store. Falcon took them in two bounds. He tried not to jostle the baby too much in the process. The door was closed. He jerked it open and stalked inside.

Instantly he saw that there was a standoff. Hardpan and Twister were backed against the counter at the rear of the store. Twister's round face was set in grim lines, instead of his usual affable expression. He had his Winchester leveled, menacing the three men who crowded in front of the old prospectors.

Hardpan was turned the other way, facing a couple of men behind the counter and brandishing an ax he obviously had grabbed up from a nearby display. The two men, wearing clerk's aprons, kept their distance and had their hands half-lifted to show that they weren't threats. They didn't want Hardpan swinging that ax at them.

The three men confronting Twister weren't store clerks, Falcon was sure of that. They wore range clothes and had hard-planed, beard-stubbled faces. Hardcase drifters. Falcon had seen scores of them. He would have taken them for outlaws, if not for the deputy marshal badges pinned to their shirts.

Of course, a man could wear a tin star and still be nothing but an owlhoot . . .

The three men hadn't noticed him come in. One of them blustered, "Put down that gun, you crazy old coot. Your friend could've killed one of us, shooting like that, so we ain't in the mood to be patient with you."

"Yeah, if I put down this rifle, you'll ventilate both of us," Twister shot back at him. "We ain't fools."

"Yeah, you are. The boss says if you leave town peaceable-like, you're free to go. Nobody's gonna hurt you."

Hardpan rasped, "We're not leavin' without the supplies we need. Anyway, you're lying. That bald baboon sent you over here to kill us."

"You shot our boss!" one of the other men said angrily.

"No, he didn't," Falcon said, interjecting himself into the confrontation as he slid his gun from its holster. "That'd be me. And it seems to me like an honest marshal wouldn't have been acting like a bushwhacker."

The three men tensed and looked over their shoulders at him. Now that Falcon got a better look at their faces, he was more convinced than ever that they were hired guns.

The one who'd been talking to Hardpan and Twister had a scar on his cheek that ran down to the corner of his mouth and twisted it into a permanent sneer. He said, "You'd be MacCallister."

"That's right," Falcon said as he held his Colt steady on the three men.

"Heard of you. My name's Briggs. Anse Briggs. Could be you've heard of me."

"No," Falcon said slowly, "can't say as I have."

He knew that would annoy the man, but it also happened to be true. Gun wolves like this were the proverbial dime a dozen. They could still be dangerous, though.

"You're under arrest," Briggs said.

Falcon smiled thinly. "For what? Shooting that so-called *marshal*?"

"Duly appointed marshal," Briggs snapped.

"Appointed by who? Otto Kramer?" Without taking his eyes off the three "deputies," Falcon continued speaking. "You boys behind the counter . . . tell me, was there ever an election where Kramer was elected mayor, or did he just declare that he was?"

Briggs glanced at the clerks and barked, "Don't answer that."

"Well, that pretty much gives me the answer, anyway, doesn't it?" Falcon mused. "Kramer's not the legally elected mayor any more than I am."

One of the men behind the counter cleared his throat and said, "Well, he, uh, sort of started the town, so everybody figured he had the right to, uh, call himself whatever he wanted to . . ."

"What that amounts to is that, badge or no badge, your *marshal* didn't have any legally constituted authority, and neither do these would-be deputies." Falcon's tone dripped contempt. "So they can't arrest me and my friends, and they can't tell *you* what to do, either. So if they claim you can't sell any supplies to us, they're lying. You can do whatever you want."

"You'll be sorry if you do," Briggs blustered. "You've still got to live here. These men'll ride out and not give a hang what happens to you."

Falcon didn't like it. Briggs had a point. Not that he and Hardpan and Twister wouldn't care what happened to the storekeepers, but once they had left Carlsburg, they wouldn't be able to do anything about it.

Unless . . .

He had an idea, and although he didn't like *it*, either, he didn't see any other better options at the moment.

"Let's go see your boss," he said.

It was a toss-up who looked more surprised: the three gunmen, the two clerks, or Hardpan and Twister. But after a moment, Briggs's sneer turned into a smirk, and he said, "Sure. Let's do that."

"Twister, keep your rifle on these boys, just so they don't get any ideas," Falcon said as he backed toward the door.

Once they were all outside, Falcon made Briggs and the other two gunnies walk in front of him toward the Ace-High Saloon. Hardpan and Twister flanked him.

"What in blazes are you up to?" Hardpan asked quietly.

"My neck in trouble, most likely," Falcon replied.

Eleanor came out of the livery stable, leading a saddled horse. When she saw the procession going along the street, her mouth opened and she stared in confusion.

So did the townspeople who were around. More than likely, they had never seen anybody stand up to Kramer and his henchmen before. They didn't look too happy about seeing it now. Most people didn't like it when what they considered the natural order of things were upended, even when they weren't particularly happy with the way things were.

Eleanor waited until they were going past the livery stable and then fell in with them. "What are you doing, MacCallister?"

"I'd just as soon not bring any more trouble down on this town than I have to," Falcon said. "So I'm going to make Kramer a little wager. Is he a gambling man?"

Eleanor thought about it for a second. "I'd say so. He likes a good game of poker."

Falcon nodded. "We'll see if he takes the bet, then."

At Falcon's command, the little group came to a stop in front of the saloon. He raised his voice and called, "Kramer! You in there, Kramer?"

The batwings were fastened back against the walls and the inside doors were closed now, since the day was getting chillier. A moment after Falcon's hail, one of the doors was jerked open and Otto Kramer stepped out onto the boardwalk. His big hands clenched into fists at his sides as he saw Falcon, Hardpan, and Twister holding guns on his so-called deputies.

"I sent you to do a job, Anse," he rumbled.

"MacCallister got the drop on us," Briggs said. "You know his reputation, boss. We couldn't buck him when his gun was already in his hand."

"And it's a good thing they didn't," Falcon said, "or else you'd have been short three more phony marshals, Kramer. Those badges they're wearing are just meaningless pieces of tin. I happen to know that nobody ever elected you mayor, so you don't have the authority to appoint anybody. The only reason you run things around here is because you figure you're bigger and stronger than everybody else."

"*Ja*. I am." Kramer thumped a fist against his own chest, reminding Falcon of pictures he'd seen of gorillas doing the same thing.

"I don't think so," Falcon drawled. "In fact, I aim to prove that you're not."

Beside him, Eleanor whispered urgently, "MacCallister, what are you doing?"

Kramer wanted to know the same thing. Glowering down from the boardwalk, he demanded, "What is it you propose?"

"A bet," Falcon said. "We settle this between us, just you and me, man to man."

Kramer snorted. "You are a notorious gunfighter, my men tell me. I'm not foolish enough to think that I can outdraw you."

"Not with guns, then," Falcon replied with a shake of his head. "You decide how we go about it. One hand of poker, or—"

"Fists," Kramer said. "Man to man, as you say. No holds barred."

That was exactly the response Falcon expected. He would have risked a hand of cards, if Kramer had gone for that, but really, Falcon had had a hunch ever since he got the idea that it would come down to this.

Eleanor clutched his arm. "He'll kill you," she warned. "I've seen him nearly break men in half, and they were big men, too."

Falcon ignored that, nodded to Kramer, and said, "All right, but you've got to agree to my conditions. If I win, Miss Marshall gets that horse free and clear, no charges of stealing it hanging over her head. My friends and I are allowed to buy whatever supplies we need at the store, and you won't take any action against the clerks who sell them to us. Then we have safe passage out of town, along with your word that you won't come after us"—he glanced at Briggs and the other two gunmen—"or send anybody after us. Do you agree to all that, Kramer?"

"And if *I* defeat you?"

Falcon shrugged. "Then I probably won't be in any shape to stop you from doing whatever you want, will I?"

"You will be a broken husk of a man," Kramer said. "And I will take great pleasure in breaking you."

He started taking off his coat, obviously getting ready to fight.

"You didn't actually give me your word that you agree to those conditions," Falcon pointed out.

"Bah! You have my word. You take what you need and get out of my town." Kramer began rolling up his sleeves.

Eleanor shook her head and said, "This is a mistake. And it's not just your life you're playing with, MacCallister."

"I know that," Falcon told her. "But I don't intend to lose."

Her attractive face was set in bleak lines despite his assurances. He motioned with his gun and told Briggs and the others to go up on the boardwalk and stay there.

"Keep an eye on them," he said to Hardpan and Twister. "And don't hesitate to pull the trigger if it looks like they're going to try anything."

"Those are professional gunmen," Hardpan complained. "Twister and I won't be any match for them."

"They're not likely to make a move as long as you're covering them."

The two old-timers didn't look convinced, but they leveled the Sharps and the Winchester at the gun wolves.

Falcon pouched his iron, unbuckled his gun belt, coiled it, and handed it to Eleanor.

"You know how to use a Colt?" he murmured to her.

"Yeah. Point it, cock it, and pull the trigger."

"Well, I hope you don't have to, but . . ."

"I'll be ready if I do," she said.

Falcon nodded. He hung his hat on the horn of Eleanor's saddle and unwrapped the sling from around his neck. Gently he held out the baby to Eleanor.

"You mind hanging on to him for a little bit?"

She looked distinctly uncomfortable as she took the infant. "I'm not exactly the maternal type," she muttered.

"Maybe not, but you'll do all right," Falcon told her. Eleanor held the baby in one arm and hung on to the horse's reins with her other hand.

Falcon took off his coat and folded it to drape it over his saddle. He was unbuttoning his shirtsleeves as he walked over to face the steps leading up to the boardwalk where Kramer waited.

Kramer didn't wait, though. Falcon was still fiddling with one sleeve when Kramer suddenly launched himself off the boardwalk in a diving tackle.

Chapter 24

Falcon saw Kramer coming at him and tried to brace himself, but Kramer was fast for such a big, bulky man. He crashed into Falcon before he could get his feet set. Both men went down hard in the street.

Falcon knew what Kramer was trying to do. Kramer wanted to use his heavier weight to pin Falcon to the ground and hammer him into submission. Falcon already couldn't breathe because of the mass pressing down on his lungs.

Kramer groped for Falcon's throat with his left hand. His right closed into a fist. He raised it high, ready for a sledging blow into Falcon's face.

Before that blow could fall, Falcon lowered his head and hunched his shoulders so Kramer couldn't get hold of his throat. At the same time, he bent his knees and jackknifed his legs up. He was able to get both legs around Kramer's neck and lock them at the ankles. When he straightened his legs, Kramer toppled backward.

That gave Falcon the chance to kick and twist free of the big man. He rolled away, slapped his hands on the ground, and pushed up to his knees. Kramer had already caught himself and tried to tackle Falcon again, while both of them were still down.

This time, Falcon was ready. He clubbed both hands together and swung them in a crushing blow that caught Kramer on the side of the head and drove him down.

For a second, Falcon hoped that would be enough to end the fight. It would have put most men down and out.

No such luck where Otto Kramer was concerned. The impact barely slowed him down. He scrambled up onto hands and knees and reached out to snag Falcon's ankle as Falcon tried to stand. Falcon went over backward again.

Falcon let the momentum of his fall carry him into a somersault that put a little more distance between him and Kramer. He and Kramer were about the same height, but Kramer had the advantage in weight. Falcon had a longer reach, though, and he needed space if he was going to be able to use that.

He made it to his feet this time. Facing an evil bruiser like Kramer, he wouldn't have hesitated to kick the varmint while he was down, but Kramer was too fast. He sprang up like a jack-in-the-box, bouncing a little on his toes as he advanced with his fists cocked, ready to box now.

Falcon lifted his arms. With four older brothers, he had learned how to wrestle and box at an early age. It was a matter of self-defense. He swayed a little as he watched Kramer, waiting for the inevitable signs that would tell him what the big man was going to do.

Kramer feinted to his left, but Falcon didn't fall for it. He darted to his own left and beat Kramer to the punch. His fist shot in and landed a sharp jab on Kramer's nose that rocked his head back a little. Blood spurted hotly over Falcon's knuckles.

Kramer growled and swung a looping right. The punch was too wide. Falcon stepped inside it and hooked a left and a right into Kramer's midsection. His fists sank into the layer of fat that overlaid the thick slabs of muscle on Kramer's belly.

Even though Falcon put a lot of power into the blows, Kramer didn't react much. He moved back a single step. That put him in position to lift his left in an uppercut. Falcon tried to jerk his chin out of the way, but Kramer's fist clipped him, anyway.

Falcon stumbled backward. Even that glancing blow had been enough to shake him. Kramer was strong enough, Falcon realized, that if the man ever landed a punch with full force, it might just take his head off.

Since that was the case, Falcon would just have to make sure Kramer didn't land any solid punches.

Kramer bored in at him. Falcon ducked and weaved and darted, blocking some punches and slipping others. He didn't get a chance to throw many of his own. But he circled as he fended off Kramer's attack, and Kramer moved to follow him until Falcon had the big man where he wanted him.

Falcon crouched to let a fist whip past above his head, and in that split second, while Kramer was off-balance, Falcon lunged forward, wrapped his arms around the man's waist, and drove with his legs as hard as he could.

An empty hitch rail was only a couple of feet behind Kramer, who was unable to stop before Falcon rammed him into it. Kramer bellowed in pain as the force of Falcon's charge bent him backward over the rail. Sturdy enough to hold spooked horses, the rail didn't go anywhere. While Kramer was trapped against it, Falcon slammed punch after punch into his belly, trying to soften him up.

Kramer roared, got hold of Falcon's shoulders, and flung him away. Falcon stumbled, lost his balance, went down, but rolled and came right back up again.

Kramer was hanging against the hitch rail with his right arm hooked over it to hold him up. His face was gray. Falcon had hurt him that time. He didn't want to lose even the slightest advantage, so he rushed in, ready to hammer his fists to Kramer's face.

Kramer might not have been hurt as bad as he appeared to be, though. He twisted away at the last second and swung a backhand that landed on Falcon's left shoulder and sent him rolling in the street.

Falcon came to a stop on his back and threw his hands up just in time to grab Kramer's boot as it came toward his face. With a grunt of effort, Falcon heaved, hoping to throw Kramer off his feet again.

He wasn't able to do that, but Kramer had to reel backward to catch his balance. Falcon rolled, came up against the back wheel of a wagon parked next to the boardwalk, and used the spokes and rim to brace himself as he climbed upright again.

This was a strange fight. Quite a few people were watching, but no one shouted encouragement to either of the combatants. Evidently, the townspeople couldn't bring themselves to support Kramer, and they were too afraid of him to cheer for Falcon. So the slugfest continued in eerie silence, broken by the harsh breathing of the two men and the meaty thuds of fists against flesh.

Falcon caught a glimpse of Eleanor as he ducked another roundhouse swing by Kramer. She stood holding the baby and the reins of the horse she had brought from the livery stable. Her bottom lip was caught between her teeth as she watched the battle anxiously. He knew she was probably thinking about what might happen to her if Falcon lost this fight. She would be back at Otto Kramer's mercy again—and Kramer wouldn't be inclined to be merciful.

Not far away, Hardpan and Twister had moved so that they could cover Anse Briggs and the other two gunmen on the boardwalk, while still being able to see what was happening between Falcon and Kramer.

That proved to be too much of a distraction. Even in the midst of the desperate struggle against Kramer, Falcon saw that happening, even though the two old-timers didn't. He realized he should have disarmed Briggs and the others. He shouted, "Hardpan! Twister! Look out!"

Briggs had his gun out and coming up fast. Hardpan jerked

the Sharps toward him and pulled the trigger. The boom was nearly deafening, even out here in the open. The heavy slug missed Briggs, but struck a post right beside his head. Flying splinters stabbed into his cheek and made him flinch as he pulled the trigger. His shot went wild.

Twister flung the Winchester to his shoulder and yelled at the gunmen, "Don't do it!" They froze with their guns not yet out of their holsters. "Drop your gun, Briggs!"

Hardpan had the Sharps reloaded with the swift efficiency of a man who had performed the action thousands of times. He lined the heavy rifle on Briggs's head and said, "This gun'll blow your head clean off your shoulders, mister!"

Grimacing, Briggs, with his free hand, wiped at the blood trickling down his cheek from the cuts; meanwhile he dropped the gun in his other hand. It thudded onto the boardwalk planks at his feet.

"Kick it away!" Twister ordered.

Falcon would have appreciated the prompt, cool-under-fire actions of the old prospectors if he'd had a chance to observe them. At the moment, however, he still had his hands full with Kramer, who bulled in and sledged punches at Falcon's head as if he were a nail and Kramer wanted to drive him into the ground. Falcon's left arm still wasn't working quite right because of the blow he had taken on it that had numbed his whole arm for a moment. He avoided the pile driver blows and flicked a few punches at Kramer's face, but he could tell he was losing strength.

So was Kramer, and he was slowing down, to boot. He failed to block one of Falcon's punches that landed cleanly on his mouth and split both lips. Blood welled down over Kramer's chin.

Kramer swayed a little. Was he actually giving out? Or was it just another trick to lure Falcon in?

Falcon didn't know—and didn't really care, either. *He* was

giving out, and Falcon knew he had to end this fight soon, if he was going to end it at all.

If Kramer ended it, that wouldn't be good . . .

Roaring so that blood sprayed from his busted lips, Kramer charged in again. Falcon summoned up some of the last bits of his speed and strength to dart aside. Kramer lumbered past him. Falcon laced his hands together again and smashed them on the back of Kramer's neck. The blow sent Kramer stumbling toward the wagon. Falcon pounced, got a hand on the back of Kramer's head, and shoved it into the wheel.

The sound Kramer's head made as it hit the iron-tired wheel was like an ax biting deep in a chunk of wood. His knees buckled. He fell against the wheel and slid down it, trying feebly to catch hold of the spokes. He failed and crumpled all the way to the ground.

Falcon had to hang on to the wagon's side boards to steady himself as he stood there breathing hard. His hair hung in his eyes as he looked down at Kramer. He lifted a shaking hand and pushed it out of the way. As hard as Kramer's head had hit that wheel, Falcon wouldn't have been surprised if the man was dead.

He wouldn't care if that turned out to be the case, either.

Kramer was breathing. Falcon heard the man's nose bubbling and wheezing as the air went in and out. He appeared to be out cold, and there was no telling how long he would remain that way.

The street was still strangely quiet. As he continued leaning on the wagon, Falcon lifted his head to look around. The townspeople, including Anse Briggs and the other two gunmen, were all staring as if they couldn't believe their eyes. Someone had actually defeated Otto Kramer. Not just defeated him, but knocked him unconscious.

Falcon's heart still slugged heavily in his chest, and his pulse pounded a steady rhythm in his head. He had recovered enough to push away from the wagon, though. He didn't feel too shaky as he walked toward the hotel, flexing fingers sore from hammering Kramer's thick skull.

"All right, Briggs, you heard what your boss said. If I beat him, we get our supplies—which we'll pay for, by the way—and nobody bothers us or comes after us. That was the deal, and I expect you and your pards to live up to it."

It was obvious from Briggs's expression that he wanted to argue, but everybody on the street had heard Kramer's arrogant agreement to the deal. Even in a place like this, a man's word had to be worth something.

Briggs wasn't quite ready to give up. He poked a finger toward Eleanor and said, "What about that horse the girl's stealing?"

Eleanor began hotly, "I told you, he owes me—"

"Hang on," Falcon interrupted. He reached in his pocket, came out with a twenty-dollar gold piece, and flipped it toward Briggs. The gunman caught it instinctively.

"There you go," Falcon went on. "Kramer's been paid. If you don't pass it on to him, that's your lookout, not ours."

Briggs sneered at the double eagle. "That horse and rig are worth five times that, at least."

"Maybe, but nobody can say he didn't get paid. That makes it legal. In fact, it'd be a good idea if you were to write out a bill of sale."

"I can't do that!"

Falcon took the coiled gun belt off his saddle and bucked it around his hips, then settled the Colt in the holster.

"I reckon you can," he said. "Unless you want to settle up, man to man, too."

He meant with guns this time, not fists. Briggs knew it. He hesitated, grimacing even more than the scar on his cheek made him do all the time. Finally, he said, "All right, I'll fix your blasted bill of sale. Unless the boss wakes up first. Then I'll do whatever he tells me . . . and you might not like it, mister."

"I don't like anything about this town," Falcon said. "So a threat like that doesn't mean much to me." He drew his gun and told Hardpan and Twister, "Go get those supplies. I'll watch these fellas."

He gave them another double eagle to pay for the purchases. "Be careful," Hardpan said. "Could be somebody else might try to bushwhack you."

"I'll watch his back," Eleanor said. She shifted the baby in her arms. He was starting to fret a little. The small, restive cries sounded surprisingly loud in the hushed street. Eleanor wrapped the horse's reins around her hand so she could use both hands to hold the baby and bounce him up and down as she tried to comfort him.

Falcon saw that from the corner of his eye, even though he was concentrating on Briggs and the other two gunmen.

"Not exactly the maternal type, eh?" he said with a slight smile.

"Shut up, MacCallister, and pay attention to what you're doing." Eleanor paused, then added, "I've been around a few babies before, you know."

He didn't press her for details. It was enough that she was holding the kid and keeping an eye out for any signs of further trouble.

Hardpan and Twister returned a short time later, leading the pack mules. The packs were bulging with supplies.

"We paid for the provisions, like you said," Twister reported.

"Although it's a blasted shame to put any money in that varmint Kramer's pocket," Hardpan added.

"All legal and aboveboard," Falcon said. He looked at Kramer, who was still breathing but otherwise hadn't budged. After a wallop to the head like that, there was no telling how long it would be before he woke up.

He slid his gun back in the holster and reached out to take the baby from Eleanor. Instead of giving him back, she held on to him and said, "That's all right. I can carry him for a while. This sling looks like it ought to be fairly comfortable."

"Are you sure?" Falcon asked.

"If there's any gunfighting to be done, you don't need an infant getting in your way. If you'll just hang on to him for a minute while I get mounted . . ."

Falcon took the kid. Eleanor pulled up her dress, revealing boots and a pair of canvas trousers underneath it. She put her foot in the stirrup and swung up into the saddle like a man.

She looked down at Falcon, who appeared mildly surprised, and said, "What, you didn't expect me to be a delicate flower who needs a sidesaddle, did you?"

"I reckon not," he said. He handed the baby up to her and watched to make sure she had figured out how to arrange the sling in which the infant rode. Satisfied that the baby had a secure perch, he climbed onto his own horse; then Hardpan and Twister did likewise. The two old-timers had been covering the gunmen. Now Falcon took over that chore again.

"Listen to me, Briggs," he said. "The deal was that nobody would come after us. Kramer had better honor that. Because if I lay eyes on him, or any of you boys, I'm not going to ask any questions. I'm just going to shoot to kill. Understood?"

"Understood," Briggs practically snarled. Whether or not that meant he and the other gunmen would hold up their end of Kramer's bargain, Falcon didn't know.

But he knew that *he* had meant every word he'd said. If Kramer, Briggs, or any of the other hard cases from Carlsburg showed up on their backtrail, Falcon was going to do his best to see that they caught bullets for their trouble.

Chapter 25

Chugwater

"God bless us, everyone!"

"Excellent job, Tim! I mean, Roscoe," Andrew told the little boy who had just delivered the line in a reedy voice.

After a number of youngsters had tried out for the part of Tiny Tim, most of them pushed to do so by their parents, the role had finally gone to Roscoe Mullins. Tall for his age, skinny, and carrot-topped, he didn't really match the description of Tiny Tim in Mr. Dickens's novel, but as Andrew put it discreetly to Duff, Meagan, and Rosanna, "He seems to be the only lad in Chugwater who's not absolutely terrible when it comes to acting."

"All right, Bob and Mrs. Cratchit," Andrew said as the rehearsal continued, "the two of you move up behind Tiny Tim, and each of you rest a hand on one of his shoulders. Duff, you take your position on his right, and, Fiona, you'll be on the left."

Roscoe stood there, leaning on Tiny Tim's crutch, as Duff and Fiona took their places behind him. Duff cleared his throat and rested his left hand on Roscoe's right shoulder. Fiona moved into position on the boy's other side, but instead of putting her right hand on his left shoulder, she used her left hand for that and raised the right so that she could rest it possessively on Duff's left shoulder. She stood so close that her hip touched his.

Duff glanced over at her. Instead of looking at Roscoe, who was playing her son, she gazed at Duff instead. Her eyes shone soulfully with affection.

"Well," Andrew said, "I didn't specify that particular bit of business, Fiona, but, actually, it works. It seems like just the sort of thing that Mrs. Cratchit might do under the circumstances."

Duff saw Meagan watching from the back of the room with an unreadable expression on her face. He wanted to say to Andrew that what Fiona had just done didn't work, didn't work at all, but he didn't want to argue with his cousin, who was directing this play, after all.

"Now the carolers begin," Andrew said, half-turning to point to a group of a dozen townspeople, equally divided between men and women, who stood to one side. During the actual performance, they would be visible through a window in the "wall" of the Cratchit residence. All those scenery flats were being constructed in the vacant lot behind the town hall. The sound of hammering from back there could be heard inside the building, but it wasn't too distracting.

While the carolers crooned "Hark! The Herald Angels Sing," Andrew said, "Now, as Scrooge, I'll join the happy family to celebrate Christmas morning." He moved to do so, standing on Duff's right side and beaming with the joy of having understood the holiday at last. From the corner of his mouth, he said, "Annnnnd . . . curtain!"

The curtain didn't actually close for this rehearsal. The mere mention of it made Duff look up at the sandbag that had come close to injuring Meagan—or worse.

Since that incident a couple of days earlier, nothing else un-usual had happened. Casting and early rehearsals had gone smoothly. Duff was still wary, though. If nothing else, the at-mosphere took on a little chill whenever Meagan and Fiona were around each other. When they had to interact, they were stiffly polite. Mostly, they each pretended the other didn't exist, except when they thought no one was looking and they glared at each other.

Meagan was certainly attentive, touching Duff on the fore-arm or shoulder and smiling at him a lot, but Fiona was the same way. Duff supposed he could understand why some men enjoyed having two women vying for his attention. It was flat-tering, no doubt about that. But at the same time, it just made him uncomfortable.

"All right, everyone," Andrew continued. "Let's take a break, and then we'll run through the blocking again."

No groans of dismay sounded. Andrew was a stern task-master when it came to directing, but this experience was still enough of a novelty to the people of Chugwater that they were enjoying it and didn't complain about the long hours they were putting in.

Duff turned away from Fiona, intending to go talk to Mea-gan, but she hurried to step alongside him.

"'Tis going splendidly, dinna ye think?" she said.

"I suppose. I dinna have all tha' much experience wi' puttin' on plays, so I canna really say whether 'tis goin' well."

"I think 'tis. I'm for thinkin', too, tha' this will be a Christ-mas the likes o' which Chugwater will ne'er forget."

Duff grunted. "Tha' could be a good thing . . . or a bad one."

"Oh, 'twill be good. Verra good."

Fiona had slowed him down enough that by this time, An-drew had gone over to Meagan and was talking to her. Judging by his animated gestures, he was telling her how he wanted her to play the part of the Ghost of Christmas Future. Duff didn't want to interrupt that. His hesitation gave Fiona the chance to slip her arm through his.

"Why don't we go out and see how the scenery construction is comin' along?" she suggested.

Duff couldn't think of any way to refuse without being rude, so he nodded and said, "I reckon we can do that."

They left the town hall through a rear door and stood on its back stoop, watching the men who had volunteered to build the sets. The flats were constructed of lightweight lumber and weren't built to last. In fact, once the play was over, they could be knocked apart and some of the lumber used for other things—unless the town decided to keep them on hand and use them in other productions in the future. Some frontier communities did such things, using theater to help bring everyone in the area together.

"My, they're comin' along well, are they not?" Fiona said as she hugged Duff's arm tighter and leaned against him.

"Aye." He saw Elmer and Wang working on one of the flats, and a couple of the hands from Sky Meadow were hammering together another one. Luckily, there wasn't quite as much work to do on that ranch at this time of year, so he was able to spare a few members of the crew to help out here in town.

"Duff, look at me."

He turned his head and looked down into her eyes, which gleamed strangely.

" 'Tis fate, ye ken, tha' brought us together like this," Fiona went on. "We were cast as husband an' wife in this play because that's wha' we're intended t' be in real life."

Duff said, "This play is just fiction. 'Tis nothin' to do wi' real life, only a story."

"Stories come true, as I've told ye before. All ye have t' do is let go o' yer stubborn ways and enjoy them . . ."

She was lifting herself on her toes as she spoke. Duff knew she was about to kiss him. He ought to push her away—gently, of course—or at least turn his head so that she wouldn't be able to reach his mouth with her lips. He had no romantic interest in Fiona. He didn't even fully trust her—

The sound of a throat being cleared made both of them turn sharply toward the door. Meagan stood there, arms crossed, not glaring at them, exactly, but certainly giving them an intent look.

"Rehearsal will be starting again soon," she said. "I thought I saw the two of you come out here and figured I'd better let you know."

"An' 'tis thankin' ye for your consideration, we are," Fiona replied with one of her usual sweet smiles. "Come along, Bob Cratchit, my love."

"I'll, uh, be along in a moment," Duff said as he disengaged his arm from hers.

Fiona looked like she wanted to argue, but then she shrugged and went back into the town hall, leaving Duff and Meagan on the rear stoop.

"She was about to kiss you," Meagan said.

"Aye, she might've had some idea o' doin' that, but I dinna intend for it t' happen."

Meagan smiled, but sadly, and shook her head. "Duff, you really have no idea. It's not what *you* intend to happen that matters here. It's what *her* intentions are. And I don't trust them, not for one minute."

"Ye've no need t' be jealous—"

"*Jealous?*" Meagan repeated as she interrupted him. "I'm not *jealous*, Duff. I'm worried. That girl has something up her sleeve, something that's going to cause trouble for all of us. As Elmer would say, I'd bet a hat on that."

Duff felt compelled to defend Fiona. She had been through a great deal, after all, being kidnapped from the train and everything. He said, "She just has some wild ideas in her head—"

"There's nothing wild about the idea of getting you to fall in love with her. That's what she's after. For goodness' sake, Duff, she even claims to be a witch and says that she cast a spell on you! Someone who would believe that . . . Well, you just can't tell what else they might do."

"I suppose not. But I dinna believe ye need to worry about Fiona. After the holidays, when Andrew and Rosanna leave and go back to their normal life, I plan to see to it tha' Fiona goes wi' them. My cousins have agreed tha' she can continue to work for them."

"I *hope* that's the way it turns out." Meagan came up on her toes, and Duff did nothing to discourage her as she gave him a quick kiss. "But call it *female intuition* if you want . . . *I* still believe that girl is up to no good."

Rehearsals had run fairly late, and at this time of year, darkness closed in early, especially on cloudy days, as most of them were. Quite a bit of gloom had gathered already as Fiona Gillespie walked toward the hotel by herself.

She had planned to ask Duff to walk her back, but that Parker hussy had moved in and claimed him before Fiona was able. She could have waited until Andrew and Rosanna were finished going over the notes Rosanna had made during the rehearsals. They would have been happy to walk with her, but she'd been in such a huff that she hadn't felt like lingering in the town hall.

So now she was walking by herself on a rapidly darkening evening with a chilly wind blowing down the street that made her tighten her shawl around her shoulders.

She was brooding over how her plans had gone awry and how circumstances were going to force her to take even more extreme measures. With that on her mind, she almost didn't notice when the man wearing a long duster stepped out of an alley mouth to block her path. She nearly ran right into him before she jumped back.

"That's far enough, lady," he rasped in a low voice. The bandanna tied across the lower half of his face as a mask muffled his words.

Fiona gasped. "You're . . . you're tha' outlaw! The one who carried me off!"

She turned as if to run, but his left hand fell on her shoulder and jerked her around. With his right hand, he swept the duster aside and came up with the revolver from his holster. He put the muzzle under her chin, tipped her head back, and growled, "Don't scream or I'll blow your head off."

"I . . . I won't," Fiona managed to get out.

With his grip still cruelly tight on her shoulder, he pulled her into the alley. Shadows folded around them so thickly that anyone passing by on the street would have had a hard time seeing them. Fiona's captor seemed to know where he was going, though. He tugged her along the alley and then through other passages until they reached a small barn on the outskirts of the settlement. He had taken the gun away from her chin, but kept it pressed into her side. Fiona didn't cry out.

The outlaw let go of her long enough to jerk open a small door, then shoved her into the barn. She stumbled into the darkness. He followed, heeling the door closed behind them.

The sudden flare of a match was almost blinding in that gloom as he flicked it to life with his thumbnail. Clearly, he had prepared, because a lantern was hanging from a nail driven into a post. He held the match flame to its wick, then lowered the lantern's glass chimney over it once the wick had caught.

A yellow glow welled up. It didn't *actually* do much to alleviate the chill in the barn, but it seemed to. Fiona shivered, anyway, as she stood there and stared at the grim, masked figure in front of her.

"Wh . . . what are ye goin' t' do to me?" she asked.

"It doesn't matter," he said. "You can't stop me from doing whatever I want."

He holstered his gun and stepped closer to her. He lifted his left hand, cupped it under her chin, and held her motionless as his right hand lewdly explored her body. She shuddered at his bold touch.

"If you're thinking about trying to grab my gun out of its holster, I wouldn't if I were you," he told her. "You'd be mighty sorry if you did."

"What would ye do . . . if I tried?"

His hand slid down and tightened, bringing another gasp from her.

"You don't want to find out."

"I . . . I'm no' afraid o' ye. You're naught but a . . . a scurvy highwayman. Ye wouldna dare . . . harm me . . ." Her hand suddenly flashed up, grabbed the bandanna mask, and jerked it down, revealing the hard planes of his face in the lantern light. "Nick Jessup!"

His mouth twisted in a snarl. He spat out an obscenity, jerked her against him, and brought his mouth down on hers. She tried to pull away from the savage, urgent pressure of his lips, but he was too strong for her.

After a moment, she stopped struggling. Her arms came up and wrapped around his neck as she returned his kiss with just as much passion and intensity as he brought to it. Her body molded to his. She trembled as he caressed her, but in excitement this time.

"Ah, Nick, me lad," she whispered as she broke the kiss, "I was for startin' to think tha' ye'd never get here!"

Chapter 26

Later, they lay side by side on a pile of hay in the barn. Neither of them was sure to whom the place belonged, but no animals were kept in it and no one ever seemed to come near it, which made it a good meeting place for them.

Nick propped himself up on an elbow so he could look down into her face. Fiona knew she wore a satisfied expression. She could tell that he was pleased by that. He was so easy to manipulate—but then, most men were.

He moved aside a strand of red hair that had fallen over her eyes and said, "There. I never saw such pretty green eyes. They don't need to have anything in front of them, even such pretty red hair."

His words had no poetry to them, no beauty to inflame a woman's senses and sweep her away, but Fiona didn't really care about that. All that really mattered to her was that Nick Jessup was going to help her get what she wanted more than anything else in the world.

Vengeance on the hated Duff Tavish MacCallister.

"What are you thinking?" Nick asked.

"About how lucky 'twas tha' ye carried me away from tha' train, like some highwayman of old," Fiona lied easily.

"You were really scared, weren't you?"

"*Scared?* I was frightened out o' me wits, truly!"

An anxious frown creased Nick's forehead. "But you weren't scared a while ago when I pretended to kidnap you again, were you?"

"Och, nae!" She smiled and pushed a hand against his shoulder. "As soon as I laid eyes on ye, I knew what ye were up to. And I played along just fine, did I not?"

"Yeah, it was really good." Nick leaned down and nuzzled his lips along her jawline and then into the hollow of her throat.

A little shiver went through her, and this time it had some genuine feeling to it. He was a passionate young man, with some rudimentary skills and plenty of energy and enthusiasm.

"Now that we're . . . you know . . . friends . . . I'm sorry I really scared you, that day on the train. I promise, I never intended on hurting you."

He's lying, she thought, *if not to me than to himself.* When he kidnapped her, he'd had every intention of forcing himself on her, and when he was done, he might have even let the rest of the outlaws have their way with her. And then, sooner or later, one of them would have killed her so she wouldn't be an inconvenience. Fiona didn't doubt any of that.

Nor did she care, because as soon as she'd found out that Nick also had a grudge against Duff MacCallister, she had seen clearly—bursting in her brain like fireworks—that she could turn him into an ally and make use of him. All she had to do was promise him that if they worked together, it was absolutely certain that Duff would die.

Well, that, and give him freely what he would have taken, anyway . . .

For a time, it had looked like Duff and his friends were going to ruin everything by rescuing her. Fiona had already decided that she would convince Nick to let her go, so that the posse would find her and she could tell them that she'd "escaped" from the gang of train robbers. It might not have been easy to get the rest of the outlaws to go along with that, but she was sure she could have persuaded them by promising she would help them come up with a way to loot the entire town.

Then, during the posse's attack on the hideout in Badwater Canyon, for all she knew, Nick and the rest of the gang would be wiped out. She would have had to start over with her plans.

But she'd consoled herself with the knowledge that she would be no worse off than she was when she started. All she'd ever figured on doing by befriending Andrew and Rosanna MacCallister was getting to Chugwater. She would come up with a scheme then to get her revenge on Duff. Nick Jessup was just a stroke of luck that had fallen into her lap, so to speak.

Then that possible advantage had been yanked away from her by the posse's attack. But the outlaws had escaped, losing a few men in the process, but remaining a formidable force for her to make use of. And Andrew had presented her with another bit of luck on a silver platter by coming up with the idea of staging a production of *A Christmas Carol*.

When Nick had shown up after that, sneaking into town to see her, spying on her until it was safe to approach her, she had known beyond a shadow of a doubt that fate actually was on her side. If she hadn't known that this business about being a witch and casting a spell on him was just a story she'd made up to get under Duff's skin, she might have started to believe that there really was something to it.

"You know," Nick mused, making conversation now that they had finished making love, "you never have told me just why it is that you hate Duff MacCallister so much. You know why I want to see him dead. He killed my brothers. Did the varmint hurt somebody who was important to you, too?"

"Aye," Fiona said, hesitating to answer the question beyond that. Her hatred was her own, and she had nursed it to her bosom for so long, nurturing it and letting it grow, that sharing it with someone else seemed almost like a betrayal.

At the same time, that much hate was a burden. It might feel good to lighten that load a bit by telling Nick what had happened. Besides, he and his brother and the rest of the gang were going to help deliver the vengeance that Duff MacCallister so richly deserved. Maybe Nick had a right to know.

"Me name is Fiona Gillespie, as ye ken," she began, "but me mother was a Somerled."

Nick frowned slightly and shook his head, indicating that the name meant nothing to him.

"Her brother, me uncle, was Angus Somerled, Lord High Sheriff of Argyllshire, the part of Scotland we come from," she went on.

"A badge-toter, eh?"

"Well . . . a sheriff in our part o' the world isna exactly the same as the position here in America, but certainly similar. The Somerleds are an important, highly respected clan. And as far back as any can remember, they've hated a batch of craven, ill-bred louts known as the MacCallisters."

"A feud!" Nick exclaimed with excitement in his voice. "I know about feuds. We've had a bunch of 'em here in the West. Why, down in Texas, they're feudin' fools. Families war with each other for decades. Hundreds of men killed on both sides."

"There be no feud like a Highland feud," Fiona insisted. "His name alone would be reason enow for me to hate Duff MacCallister, but there be more. Ye see, Duff MacCallister killed me beloved uncle Angus, as well as his sons, Alexander, Donald, and Roderick, me cousins."

Actually, some of the details of those deaths were a wee bit fuzzy. MacCallister's intended, Skye McGregor, daughter of Ian McGregor, owner of the White Horse Pub, had been killed in the conflict, too. But what was important was that Fiona's relatives had died and Duff had fled to America with murder charges hanging over his head. Angus Somerled, grieving over his dead sons, had followed Duff and wound up dying in this godforsaken country, no doubt murdered by Duff just like his boys had been.

Ever since she had watched her mother crying bitterly over what had happened, she'd sworn vengeance on Duff MacCallister. She already bore a grudge against him because, as a girl, she had gazed at him with longing from the age she became aware of just how big and handsome he was. And he had ignored her completely, the scoundrel. That part of her story was true. True love spurned could do naught but turn sour and spoil. Duff had had eyes only for Skye, so Fiona had felt pangs of glee when she heard that the McGregor wench was dead. Duff's part in the deaths of her uncle and cousins just deepened the hate she felt for him.

She sketched in the details of that background for Nick without revealing too much of herself. By the time she was finished, he knew she had good reason to hate Duff MacCallister. His eyes burned with righteous anger as he said, "I'll help you pay him back. You can count on that, Fiona. And so will my brother, Logan, and Hank Spalding, and the rest of the bunch . . . as long as there's enough loot to make it worthwhile for 'em."

"How about the loot of an entire town?" she asked.

His eyes widened at the thought. "The whole town? How do you figure we can pull that off?"

"Ye ken about the play we're puttin' on?"

"*A Christmas Carol.* Sure, you told me about it."

"Between the people who are actin' in the play and those workin' on it, and the audience who'll come t' see it, just about everybody in Chugwater will be in the town hall that night. I'll slip away durin' the performance and bar th' doors, so tha' no one can get out. Ye and your friends will be free to loot the bank and take any money or valuables ye find in the other businesses in town, too."

Nick shook his head. "Once folks realize they've been locked in and something bad is going on, they'll bust out. They'll knock the doors down or break the windows or both."

"They may try, but if ye have men posted around the building, in good cover, to shoot at anybody who dares poke his head out, 'twon't be long afore they realize they're stuck in there."

Nick frowned in thought for a long moment, then said, "It might work."

" *'Twill* work, I promise ye. Do wha' I say, and ye'll all be rich men." Fiona paused. "And ye the richest o' all, Nicholas Jessup, because ye'll have me in addition to your share o' the loot."

She reached up, put her hand behind his neck, and pulled his head down to hers. Their mouths came together again, and as Fiona felt the heat and urgency of Nick's kiss, she knew that he would do absolutely anything she told him to do.

What he didn't know—and what he didn't *need* to know until the time came—was that her plan had one more step to it. Yes, she was going to trap everyone in Chugwater inside the town hall while they were celebrating Christmas . . . and then she was going to set the place on fire. She planned to hide tins of coal oil underneath the building to add to the inferno that would consume not only Duff MacCallister, but also everyone he cared about. She just wished there were a way to let him know, as the flames melted the flesh off his bones, just why he and all the others were dying.

But if she couldn't figure that out, he would still die.

She laughed, couldn't keep from laughing, and Nick raised up a little and asked, "What is it?"

Fiona cupped her hand on his cheek and said, "Beautiful thoughts, me bonny lad, beautiful thoughts."

And the light of madness burned brighter in her eyes than any flames.

Chapter 27

Carlsburg, Utah

"Set him down careful-like," Anse Briggs told the three towns-men he had drafted to carry Otto Kramer back into the Ace-High Saloon. Kramer's living quarters were upstairs, but Briggs didn't think the men could haul his massive weight up there. However, the saloon had a back room with a cot in it, where drunks sometimes slept it off—when Kramer didn't just toss them out into the street—so Briggs figured that would do for now.

Grunting with effort, the townies lowered Kramer's sense-less form onto the cot. They let go of him and stepped back. Their chests heaved from the exertion. As the other two deputies, Trent and Clive, stepped into the room, one of the townsmen asked, "Can we go now, Deputy Briggs?"

"Yeah, go on," Briggs replied as he jerked a thumb curtly at the door. "And don't go running your mouths about this. The boss is fine."

The men nodded and shuffled out. Briggs hooked his thumbs in his gun belt and frowned down at Kramer. Trent said, "Shouldn't he have woke up by now, Anse?"

"He will," Briggs snapped. "That was quite a wallop he took from MacCallister."

Clive said, "We should'a gunned down MacCallister's friends while we had the chance and then bushwhacked him when he come a-runnin'."

"Mighty smart after the fact, ain't you?" Briggs asked with his upper lip curling into a sneer.

Clive didn't cotton to being talked to like that. His hand twitched a little toward his gun. He saw that Briggs was ready to draw, though, and he knew he wasn't as fast as the lean, scar-faced man. Instead of slapping leather, he muttered, "I was just sayin', that's all."

Briggs ignored him, once he saw that Clive wasn't going to push things. Instead he watched the steady rise and fall of Kramer's barrel chest. The boss of Carlsburg was alive, no doubt about that. So, why didn't he go ahead and wake up? Despite the confident answer he had given Trent, Briggs wasn't completely sure Kramer would *ever* regain consciousness.

But as if Kramer somehow sensed that doubt, a groan came from deep within him. It ended in a chuffing sound that reminded Briggs of a grizzly bear, which was appropriate, since Kramer was kind of built like a griz. Kramer turned his head from side to side. He blinked rapidly for a moment. Then his eyes stayed open and he rumbled, "Wha . . . what . . ."

Briggs rested his left hand lightly on Kramer's shoulder and said, "Take it easy, boss."

Kramer's shoulder twitched. "Get your . . . hand off me," he rasped. "Help me . . . sit up."

Did he want help, or did he want Briggs to keep his hands off? *He can't have it both ways,* Briggs thought. But then he motioned for Trent to help him and they both got under Kramer's shoulders and pushed and shoved until Kramer was sitting up on the cot. Kramer swung his legs off and let his feet drop heavily to the floor. He leaned forward, covered his face with his hands, and sat there, obviously trying to get oriented again.

Finally he lowered his hands and raised his head to glare at Briggs. "What happened?"

"MacCallister got lucky and—"

"Bull! He *beat* me. Me, who's never been beaten by any man." Kramer's face darkened with seething rage. "He won't get away with it."

Trent said, "You made a deal with him, boss—"

Kramer came up fast off the cot. He swung his left in a back-handed blow that smashed Trent's jaw and flung him against the wall. Trent slumped there for a moment, looking sleepy and stupid, before he was able to brace himself against the wall and straighten up again.

"Sorry, boss," he muttered.

Kramer looked over at Briggs again. A vein stood out in his temple and throbbed in time with his pulse.

"Why didn't you kill them?" he demanded. "Including that slut Trixie."

"Because, like Trent said, you made a deal with them," Briggs grated. He hoped Kramer wouldn't swing on him. He wouldn't take that from any man, not even the one he worked for. "Besides, MacCallister and those two old coots had the drop on us."

"Mighty sorry gunmen the lot of you are," Kramer said. "Letting one man and a couple of old buzzards get the best of you."

"Falcon MacCallister may be one man, but he's not some-body you'd want to underestimate. Not many are faster on the draw or better shots."

Kramer made a slashing motion and said, "Forget it. What's important is that, deal or no deal, I will not allow MacCallister to get away with this. Saddle horses and gather supplies. We are going after them."

Briggs started to object. Even though he'd never been overly burdened with morals—his gun was for hire, after all—it went against the grain to back out of a bargain. Reneging on a bet, that was what it amounted to.

On the other hand, Kramer was the one who'd made the deal with MacCallister. Briggs himself hadn't promised anything. So in one way of looking at it, even though Kramer might be reneging, Briggs could follow his orders with a clear conscience. Trent and Clive looked to him; they would do whatever he did.

The matter had some practical considerations to it, though, even if he didn't mind going along with what Kramer wanted.

"You were out for a pretty good spell, boss," Briggs said. "It's late in the day. By the time we got ready to ride, there wouldn't be much light left. Wouldn't it be better to wait and get an early start in the morning?"

"And allow MacCallister and the others to get that much more of a lead?" Kramer said with a scowl.

"Not that awful much more. They'll make camp when it gets dark, I reckon. Maybe even before then. We'll be able to pick up their trail."

Kramer stared at him with narrow, hate-filled eyes. "You had better hope things work out like that," he said. "If MacCallister escapes my vengeance . . ."

Kramer left the rest of it unsaid, but Briggs didn't need him to finish the veiled threat. Briggs knew good and well what he meant. Briggs needed to make sure MacCallister and those two old-timers wound up dead, and that Trixie was hauled back here to suffer whatever punishment Kramer wanted to dole out to her. Otherwise Briggs's own life might be forfeit.

Briggs wasn't going to let that happen, no matter who else had to die.

Wyoming

A couple of days had passed since the ruckus in Carlsburg. During that time, Falcon and his companions had crossed the border from Utah to Wyoming. He hoped that two or three more days would find them arriving in Chugwater for that visit with his cousin Duff.

Falcon was still pretty sore from that tussle with Otto Kramer, but his bruises faded and his muscles were less stiff with each day that passed. He kept a close eye on their back-trail, just in case Kramer didn't keep his word and sent those gunmen after them. Kramer might even come himself if his pride was wounded enough. Falcon warned Hardpan and Twister to keep their eyes open, too, but didn't say anything about it to Eleanor.

She had her hands full taking care of the baby. She might have claimed not to have any maternal instincts, but as far as Falcon could see, that wasn't true. She kept the baby with her most of the time while they were riding, snuggled against her chest in the sling arrangement.

After making camp that evening, they were sitting around the campfire, which Eleanor had started by snapping a match to life with her thumbnail, just like a man. That was just one of the skills she had picked up, she'd explained dryly.

As they lingered over cups of coffee, Twister said, "You know, I've been thinkin'—"

"That's never a good sign," Hardpan put in.

"No, just listen. Maybe it's just the season, but I've been thinkin' that whenever I look around at us, I'm reminded of a familiar story."

"What story would that be?" Falcon asked.

"Well . . . here it is, not long before Christmas, and we're travelin'. We got a baby, we got a young woman, and we got three fellas lookin' out for 'em—"

"By grab, if you're comparing you and me and Falcon to those three Wise Men in the Good Book, you're loco!" Hardpan said.

Eleanor let out a quiet laugh edged with bitterness. "And I'm about as far away from a virgin bride as you could find, Twister.

About the only thing you've got right is that there's a baby involved."

"I'm sorry, Eleanor," Twister said hastily. "I didn't mean to offend you—"

She smiled at him. "It's all right. I'm not offended. Actually, that was quite a compliment you just paid me, whether I deserved it or not."

"Well, as far as I'm concerned, I haven't seen one thing about you that I don't find honorable, no matter what might have . . . I mean . . ."

"Just let it go where you are, pard," Hardpan advised.

Falcon smiled. He had also found Eleanor to be smart, good company, and seemingly devoted to taking care of the infant. Working as a soiled dove hadn't coarsened her, as it did with so many unfortunate women. She hadn't picked up an opium habit, either, and didn't roll cigarettes or chew tobacco. Falcon enjoyed being around her.

Later, after he had checked on the horses and taken a quick walk in the darkness around the camp to make sure nobody was trying to sneak up on them, he came back to the fire and sat down next to her. The flames had burned down to little more than orange glowing embers. Hardpan and Twister were snoring in their bedrolls. The kid was asleep, too, in the nest of blankets Eleanor had made for him.

Falcon clasped his hands together in front of him and said quietly, "Sorry if Twister got to talking out of turn a while ago. He didn't mean anything by it."

"I know that," Eleanor said, equally softly. "I suppose it's a compliment that he seemed to forget what I was doing for a living *before* I left Carlsburg."

"That wasn't your fault. I may not be a wise man, but I know that much." Falcon cleared his throat. "Life just sometimes takes us down trails we'd rather not follow. We don't always have much choice about it, though. Or any."

She slipped her arm through his and leaned her head against

his shoulder. "And you claim not to be a wise man. You couldn't prove it by me, MacCallister." They sat there in companionable silence for a moment, until Eleanor added, "Don't let this give you any ideas."

"No, ma'am," Falcon said. "There's not an idea in my head right—"

He stopped short and stiffened, for in the dim light from the campfire, he saw his horse raise its head and prick its ears.

Eleanor must have noticed his abrupt silence and the way his muscles tensed. "What is it?" she whispered.

"My horse scented something out there," Falcon said, keeping his voice low, too. "Might be a big cat hunting. They start to get hungry this time of year. Or it might be another horse." He paused. "I think I'd rather it was the cat."

"Because a horse could mean it's a man doing the hunting."

"Or men," Falcon said. "I haven't asked you this, but are you packing iron?"

"I have a little Smith and Wesson .32 in a holster on my leg, under my dress."

"Are you any good with it?"

She laughed softly. "I don't know. I've never really used it. I just thought it would be a good thing to have if . . . if I was going to work in a saloon like that."

Falcon suppressed a sigh of exasperation and asked, "Is it loaded?"

"Yes, it is. I suppose it'll shoot, but I don't actually *know* it will."

That was better than nothing. Maybe.

"I want you to go ahead and lie down next to the kid. Curl up in your blankets and pretend to go to sleep. But move your hand around, slow and careful-like, until you can get on that gun in a hurry if you need to."

She nodded and whispered, "I understand. What are you going to do?"

"After you lie down, I'm going to wait a couple of minutes

and then drift over to the horses and mules, like I'm checking on them. That'll give me a chance to slip off into the shadows and take another look around."

"You didn't see anything earlier when you were out scouting?"

Falcon still had his eye on his horse. The animal continued to seem interested in something out there in the night.

"Nope," he said to Eleanor, "but that doesn't mean nothing was there."

She yawned as if she were about to doze off. He had to give her credit for not overdoing it. She still had her arm linked with his. She raised her head and brushed a kiss across his cheek.

"Just making it look realistic," she murmured.

"Sure," he said.

She let go of his arm, stretched for a moment, and then arranged her blankets on the ground next to the baby. She folded up one of them to serve as a pillow, then stretched out and wrapped the others around her. Falcon sat there, not moving, apparently at his ease, until her breathing settled into a regular pattern.

She is pretty good at acting, he thought fleetingly. Maybe one of these days, he'd introduce her to his brother and sister. Duff had planned to invite them to Sky Meadow for the holidays, so maybe he'd see them in Chugwater.

Assuming they all made it there alive.

When he judged that enough time had gone by so nobody watching the camp would get suspicious, he stood up and moved toward the horses. He slid around the animals, patting them and murmuring to them. Using the horses to shield his actions, he reached down to where the saddles rested and slid his Winchester from its sheath. Then, as silent as the chilly breeze blowing across the Wyoming landscape, he drifted away from the camp into the shadows.

He gauged the wind and cat-footed into it, knowing that whatever his horse had scented was in that direction. He sniffed the air himself, but didn't smell anything out of the ordinary. He also stopped every minute or so and stood absolutely still, listening as hard as he could. The night was quiet.

Then, during one of those halts, he heard a faint clinking sound. It was a bit chain, and the sound had been caused when the horse that was attached to the bit had moved its head. Somebody was out there, all right, somebody human—and probably dangerous.

Falcon eased ahead, moving through the cloaking darkness like a phantom. The overcast meant there were no stars and moon to worry about tonight. Unfortunately, that also meant he was just as blind as anybody else who was out and about.

He hoped he wouldn't bump right into some trigger-happy lurker.

Instinct made him drop to a knee just below the top of a grassy swell. He leaned forward and peered into the shadows, trying to penetrate them. He thought he saw several thicker patches of darkness on the other side of the little rise. One of those vague black shapes moved, and he heard another clink. Those were horses down there, all right.

They weren't unattended, either. Somebody whispered, "Keep those . . . still . . . Sound . . . at night."

Falcon caught only some of the words, but he knew what the man was saying. At least two men had been left here to watch the horses. He made a rough count—that was all he could do in such bad light—and decided at least six or eight mounts were down there in the little depression.

That meant there could be half a dozen men—or more—sneaking up on the camp right now.

Falcon considered jumping these two hombres and trying to take them prisoner without raising a commotion and alerting their friends. That would be almost impossible, but if he could manage it, he could question the varmints and find out who they were and what they were up to.

222 *William W. Johnstone and J.A. Johnstone*

The next moment, however, the decision was taken out of his hands. A gun went off, back there toward the camp. He recognized the sharp pop of a small-caliber pistol—like that .32 Eleanor claimed to be carrying.

That answered one question, anyway: The gun worked.

And hard on the heels of that report came more gun thunder, blasting through the night as Falcon surged to his feet, turned, and headed back toward the camp at a dead run.

Chapter 28

He saw spurts of orange muzzle flame splitting the darkness as he pounded toward the camp. Curses welled up in his throat, only to be bitten back as futile. He didn't think the attackers had deliberately lured him away from the camp—but that was the way it had worked out, wasn't it?

He bounded past some brush. Someone hidden in the scrubby growth launched out at him, tackling him and driving him to the ground. The impact jolted the Winchester out of Falcon's hand. His hat flew off his head.

He rolled over when he landed and looked up in time to see a figure silhouetted against the muzzle flashes. The garish, on-and-off illumination made the whole thing seem like a nightmare. Falcon caught a glimpse of an upraised gun that slashed down at him. He jerked his head to the side and heard the weapon hit the ground inches from his ear.

He shot a short, sharp punch upward at what he hoped was the attacker's jaw. The blow landed with a satisfying impact that shivered up Falcon's arm. The man had been trying again to hit him with the pistol, but the punch rocked him back. Falcon grabbed him and rolled again, taking the man with him as they wrestled.

He lifted his leg and rammed his knee into his opponent's belly. At the same time, he sledged the side of his fist into the man's face and felt something crunch. The man went limp underneath him.

Falcon scrambled up. The chances of him finding his rifle in this darkness were pretty slim, but he still had his Colt. He slapped his hand against the holster on his hip to make sure of that. Finding the gun there, he drew it and hustled forward again, leaving the unconscious man behind him.

He could tell from the muzzle flashes that the camp was almost surrounded. The man he had just tangled with had been part of that circle, but he had heard Falcon coming and broken off his attack to try to stop him from helping the others.

The rest of the bunch wouldn't know that one of them was down. Falcon realized that and slowed his charge, then stopped as he saw a way he might be able to turn this to his advantage.

He dropped to a knee again and studied the scene, his keen eyes and brain taking in the details in a heartbeat. He could see the faint orange glow—all that was left of the campfire. In the thick darkness, it seemed brighter than it actually was.

By its dim light, he saw Eleanor stretched out on the ground, her left arm cradling the baby underneath her, while she propped herself up on that elbow. She was shielding the infant with her own body. In her other hand was the little pistol, and as Falcon watched, it popped again and jetted flame as she fired at the attackers. He didn't know if she had a target or was just shooting blindly, but at least she was putting up a fight.

So were Hardpan and Twister. The two old-timers had crawled into some rocks on the other side of camp that gave them some protection from the flying lead, even though they were still caught in a cross fire. Twister's Winchester cracked steadily, punctuated by the regularly spaced booms of Hardpan's Sharps.

Almost as soon as Falcon knelt, he was back up again, gliding through the shadows to his right. He closed in on the next attacker in the circle. The man didn't hear him coming. He was too busy trying to kill Falcon's friends.

Falcon reversed the Colt, lifted it, and aimed as carefully as he could in the bad light. He brought the gun butt crashing down on the bushwhacker's head.

The man slumped forward, but his hat cushioned the blow to a certain extent, so he wasn't knocked cold. He managed to half-turn and swipe the rifle he held at Falcon. The barrel cracked against Falcon's left arm.

Falcon grunted in pain but stepped in and struck again. This time, the gun butt landed above the man's left ear and stretched him out on the ground. Falcon dropped to a knee beside him and walloped him again, just for good measure.

He knew he risked killing the man with another blow to the head like that, but at the moment he didn't care. He figured these men were some of Otto Kramer's gunnies, and they were doing their best to kill Eleanor, Hardpan, and Twister, and putting that baby in deadly danger, too. Whatever happened to them, Falcon wasn't going to lose any sleep over it.

Confident that this hombre was out of the fight for a while, if not for good, Falcon rose to his feet and stole toward the next bushwhacker. He knew he had to hurry. The guns continued to roar, and with every moment that passed, the risk to his friends grew greater.

The situation changed abruptly as a swift rataplan of hoof-beats swept through the night. Falcon heard the horses pounding over the ground right behind him, and desperately flung himself to the side to keep from getting trampled. The gunfire must have spooked the first two men he had seen, the ones holding the horses, and they were joining the fight by stampeding through the camp, leading the other mounts.

Falcon jumped up and sprinted toward the camp. His plan to

whittle down the odds was over now, but at least he had taken care of two of the bushwhackers.

"Eleanor, look out!" he shouted, not knowing if she could hear him over the hoofbeats.

A gun barked to his left. He felt the wind-rip of a slug close beside his head. Twisting, he fired as he ran, aiming by instinct at the glimpse of muzzle flame he'd caught from the corner of his eye.

Somewhere off in that direction, a man howled in pain. That brought a grim, fleeting smile to Falcon's lips.

Then he saw sparks fly and swirl as the riders pounded through what was left of the campfire. Eleanor screamed. The spiteful pop of her little pistol mixed with rifle cracks and the booming reports of heavier handguns. Chaos reigned in the camp, and as Falcon plunged into the middle of it, a man shouted, "I've got the girl!"

That made Falcon's pulse hammer. He swung his Colt in the direction of the voice, but didn't squeeze the trigger. He couldn't shoot, not knowing where Eleanor and the baby were. Cursing the darkness, he jammed his gun back in its holster and ran toward the man who had shouted, intending to drag him out of the saddle.

A charging horse came out of nowhere and clipped him with its shoulder. That collision sent Falcon spinning off his feet and left him lying stunned and breathless on the ground.

He tried to push himself up, but his muscles refused to cooperate. Even the embers of the fire were scattered now, and he couldn't see a thing as the hoofbeats faded. Men yelled back and forth, but he couldn't make out the words.

"Eleanor!" he finally gasped. "Eleanor, are you still here?"

She didn't answer, but a tremulous wail sounded not far away. Falcon was relieved that the attackers hadn't carried off the baby, but as the kid's squalling grew in volume, he started to worry that the infant was hurt.

That worry spurred his muscles and nerves to start working again. He crawled toward the crying and after a moment touched a blanket-wrapped bundle. Falcon scooped up the baby as he raised himself onto his knees. Holding the infant firmly in the crook of his left arm, he used his right hand to explore the sturdy little body. The baby quieted down, evidently soothed by Falcon's touch.

He didn't feel any blood, and the kid's arms and legs, waving around like they often did when he was awake, seemed to be working all right. If the bushwhackers actually had carried off Eleanor, they either hadn't known about the baby or hadn't wanted to take it along.

The shooting had stopped, and as the hoofbeats dwindled off in the distance, an ominous quiet fell in their place. Twister broke that brooding silence by whispering, "Falcon! Falcon, are you around?"

"Here," Falcon replied quietly. If any of the attackers had remained nearby, he didn't want to draw a shot, but he had to find out if the two old-timers were hurt. "I'm all right, and the baby seems to be also. How about you and Hardpan?"

"We're fine," came a growl from Hardpan in response. "Did they really get the girl?"

"I think so." Falcon whispered urgently, "Eleanor! Eleanor, can you hear me?"

Nothing. She was gone, all right.

Or dead.

He didn't want to think about that. Instead, holding the baby against him, he crawled toward the rocks where Hardpan and Twister had taken cover.

"I'm coming toward you fellas with the kid," he told them. "Don't shoot us."

"Come ahead," Hardpan told him grimly.

Once Falcon reached the relative safety of the rocks, he placed the baby against one of them and then twisted around to face outward with his gun in his hand. He didn't think the bushwhackers were going to come back, but he wanted to be ready if they did.

"Were you hit?" he asked.

"We were lucky, I guess," Twister replied. "With all that lead flyin' around, it's a wonder neither of us got tagged."

"They grabbed Eleanor, though, didn't they?" Hardpan said.

"Seems like it," Falcon said. "But that doesn't mean they're going to get away with it. We can't track them in the dark, but at least we know where they're going. And first thing in the morning, we'll be headed back to Carlsburg."

That would probably mean missing Christmas with Duff, but it couldn't be helped. There was no way Falcon was going to abandon Eleanor to whatever fate Otto Kramer had in mind for her.

"You reckon it was Kramer's men who jumped us?" Twister asked.

"Who else could it have been? I halfway expected him not to live up to his word. Maybe more than halfway, really."

"Yeah," Hardpan said. "He didn't seem exactly like the trustworthy sort."

Something about the voices of both old prospectors struck Falcon as odd, as if they weren't completely convinced Kramer was behind the attack tonight. Falcon couldn't think of anybody else who would want to kill him, Hardpan, and Twister and kidnap Eleanor.

The baby started fussing again. *Probably misses Eleanor,* Falcon thought. Already, just in the few days they had traveled together, the kid had gotten attached to her. He recalled the way she had hovered over the infant, protecting him from bullets with her own body. And she claimed not to have any maternal instincts. Falcon was more convinced than ever how that wasn't true.

He tried to calm the kid down, and eventually the baby dozed off again. Enough time had passed that Falcon judged it safe to go check on the horses and pack mules. He hoped none of them had pulled loose from their pickets and bolted during all the gunplay.

The animals were still there and all right. They were picketed, well off to the side of the camp, and hadn't been too much in the line of fire. When he was satisfied, Falcon returned to the camp and found Twister kindling a small fire.

"I don't know if that's wise," he said.

"Neither is freezing to death," Hardpan said. "And let's face it, those varmints know where we are. Anyway, you said yourself that they'll be heading back to Carlsburg."

"Yeah," Falcon said slowly. A frown creased his forehead. He hunkered beside the fire as the flames began to dance a little higher. Hardpan was right about one thing: The warmth felt good.

But not knowing if his companions were telling him the truth—or the whole truth, anyway—didn't.

Chapter 29

Nobody slept much that night except the kid. Falcon, Hardpan, and Twister took turns dozing, but too much had happened and they were too keyed up to fall into a sound slumber. By morning, weariness had a strong grip on Falcon, and his eyes felt gritty, as if their sockets were lined with fine sand.

Coffee would help, he knew. Twister had a pot brewing by the time the eastern sky was just starting to turn gray.

The coffee wasn't done yet when the sound of a horse slowly approaching the camp from the west made all three men reach for their guns. Falcon had found his rifle where he had dropped it the night before. It felt good to have the Winchester in his hands again—as good as anything could feel under the circumstances.

As the hoofbeats stopped, a voice hailed them through the predawn gloom. "Hello, the camp! Hold your fire!"

Hardpan and Twister withdrew into the rocks, taking the baby with them. Falcon moved off to the other side of camp and dropped to one knee, holding the rifle ready. The man's voice was vaguely familiar, but Falcon didn't really recognize it.

"Stay where you are," he said. "Who are you, and what do you want?"

"My name's not important," the man replied. "And what matters is, what do *you* want?"

Falcon thought he had the rider located now, about fifty yards west of the camp. Well within range, but Falcon didn't want to start shooting until he knew whom he was shooting at—and why.

"I don't follow," he said in reply to the man's enigmatic question.

"It's simple. Do you want that girl back safe and sound?"

That deepened the frown on Falcon's face. It sounded like the man wanted to trade Eleanor back to them. That didn't seem like something Otto Kramer would do. Once again, his eyes narrowed in suspicion as he glanced toward the rocks where Hardpan and Twister crouched.

"Of course, we want Eleanor safe. What do you want in return?"

As he waited for the answer, he listened intently for the sound of anyone trying to creep closer to the camp. It was possible the rider was just trying to distract them as men snuck in to attack again.

Falcon didn't hear anything, though, and the response from their early-morning visitor came back quickly.

"All you have to do to get the girl back is turn over those two old codgers. Send them out, on foot, and we'll send the girl to you."

Falcon stiffened. If he needed more proof that Hardpan and Twister were up to something he didn't know about, he'd just gotten it.

The two old-timers had heard what the stranger said and had to have a pretty good idea about the thoughts going through Falcon's head right now. Hardpan called, "Falcon, don't jump to any conclusions now—"

"Shut up," Falcon snapped. He had to think about this, and while he did, he asked the man lurking out there, "How do I know I can trust you?"

"You can trust this," the man replied. "If you don't give us what we want, you won't like what happens to that pretty little blonde."

The eastern sky had lightened even more. Although Falcon still didn't have a good view of the rider, he felt pretty sure he could knock the varmint out of the saddle with his Winchester anytime now. But that wouldn't do Eleanor any good, and judging by the man's confident—even arrogant—tone, the same thought had occurred to him.

"We've got to talk about this," Falcon said, stalling for more time.

"Well, don't talk too long. You'll be sorry if you do." The man wheeled his horse. "Not as sorry as that blonde, though!" he flung back over his shoulder as he heeled the animal into a run. Instinct made Falcon want to throw a shot after him, but he controlled the urge.

The hoofbeats faded away. Falcon stayed where he was for several long minutes, wary of a trick, even though the man had sounded completely sincere. When he finally stood up and moved back over by the campfire, Twister greeted him from the rocks by saying, "Falcon, it's not what you think."

"What I think is that you two have been lying to me all along," he said. "And now it's time for you to come out here and tell me the truth."

He heard one of the old-timers sigh. "He's right," Hardpan said to Twister. "I guess we've got to tell him the whole story."

Whatever they told him, Falcon thought, he was going to be a mite leery of believing it. Right now, though, he didn't have any choice but to listen to what they had to say.

They emerged from the rocks. Twister had the baby in his arms. As the infant fretted, Twister said, "I think he's hungry."

"More than likely," Falcon said. "You can hang on to him

and try to keep him happy while Hardpan rustles some breakfast for all of us."

"Sure, sure," Twister muttered. Carefully he sat down cross-
legged on the ground, close enough to the fire to get some of
the heat from it.

When Hardpan began cooking flapjacks and frying bacon,
Falcon said, "You can talk while you're working."

"Sure. Twister ought to tell you the story, though. He's better at talking than I am."

"I'm sure I'll be hearing from both of you. Go on."

"All right. You ever hear of a man named John Henry Stillwater?"

The name was familiar to Falcon, but it took him a moment
to recall where he had seen it before. He had read it in various
newspaper articles, he realized, mostly in the Denver paper.

"He owns a mine, doesn't he?"

Twister grunted and said, "A mine . . . not exactly. He owns
half a dozen that we know of, and maybe more by now, the
way he gobbles up claims."

"Yeah, I remember now," Falcon said, nodding. "He's supposed to be one of the richest men west of the Mississippi."

Hardpan said, "If he went *east* of the Mississippi, he'd still be
one of the richest men."

"He's rolling in loot," Twister added.

Falcon cocked his head. "You're not going to try to tell me
this fella Stillwater was behind those men trying to jump that
worthless claim of yours, back where we first met."

"No, Stillwater wasn't interested in that claim," Hardpan
said.

"It was us he wanted," Twister said.

"Why would a tycoon like Stillwater want a couple of old
pelicans like you two dead?" Falcon didn't bother to frame the
question with a *No offense* preface. Right now, he didn't care if
he offended them.

"He doesn't want us *dead*, exactly . . . ," Hardpan said.

Falcon's mind went back to the day he had met the two old-timers. The so-called claim jumpers had sounded like they didn't want to kill Hardpan and Twister, which explained why they had been reluctant to blast them out of the mine tunnel with dynamite.

"So Stillwater needs you alive, does he? Why would that be?"

"Because we were his partners," Twister said.

"*Are* his partners," Hardpan added.

Falcon scrubbed a hand over his face. "You're going to have to explain that. If you're partners with a man as rich as John Henry Stillwater, then why are you wandering around and grubbing at claims that don't even pan out?"

"It's been a long time since we actually worked with him," Hardpan said. "We were all just starting out when we met each other. Since none of us really knew what we were doing, we figured it might not hurt to have somebody else along on our prospecting trips."

"You know, like they say, 'Two heads are better than one,'" Twister put in. "There were three of us."

Hardpan picked up the story again. "We had a little luck, turned up some color here and there. When that happened, John Henry started thinking it might be a good idea if we drew up some sort of agreement and signed it."

"'Share and share alike,'" Twister elaborated. "No matter which one of us actually found anything worth finding."

"John Henry drew up the paper. He worded it so things would stay the same among us from then on, unless we all agreed to end the partnership. That was important to him, that it had to be, what's the word, *unanimous*."

"If you ask me," Twister said, "John Henry had decided that he'd never be any great shakes as a prospector, but he thought that Hardpan and me might actually get lucky and find a real strike. I hate to speak poorly of anybody, but he was a pretty greedy fella."

Falcon said, "So this partnership the three of you had was never dissolved?"

Hardpan shook his head. "As it turned out, John Henry wound up going his own way, and wouldn't you know it, *he's* the one who struck it rich. Twister and I enjoyed the life we'd carved out for ourselves, though, so we kept prospecting. Never had much luck at it, but it's a fine way to live, always out in the open air, seeing the world."

"Did you forget all about being partners with Stillwater?" Falcon asked.

Twister smiled and said, "It's a plumb funny thing, but we did. For a long time, anyway."

"Then, while we were in a town picking up some supplies, we came across an old newspaper with an article in it talking about John Henry and how rich he is, and that got us to thinking."

"About how you could each claim a third of the fortune he's made," Falcon said.

"Mighty intriguin' turn of the cards, ain't it?" Twister said.

"You still have that signed partnership agreement?" Falcon asked.

Hardpan nodded. "We do. Took us a while to find it, but we turned it up among some old books and papers we had in our belongings."

Falcon was almost afraid to ask, but he said, "What did you do then?"

"Why, we went to see John Henry in Denver, to have us a fine ol' reunion," Twister said.

"And demand your shares." Falcon's words weren't a question this time.

"Well, we had 'em comin'," Hardpan said indignantly. "A deal's a deal, ain't it? And there was no way John Henry could deny we had a deal, since he was the one who'd come up with it in the first place and then put his name on it, along with ours."

"What did he do?"

Twister looked a little embarrassed as he said, "He, uh, had us thrown out of his office."

Hardpan snorted. "Tossed out, like we were nothing but tramps."

"What happened then?" Falcon asked.

Hardpan shrugged and said, "What could we do? There's just the two of us, and Stillwater's got a lot of men working for him. Hard men who don't mind hurting folks. We figured we'd given it our best shot." He sighed. "Men like us, we just ain't cut out to be rich. So we went back to what we do best, roaming around and looking for a new claim that might pay off."

"One of these days, one of 'em will," Twister insisted. "We'll make enough, we won't have to just scrape by no more."

Falcon didn't know what was more pathetic, that Twister was still telling himself that, or that he sounded like he actually believed it. But who was to say he was wrong? Maybe fate was just biding its time, waiting for the right moment to deal these two old desert rats a good hand.

"It sounds to me like after you left, Stillwater got to thinking . . . and worrying," Falcon said. "If he knew you had that old document, he might be afraid that you'd come back again, maybe with some fancy lawyer the next time."

"*A lawyer!*" Twister said. "By golly, Hardpan, we never thought of that!"

"We didn't have the money to hire one, even if we had thought of it," Hardpan said.

Falcon knew some lawyers, including one of his own brothers. He might be able to help these old codgers get what was rightfully theirs—although it was a stretch to say that they deserved any of John Henry Stillwater's riches. After all, partnership agreement or not, Stillwater was the one who had done the work to amass that fortune.

However, all that could be hashed out later. At the moment, there were more important things to settle.

"Back when those gunnies jumped you, you figured they were Stillwater's men, didn't you?"

"It seemed pretty likely," Hardpan admitted with a shrug. "That claim wasn't really worth jumping."

"Why didn't you tell me what was going on then? Were you afraid I'd try to double-deal you and grab that paper, maybe sell it to Stillwater to get you off his back?"

"It could've happened that way," Hardpan blustered. "Yeah, you'd given us a hand—"

"A mighty big hand," Twister said. "Saved our bacon, even."

"But we didn't really know you," Hardpan went on. "Now that we've spent more time with you . . . yeah, I reckon we trust you now. You're a decent sort."

"Thanks," Falcon said dryly.

"But there still didn't seem to be any reason to complicate things."

"Even though Stillwater's men were still after you." Falcon looked at Twister. "It was one of them who took that potshot at you, not some Indian, right?"

Twister shrugged and said, "I reckon. The fella I saw didn't really look like an Injun. Might've been, though, I suppose."

Falcon didn't pursue that. Instead he said, "So now they've tried to grab you again. The reason none of that flying lead hit you is that Stillwater wants you alive. His men were firing high. He's afraid you've hidden that agreement somewhere, and he wants it in his hands before he kills you."

"That's the way it lays out to us," Hardpan agreed.

"But he doesn't care about Eleanor, and when that bunch wound up with her as a prisoner, instead of you two, they figured they could trade her and get what they really want."

"That makes sense. So, what are we going to do about it?"

"That's the simplest question of all," Falcon said. "I'm going to give the two of you to them."

Chapter 30

The sun was peeking over the horizon by the time the rider approached the camp again and called, "MacCallister!"

Eleanor must have told them my name, Falcon thought. Otherwise they wouldn't know who he was. More than likely, she'd warned them that the famous gunfighter Falcon MacCallister was her friend.

That probably hadn't done much good. Falcon might have a reputation—but John Henry Stillwater, the man they worked for, had a few mountains of gold.

"I'm here," Falcon said. He had pulled back into a little gully that gave him some cover as it curved around through the shallow, rolling hills. The horses and mules were picketed behind him. He had his Winchester thrust over the lip of the gully in front of him. "Keep coming so I can see you."

Fifty yards away, the rider came into view at the top of a rise that was thick with dead grass at this time of year. Falcon squeezed the trigger and the Winchester cracked. The bullet kicked up dirt from the ground about ten feet in front of the man on horseback, who reined in sharply.

"What the devil do you think you're doing?" he yelled angrily.

"Just keeping you honest," Falcon replied. "Also letting you know that if you try any tricks, I won't have any trouble knocking you right off that horse's back."

"No tricks, blast it. Just a simple bargain. You know the terms. The girl for those two old geezers."

"You've got a deal," Falcon called.

The rider was silent for a couple of seconds, as if Falcon's response surprised him. Then he said, "You're going to give them up?"

"You've seen them, and you've seen the girl. Who do *you* reckon means more to me?"

The man stared in his direction for a second longer, then laughed.

"I guess if you look at it that way, it makes sense."

"Only way to look at it," Falcon said. "I took those old pelicans' guns away and tied their hands, but they can still walk out to you. I'll send 'em in your direction . . . as soon as Eleanor's back here with me."

The rider shook his head. "What kind of fool do you take me for? You give me the old-timers, then you get the girl back."

Falcon laughed harshly. "Now you're trying to play *me* for a fool. How about we start 'em at the same time, the girl from your end and the old-timers from mine?"

Falcon was watching the man's reaction closely. The rider turned his head and glanced back over his shoulder, as if checking with somebody else who was out of sight on the far side of that rise. That meant he wasn't the boss of the gang that had Eleanor, just the spokesman.

Whoever was in charge, it didn't take him long to make a decision. The rider called, "All right, MacCallister. Send the old men out here. But remember, there'll be rifles pointed at them the whole way . . . and the girl . . . just in case you get to feeling frisky."

"Anybody ought to worry about *feeling frisky*," Falcon shot back, "it's you! I can drill you before you even start to turn that horse around."

The rider glanced over his shoulder again. He was nervous, and justifiably so, about being stuck out there in the open with a target on him. But now that the deal was made, his boss must have ordered him to stay right where he was.

"All right," Falcon said quietly to Hardpan and Twister, who were waiting in the gully with him. "The two of you get out there."

Twister swallowed hard. "Are you sure about this, Falcon?"

"There's no other way to do it," Hardpan said. "Come on."

They climbed out of the gully and trudged a few feet forward. Falcon told them, "Hold it. They haven't sent Eleanor out yet."

Then he saw the early-morning sun flash red and gold on her blond hair as she came over the hill next to the man on horseback. He motioned for her to keep going. She did, but Falcon saw her turn her head and look to both right and left. He thought she was trying to tell him that riflemen were hidden along that rise. He already had a pretty good idea that was the case.

"Go ahead," he told Hardpan and Twister.

They shuffled along. Their hands were tied together in front of them, clearly visible from the rise. They made steady progress despite their obvious reluctance to do this.

Eleanor stumbled a little coming down the slope, but didn't fall. Falcon held his breath until he saw that her gait was normal. He was relieved that she hadn't hurt herself. It would have made his plan more difficult to pull off if she wasn't able to move fast when he needed her to do so.

Only about twenty feet separated her from Hardpan and

Twister. If Stillwater's men were going to try anything, it would probably be when Eleanor reached the old-timers. He saw the reaction on her face when Hardpan spoke to her, although he couldn't hear the words. She had been on a course to pass them by several feet, but she veered toward them.

Behind her, the man on horseback stiffened in the saddle and called, "What are you doing, lady?"

Eleanor turned her head and said, "I just want to hug them and say good-bye. They're giving up a lot for me."

She didn't wait to see whether he approved. She hurried to Hardpan first and then Twister, throwing her arms around each of them in turn and embracing them.

When she stepped back away from them and started toward Falcon again, she had her left arm pressed against her body, holding under her coat the bottle of whiskey Hardpan had slipped to her while she was hugging him.

Falcon had known that Eleanor was smart. She was quick-witted, too. She must have understood the plan right away when Hardpan told her what to do.

Falcon was counting the steps under his breath as Eleanor continued toward him. Her former captors couldn't see what she was doing, but he had a clear view as she brought out the bottle, snapped into flame with her thumbnail one of the lucifers Twister had given her, and held it to the whiskey-soaked rag stuffed into the neck of the bottle. The rag caught fire instantly.

Then Falcon reared up out of the gully with the Winchester socked against his shoulder and started spraying bullets along that rise as fast as he could work the rifle's lever. At the same time, Eleanor whirled around and heaved the bottle with the burning rag as far as she could toward the top of the rise.

Then she did what Hardpan and Twister had just done—she hit the dirt.

The bottle with the burning rag in it turned over a couple of times in the air, then hit the grassy slope not far below the man on horseback and exploded into a ball of fire. The flames splashed over the hillside, spreading with breathtaking speed. Thick white smoke began to billow into the air.

"Now!" Falcon shouted.

He stopped shooting as Eleanor and the two old-timers scrambled to their feet and sprinted toward him. Gunfire followed them, but Stillwater's men were shooting blind now because of all the smoke in the air. They might still score a lucky hit, but Falcon's plan had tipped the odds in his friends' favor as much as possible.

Eleanor, Hardpan, and Twister reached the gully, raced into and out of it as fast as they could. Now that they were behind him, Falcon stood up and cranked off more rounds in the direction of Stillwater's men.

While he was doing that, the other three swung into their saddles. Falcon had made it look like the old-timers' hands were tied by wrapping rope around their wrists, but that was just for show. The ends were tucked in, instead of knotted, and Hardpan and Twister were able to throw off the bonds without any trouble.

Falcon had also hung the baby's sling on Eleanor's saddle, knowing that if she reached her horse safely, she would take care of the kid.

"Falcon!" Hardpan yelled. "Let's go!"

At that moment, the Winchester's hammer clicked on the empty chamber. Falcon had fired it dry, so that was good timing. He turned, bounded out of the gully, and ran toward his mount. He practically vaulted into the saddle and rammed the rifle back into its scabbard as he grabbed the reins with his other hand.

"Come on!" he barked at the others. He jabbed his boot heels into the horse's flanks. It leaped into a run, heading east. Falcon heard hoofbeats behind him and glanced back to see that his three companions were following. Eleanor was right behind him, holding the baby against her in the crook of her left arm, while she handled the reins with her right. Hardpan and Twister closely brought up the rear.

Shots still banged from the other side of the fire, which had now spread to engulf the entire rise for at least a quarter of a mile. It grew with each passing second. Falcon, like most frontiersmen, hated and feared an out-of-control blaze more than almost anything. He hadn't seen any other way to free Eleanor and protect Hardpan and Twister, though.

Anyway, out here in this isolated region, no settlements would be threatened. The fire might force some wildlife to flee, but it wouldn't harm any humans.

Every so often, he heard a bullet hum past, relatively close, but that didn't last long. They galloped up and down the rolling hills and soon left their enemies behind. Falcon pushed them at a hard pace until he knew the horses couldn't take it anymore and needed to rest.

He slowed his mount to a walk and the others followed suit. As Eleanor came alongside him, he asked, "Are you all right? Those varmints didn't mistreat you?"

"No, I'm fine," she said. "Their boss wanted to keep me nice and safe so he could trade me for Hardpan and Twister." She turned her head to look back at the desert rats. "That man has a powerful hate for you two, though."

"Are you sayin' that John Henry Stillwater his own self is with 'em?" Twister asked.

"A stocky man, a little under medium height, with a face like a bulldog? Not much hair and what's left of it is gray?"

Hardpan nodded and said, "That sounds like John Henry, all right. Not when he was young, of course, but like he was when we saw him in Denver a few months back."

"He must really be mad at us if he rode all the way out here with those hired guns," Twister said.

Eleanor said, "From the way he talked, he'd be happy to string you both up over a fire and cook your brains out, the way the Indians do. But only *after* he got some sort of paper from you. He never explained what that was all about. In fact, he didn't talk to me at all except to promise that I wouldn't be hurt if you cooperated, and he was pretty gruff about that." She frowned. "What's on that paper that it's so all-fired important to him?"

"That's a long story, and these old codgers can tell it to you later," Falcon said. "Right now, we need to pick up the pace a little and keep moving. The way that fire was spreading, it's going to take them a while to go around it—at least I hope so—but they'll be picking up our trail again, I expect."

"Yeah, John Henry ain't the sort to give up," Hardpan said.

"John Henry Stillwater," Eleanor repeated. "I've heard that name before, haven't I? Or read it in a newspaper?"

"More than likely," Falcon said, "but that's part of that long story I mentioned."

"How long do you think we can stay ahead of them?" Twister asked.

"We don't have to stay ahead of them forever. Just until we get to Chugwater and meet up with my cousin Duff."

One of the men was howling in pain. He'd been shot in the gut, and it was only a matter of time until he died.

"Can't you shut him up?" John Henry Stillwater growled at Jed Pearson. Pearson was the one who'd put together this group of gunmen, and as such, he was responsible for them. "He's getting on my nerves."

"He's dying, Mr. Stillwater," Pearson said in his gravelly voice. He had been in this game for a long time and had a shock of white hair above a seamed, deeply tanned face.

"Yes, I know, but he can do it quietly, can't he?"

Stillwater saw Pearson's mouth tighten and realized that he

might have crossed a line. When you had enough money, the boundaries of acceptable behavior were a lot fewer and farther apart, but they still existed.

"I mean, give him something for the pain," Stillwater went on. "There's no need for the poor man to suffer like that."

The tension in Pearson eased. "We've been givin' him whiskey. I don't know what else we can do."

"Don't you have any opium or laudanum?"

Pearson shook his head. "Nope. Wish we did." He frowned. "But I get your point, Mr. Stillwater. The poor varmint's in a lot of pain, and there's no way he's gonna live through havin' his guts shot out like that." He nodded. "I'll be back in a minute."

"Fine," Stillwater said curtly. He turned his back, fished a cigar out of his vest pocket, and busied himself lighting it. Meanwhile Pearson conversed quietly with his men; then a single gunshot sounded. Stillwater's teeth clenched a little harder on the cheroot.

Sometimes in life, extreme measures had to be taken. The men who could tell when those moments came along, and how extreme those measures needed to be, were the ones who succeeded.

John Henry Stillwater was a successful man, no matter how anybody measured it.

Stillwater puffed on the cigar as Pearson came back over to him. "The boys will dig a grave," the gun-boss said. "Won't take long, and by then, that fire will've died down enough for us to go after that bunch again."

"I hope the next effort doesn't fail. You've been after those two scoundrels for quite a while now. I hoped that when I joined you, my presence would have a positive effect and we could bring this sorry affair to a close."

"Nobody wants that more'n me, boss. I've lost several good men to MacCallister." Pearson's voice hardened. "I've got a score of my own to settle now."

"I don't care about MacCallister, except that he's in my way."

"No, sir, I understand that." Pearson rubbed his chin. "Falcon MacCallister's got quite a reputation. At my age, I don't care so much about things like that anymore, but I'll admit, it'd be nice to be the man who took him down."

"I hope you succeed, because that means I'll get what I want, too . . . Hawkins and McCoy taken care of so that they can never bother me again." Stillwater jerked his head in a nod. "And I'll pursue them to the ends of the earth to assure that, if I have to."

Chapter 31

Chugwater

Andrew had toyed with the idea of presenting his production of *A Christmas Carol* on Christmas Eve, but finally had decided on the evening of December 23 for the performance. That would allow families from outlying ranches and farms to attend and then return home on Christmas Eve, so they could spend Christmas Day gathered around their own familiar hearths.

He wanted as large an audience as could be packed into the town hall, too, so he had decided not to sell tickets. Admission would be free to all. Andrew and Rosanna were covering the production's expenses out of their own funds.

The day before the performance was scheduled to go on, Duff offered to chip in, but Andrew refused.

"Once I've seen how the show plays here, I'm seriously considering taking it on the road next fall," he explained to Duff as they stood just inside the wings in the town hall, next to the stage. "This is, well, a practice performance, so to speak. A dress rehearsal, but only a bit more than that. I'll watch how it goes in front of an audience, and then I can make any necessary adjustments to my adaptation. You know, smooth out all the rough spots, assuming there are any."

"I'm for thinkin' ye ken wha' you're talkin' about," Duff told him. "Ye've been in this actin' business for a long time."

Andrew smiled. "That's right, and in the long run, I don't expect to lose any money on this project. Everyone loves Christmas. It's the time of year when people can put their animosities aside and come together, no matter what their differences."

"Aye. Ye'd think so, wouldn't ye?"

Duff was looking at Meagan and Fiona as he spoke. There hadn't been any more suspicious incidents, but the two young women hadn't put aside their animosities, as Andrew phrased it. They were sitting on opposite sides of the town hall, each looking over the script they held, but from time to time they shot cool glances at each other as well.

If I'd been smart, Duff told himself, *I would'a gotten Andrew to recast the role of Bob Cratchit.* Duff never had believed that it really suited him, and once Fiona finagled her way into playing his wife, that should have been enough to warrant a change. It would have hurt Fiona's feelings, and Duff was chivalrous enough that he didn't care for that idea, but sometimes a few hurt feelings were necessary to keep the peace.

Rehearsals were over for the day. The next morning, there would be a final run-through, and then that evening, *A Christmas Carol: An Adaptation by Mr. Andrew MacCallister of the World-Famous Novel by Mr. Charles Dickens* would have its world debut.

Duff had his copy of the script in his hand as he nodded a good-bye to his cousin. He rolled up the script and stuck it in the back pocket of his jeans, then walked over to Meagan. As she looked up at him with a smile, he said, "'Tis hopin' I am that ye'll have supper wi' me at the City Café."

"I was hoping you'd ask me that, Duff."

"Then you're for sayin' yes?"

"No," Meagan said. "I won't."

That blunt answer took him by surprise. "Ye won't?" he asked with a frown. "Have I done somethin' to offend ye?"

"Not at all," she said as she got to her feet. "I'd be very pleased to have supper with you. I just have somewhere else in mind."

"Oh." Duff nodded in relief. "Well, then, anywhere ye like is fine wi' me, ye ken that."

"I was thinking that we'd eat at my place." Mischief twinkled in her eyes. "I've done something very daring."

Duff's eyebrows rose.

"I've made a figgy pudding," Meagan went on.

"Oh," he said. "Ye mean, like in the song."

"That's right. Well, maybe not *exactly* the same. I don't have all the right ingredients. But I came as close as I could."

"'Tis all right. Figgy pudding is an English dish, to start with."

Meagan put a hand to her mouth. "And you don't care for the English, since you're a Scotsman. Oh, I didn't even think about that."

Duff laughed and said, "Nae, 'tis nothin' to worry about, lass. Those days are past. I can tolerate the Englishers . . . and their figgy puddin'. I'm sure 'twill be delicious."

"And that's not all I have for you," she went on. The look in her eyes got even more mischievous.

"Och, now tha' be an invitation I willna pass up." He held out his arm. "Shall we go?"

She linked her arm with his and said, "We shall."

They left the town hall together. Duff had a funny feeling on the back of his neck, the sort of feeling he'd experienced before when someone was pointing a gun at him. He had a hunch this one was caused by Fiona watching him and Meagan walk out, arm in arm, smiling and laughing.

A jealous woman wasn't a good thing, but at least it wasn't as bad as a bushwhacker drawing a bead on him.

*   *   *

Fiona tried to keep her face impassive and not glare as she watched Duff and Meagan stroll out of the town hall. Duff didn't look around. If he had caught her giving him a dirty look, he probably would have assumed she was upset because he was with Meagan. It never would have occurred to him that she had a blood debt to settle with him.

The only problem with the plan, as she had worked it out, was that she wanted him to know *why* he was dying, along with everyone else he cared about. She had a little more than twenty-four hours to come up with an idea of how to let him know.

Maybe she could write a note and give it to him just before the performance, asking him not to read it until after the play was over. Surely, once she had slipped out of the town hall and it was burning down around Duff and all his friends, he would think to pull the note from his pocket and read it.

Then he would know that the Somerled clan had had its vengeance.

As she sat there, she told herself to be patient. She would have her revenge on Duff soon enough. Let him enjoy his last night with his blond trollop. 'Twould be the last night on earth for both of them.

But she felt the hate gnawing at her guts, and without really thinking about what she was doing, she found herself on her feet, her steps carrying her out of the town hall and along Clay Avenue, a block behind Duff and Meagan.

They went through the dress shop and up the stairs to Meagan's living quarters. Duff saw the figgy pudding, which was actually more like cake than a pudding, sitting on a plate on the kitchen table, but he was more interested in Meagan. She said, "You wait out here. I'll be right back."

He nodded and hung his hat on a hook near the door. She disappeared into her bedroom. He wandered over to a desk against one wall and looked at the sheets of paper spread out on it. She had been working on dress designs, sketching them in pencil and making notations on them. He knew almost nothing about fashion, only that whatever Meagan wore looked good on her.

"Duff . . ."

He turned and saw that she was wearing her costume for the play. She was a beautiful Ghost of Christmas Future, with her golden hair down around her shoulders and the elegant white gown swooping low in the front to reveal the creamy curves of her figure.

He said, "I dinna remember that costume bein' cut quite so low in th' front."

"That's because it wasn't," she said with a smile. "I made it so that it can be changed easily from a less daring style to a more provocative one."

"And why would ye be for doin' that?"

"For you, of course. I thought you might appreciate it."

"Aye, I canna deny tha' I do. 'Tis a great deal that I be appreciatin' it."

"You can come closer and . . . take a better look at it . . . if you'd like."

"Oh, I intend to."

A moment later, his arms were around her waist, her arms were around his neck, and he was kissing her, a kiss returned with equal passion and enthusiasm. Time passed without either of them being particularly aware of it, and certainly neither of them gave a single thought to figgy pudding.

When the kiss finally ended, Meagan whispered, "Have you ever made love to a ghost?"

"Nae," he said, struggling mightily for a few seconds to control the reaction he felt when the image of his late, beloved Skye McGregor appeared in his mind. If he *could* make love to a ghost, she would be the one . . . but he would die before he ruined this moment for Meagan, whom he loved equally well. He put a smile on his face and said, "But I've a feelin' that I may be about to."

"I know it's still a few days away, but . . . Merry Christmas, Duff."

"And Merry Christmas t' ye, me darlin' Meagan. Ye canna start celebratin' too early . . ."

Watching from a recessed doorway across the street, Fiona saw the light go out in Meagan's living quarters. Duff and Meagan had just gotten up there a few minutes earlier. Fiona assumed they were going to have supper together. Why would they have blown the lamp out so soon, unless . . . ?

Her lips tightened into a grim line. Despite everything she had pretended, she had no interest in Duff MacCallister . . . except as the target of her revenge. So, why should it bother her that he was up there cavorting with that . . . that blond slut? Whatever they were doing, it meant nothing to Fiona.

She sniffed, tore her gaze away from the now-darkened window, and stepped out of the alcove into the chilly wind that swept along the main street of Chugwater. She tightened her coat around her shoulders and walked toward the hotel.

When a figure stepped out of an alley mouth and raised a hand, she stopped short and caught her breath.

"Fiona?" The urgent whisper came from Nick Jessup.

She sighed in relief, then tensed again. She hadn't expected to see him tonight. As far as she knew, everything was arranged.

"What is it?" she asked. "Is something wrong?"

"No, no." He beckoned. "Come back here out of sight. We don't want anybody noticing us together."

"Ye said 'twas unlikely anyone in Chugwater would recognize ye, since the only time any of 'em laid eyes on ye before, ye had a mask o'er half o' your face."

Despite that, Fiona moved stealthily into the alley with

Nick. He didn't offer an explanation, just led her to the shed where they had rendezvoused a couple of times before.

Once they were inside, Fiona said in a low voice, "What's this all about, Nick? I thought—"

"Hold on a minute," he said. "Let me get this lantern lit."

A match rasped to life with a spurt of flame. Nick touched it to the wick of the lantern he was holding. As light filled the little room, Fiona gasped at the sight of two men standing there with Nick.

She recognized both of them. The younger one, who bore a distinct resemblance to Nick, was his brother Logan. The older, more dangerous-looking man was Kent Spalding, the leader of the outlaw gang that had held up the train.

The gang was going to raid Chugwater the very next night, so Fiona supposed Spalding was there on a last reconnaissance. That shouldn't have needed to involve her, though.

"What is this?" she asked coldly. "You're not goin' back on our deal, are ye, Nick?"

Nick wasn't the one who answered her. Spalding did that, saying harshly, "Nobody's going back on any deal, lady . . . especially you."

Fiona squared her shoulders. Her chin jutted out defiantly.

"I dinna ken why you're talkin' t' me like tha', sir, but I dinna like it. I've given ye no reason to mistrust me."

"I've heard tell of too many gangs that waltzed right into a trap when they believed they had everything set up," Spalding said. "I'm not going to let that happen to me and my boys."

"Ye think I be a double-dealer?"

"I just wanted to see you again for myself," Spalding said. "Look you in the eye and decide whether or not I can trust you. We carried you from that train against your will, remember? You could be trying to get even with us."

"No, boss, I told you," Nick said. "Before MacCallister and that posse jumped us, Fiona and I worked it all out. We agreed to work together, and she promised she could arrange it so we get a big haul out of the deal. We can loot the whole town."

"Yeah, I know. But when it comes to a job the whole gang is going to pull, I call the shots."

"Well?" Fiona flung at him in a challenging tone. "Wha' ha' ye decided?"

Spalding gave her a hard, flat stare for a long moment. Then a smile slowly spread over his rugged face.

"You're a feisty one, aren't you? A pretty one, too, but what I like is that look in your eyes. The one that says you'd cut the heart out of a man who crossed you." Spalding chuckled. "I don't think I want to be that hombre."

"Then everything proceeds as planned?" Fiona said.

"That's right. Tomorrow night, once everybody's inside that town hall, you slip out and bar the doors, and we'll keep 'em bottled up. When we ride out of Chugwater, we'll be a whole heap richer, and it'll be a merry Christmas for me and my men."

When they rode out of Chugwater, Fiona thought, the town would be ablaze, because she meant to see to it that the fire spread. By Christmas Eve morning, Chugwater would be a pile of ashes and everyone in it would be dead.

That would be cause to celebrate.

Chapter 32

The day before Christmas Eve dawned with gray clouds scudding across the sky from north to south, arrayed in such thick battlements that it seemed like the sun wouldn't be able to peek through again until, say, March or April. As Duff rode around Sky Meadow, checking to see that the ranch would be all right during his absence the next two days, he sniffed the air. *Might be snow, might not,* he decided. But it was that time of year, so it wouldn't be a surprise either way.

Only a few men would be staying on the ranch. The members of the crew had drawn lots to see who would remain and who would be going into town to see the play and enjoy a little early celebration.

Wang had volunteered to stay behind, since Christmas wasn't a holiday where he came from. That way, another cowboy who found this time of year more meaningful would have a chance to take in the performance. Duff thought that was an admirable gesture.

Satisfied that Sky Meadow would run smoothly enough while he was gone, Duff returned to the ranch house, where he found Elmer shaving.

"Gettin' yourself fancied up, are ye?"

"I promised Vi I'd take her to the play tonight, so I figured I best look as handsome as I can." Elmer turned his head from side to side and studied himself in the looking glass that hung on the wall. "Which is mighty durned handsome, if I do say so myself."

From the doorway, Wang said, "Miss Violet is fortunate to have such an impressive suitor."

Elmer preened. "Why, thank you, Wang."

"Of course, not as fortunate as you are to have the affections of such a fine woman. A wise man would consider formalizing the arrangement into a state of matrimony."

Duff grinned, flung out a hand, and said, "There ye go! I've been tellin' him the same thing, Wang, but he doesna listen."

"Both of ya just hush," Elmer said with a scowl. "Vi and me will get ourselves hitched when we're good and ready, not because a couple o' yahoos like you two think we oughter. And here I thought you was payin' me a genu-wine compliment."

"We were, Elmer," Duff said. "We just wouldna want to see ye stand by and do nothin' while some other fella was to come in and sweep Vi off her feet."

"'Tain't gonna happen," Elmer grumbled. "Anyway, you're a fine one to talk, Duff. You don't seem to be in any hurry to waltz down the aisle with Meagan." He looked at Wang. "And you—"

"I am a Shaolin priest," Wang reminded him.

"Mebbe so, but that ain't the same as a Catholic priest, is it? You could get hitched if you was of a mind to."

Wang inclined his head. "We are devoted to things of a higher plane."

"Which means the right gal ain't come along yet. But one o' these days . . ."

Duff changed the subject by saying, "We'll be heading into Chugwater soon. Hitch up the wagon whene'er you're ready, Elmer, and let the boys know we'll be for leavin'."

Duff cleaned up and shaved, too. His costume for the role of Bob Cratchit—which was basically just a brown tweed suit—was at the town hall in Chugwater, along with the rest of the production's wardrobe. So he was wearing his regular range clothes as he went out to the barn to saddle his horse.

Elmer had a team hitched to the wagon, and several members of the crew, wearing clean clothes and with their hair slicked down and smelling of bay rum, had already climbed into the back for the trip into town. Usually, they would just ride their horses, but since there would be quite a bit of drinking being done at Fiddler's Green and the Wild Hog Saloon after the performance, Elmer had suggested it might be better to take the wagon. That way, the boys could start sleeping off their bender on the way home, and nobody had to risk riding off into a ravine while snockered.

A young cowhand came running out of the bunkhouse as he stuffed his shirttails into his trousers. "Don't leave without me, fellas!" he called. "I been lookin' forward to this for weeks."

"You danged fool," one of the men said. "The boss's cousin didn't even come up with the idea for that play until a week or so ago."

"I still been lookin' forward to Christmas," the young cowboy insisted. "It's the best time of the year."

"Yeah, if Santy Claus brings you the present you want," another puncher gibed. "What'd you ask the old feller for, one o' them gals who works at the Wild Hog?"

That brought on a round of hilarity in the wagon. Duff smiled as he walked past on his way to the barn. After all the hard work and danger these men faced on an almost-daily basis, it was good to see them enjoying themselves.

A few minutes later, he rode out of the barn and found the wagon packed with eager cowhands and a couple more crowded onto the driver's seat with Elmer, who would handle the reins. Wang had come out onto the front porch of the main house to raise a hand in farewell.

"Might be some snow tonight," Duff told him. "Keep an eye on the sky. If the weather's too bad, we may all stay in town tonight."

Wang nodded and said, "That is wise. All will be well here."

With Wang in charge, Duff was confident that was true. He waved and turned his horse toward Chugwater. Elmer slapped the reins against the backs of the team and got the horses moving. It rolled away from the ranch on this cold, cloudy day.

The snow held off during the afternoon, but if anything, the overcast got even thicker. The temperature dropped as the day went on, an almost-sure sign that a storm was coming.

That didn't lessen the steady stream of people coming into Chugwater on horseback, in wagons, and in buggies and buckboards. Most of the ranchers in the area had given at least some of their hands permission to attend the performance of *A Christmas Carol*. Entire families from the smaller spreads and the farms hereabouts traveled to the settlement, eager to visit with their neighbors, attend the play and be entertained, and celebrate the biggest holiday of the year. The looming weather was a bit worrisome, but they would deal with that problem when and if they had to.

All the people who lived in town were excited, too, especially the ones who owned businesses. All those establishments were thronged with customers.

In a thicket of trees nearly a mile north of Chugwater, nearly two dozen men waited with varying degrees of patience. They stayed well back in the trees, because with so many people roaming the range today, they didn't want to take a chance on being spotted.

Nick Jessup paced a little, unable to contain the excitement he felt. That prompted Kent Spalding to say, "If you're as nervous as you're acting, kid, maybe I'd better start to worry about this plan."

"I'm not nervous, boss," Nick assured him. "I'm just eager for everything to get started." He laughed. "I've never been as rich as I'm gonna be before this night is over."

Logan dug an elbow into his brother's ribs and said, "You never had a gal as pretty as that Scottish redhead, either."

"She's something else, all right," Nick said with a grin.

Neither brother had forgotten how Hank and Sherm had been gunned down so ruthlessly on the main street of Chugwater, only a few weeks earlier. The desire for revenge on Duff MacCallister was strong in them. Their late brothers would have wanted them to move on with their lives, though, to pull this job and get rich and blow holes in that skunk MacCallister.

The problem was, MacCallister would be penned up inside the town hall with all the other folks. In order to get at him and settle the score, Nick was going to have to get in there before the night was over. That wasn't part of Fiona's plan, but he wasn't going to let some girl tell him everything he could or couldn't do, no matter how pretty and smart she was.

"Rider coming, boss," one of the men called to Spalding.

Stepping to the edge of the trees, Spalding peered out at the lone man on horseback coming from the direction of town. "That's Bedoya," he said after a moment.

Spalding was right. A few minutes later, the middle-aged Mexican outlaw rode into the trees and dismounted to lead his horse the rest of the way. He was a small, nondescript hombre, the sort of man most folks saw and promptly forgot about before a minute had passed. That made him particularly useful when it came to scouting out a job.

"The town is full of people, Señor Spalding," he reported, "with more coming in all the time. And they have come to spend money. The stores and saloons and restaurants, they are doing the . . . what do you call it . . . the booming business."

A grin stretched across Spalding's rugged face. "That means there'll be that much more money in their coffers for us, boys.

All we have to do is be patient. What time's that show supposed to start?"

"Six o'clock, Fiona said," Nick replied.

"It'll be good and dark an hour before that, on a day this cloudy. Nobody'll see us coming into town until it's too late."

"Hey, boss," one of the men called from the edge of the trees, "it's startin' to snow."

Duff looked out the front window of Meagan's shop and saw a few flakes drifting lazily down from the cloud-laden sky.

"Och, I smelled it this mornin'," he said. " 'Tis snowing."

"With this many people in town, I hope it's not a blizzard," she replied from the table where she was sitting and making notes on a piece of paper. "They might be stranded here and wouldn't be able to get home for Christmas."

The sign in the door was turned around so that it read CLOSED now, but during the morning and the first part of the afternoon, the shop had been full of ladies wanting dresses made. Meagan had taken so many orders she would be busy with them until spring, she had told Duff. It was good to see her business thriving, although he supposed the workload would mean the two of them would have less time to spend together. Still, Meagan loved what she did, so Duff couldn't be jealous of her success.

As he watched, the snowfall became heavier, although the flakes appeared to be light and fluffy, swirling and dancing in the light breeze that blew along Clay Avenue. *'Twas pretty,* he thought, although he had seen how quickly such a delicate display of nature's beauty could turn into a roaring, blinding, choking monster.

Behind him, Meagan pushed her chair back and stood up.

"That's done," she said. "I have all the orders listed, and I've figured out what fabric I'll need to get. I know I could have figured out all of this later, but I don't like postponing chores."

" 'Tis industrious ye are," Duff told her. "Tha' be why I like ye so much."

"Is that the *only* reason?" she asked, smiling.

"Och, well, no' exactly." Duff paused. "You're strong for a woman, and ye have a good shootin' eye."

She picked up the pencil she'd been using and said, "If I wasn't afraid I'd hurt you—being so strong for a woman—I'd throw this at you, Duff MacCallister."

Duff reached back and pulled the shade down over the window in the door, said, "C'mere, lass, and I'll show ye wha' I like about ye."

Meagan laughed. "There's no time for that. We need to get over to the town hall and see if Andrew and Rosanna need any help."

Duff sighed in not-completely-mock disappointment. "Aye, 'tis right ye be." He reached for his hat. "I'll help ye wi' your coat."

A few minutes later, Meagan had locked up the shop and they were strolling, arm in arm, up the street toward the town hall. Duff's tall, broad-shouldered, brawny form made it easier for them to make their way through the crowd on the boardwalk. Duff and Meagan nodded and wished a merry Christmas to many of the people they passed.

They were passing the mouth of the alley between the town hall and one of the buildings next to it when Duff spotted a familiar figure kneeling beside the wall toward the back of the alley. He said to Meagan, "Hold on a minute, if ye dinna mind."

"Duff, what is it?"

He didn't answer. Instead he unlinked his arm from hers and took a step into the alley.

"Fiona?" he called. "Is tha' you? Are ye all right, lass?"

Fiona straightened hurriedly. "Duff!" she said. "I . . . I . . . Yes, I'm fine. I was just . . . walkin' through the alley when I . . .

stumbled on something . . ." She looked down and kicked an empty tin can, which someone had thrown there. "On this very thing. Och, a person could kill themselves if they dinna watch where they're goin'."

"Aye," Duff agreed. "But wha' were ye doin' back here t' start with?"

"I told ye. 'Twas cuttin' through the alley, I was, on my way inside t' help Andrew and Rosanna get ready for the performance tonight."

Duff frowned. He couldn't see why Fiona would have even been in the alley if she'd been going from the hotel to the town hall. He was about to ask her about that when she brushed past him and started toward the street, only to stop short and say, "Oh. Good day to ye, Miss Parker."

Duff looked around and saw that Meagan had followed him into the alley. He hadn't expected that. In a tone just as chilly as Fiona's—and appropriate to the day with the snow falling around them—she said, "Good day to you, too, Miss Gillespie."

It was amazing how *unfriendly* a supposedly friendly greeting could sound. Both young women had that down to an art.

Duff figured it best for all of them to move on and attend to the business that had brought them here, but Meagan said to Fiona, "Are you ready for the performance?"

"Of course," Fiona replied. "Are ye no'?"

"I'm completely prepared," Meagan said.

"As am I. O' course, how much preparation does it take to be the wife o' this fine, upstandin' specimen o' manhood?"

Smiling sweetly, but with daggers in her eyes as she spoke, Fiona linked her arm with Duff's, just as Meagan's had been a few moments earlier.

Meagan frowned and looked at Duff as if to ask why he wasn't jerking his arm away from Fiona's. His natural courtesy wouldn't allow him to do that. But he did try to ease his arm out of hers as he said, "We'd best get on inside—"

"Seems I'm better at pretendin' t' be wed to Duff here than ye be in real life, Miss Parker," Fiona went on.

"Whatever Duff and I have planned for the future is no business of yours, Miss Gillespie."

"I'm just for sayin' tha' if 'twas me in your place, Duff an' I would already be wed and I'd ha' given him a bairn by now, wi' another likely on the way!"

Fiona followed that bold declaration with a contemptuous sniff.

The light wasn't very good in the alley under the best of circumstances. It was even gloomier on this snowy, overcast day. But despite that, Duff had no trouble seeing the anger that suddenly blazed to life in Meagan's eyes, or the furious expression that came over her face.

"How dare you say a thing like that?" she burst out. "I can see why Duff never had anything to do with a hussy like you."

"Ladies . . . ," Duff said, lifting his hands and making little patting motions at the air—as if that would soothe the ruffled feelings on display.

While Fiona gasped in surprise and resentment, Meagan went on speaking. "He never even knew you were alive, but if he had, he would have ignored you. You certainly don't deserve the attention of a fine man like him, and you shouldn't be pretending to be his wife, even in a stage play!"

"Well, I notice tha' Andrew dinna cast *you*," Fiona said. " 'Tis sure and certain he knew Duff . . . I mean Bob Cratchit . . . would ne'er choose to marry such a *shrew*!"

"Oh!" Meagan stepped past Duff and advanced toward Fiona.

"Ladies, please!" he said. He tried to grab Meagan, but she moved with surprising speed. Her open hand flashed up and cracked across Fiona's face in a resounding slap.

Now that Fiona had goaded Meagan into striking the first blow, she didn't hold back. She charged, hands outstretched and fingers crooked into talons that shot toward Meagan's face. At the same time, she lowered her shoulder and rammed it into

Meagan's body, driving her backward. Duff spread his arms and tried again to catch her, but even though both young women were slender, their combined weight struck him with considerable force and knocked him back a step as well. His arms went around both of them. He might have been able to get hold of an arm each and keep them apart, but at that moment, his right boot heel came down on something slick, probably a piece of garbage someone had tossed into the alley.

Duff's foot shot out from under him and he went over backward, falling and taking both Meagan and Fiona with him.

Chapter 33

"Dadblast it," Hardpan Hawkins said as he twisted around in his saddle to gaze back to the west. "As if we didn't have enough to worry about, now it's startin' to snow!"

Falcon said, "As long as it doesn't get so thick that we can't see where we're going, we'll be all right." He pointed vaguely ahead of them as they rode. "I know we're headed toward Chugwater, and I've got a feeling we'll make it there around nightfall."

"If we see the lights, they can guide us," Twister said. "Like a star in the east."

Hardpan snatched his hat off his mostly bald head and held it as if he were about to wallop his partner with it.

"There you go again, actin' like we're some sort of Wise Men. If we were all that wise, would we have a bunch of gun wolves chasing us, out for our scalps?"

"I don't know," Falcon mused. "It's been my experience that trouble tends to crop up, no matter how smart you are." He looked over at Eleanor. "Isn't there some Bible verse about how man is born to trouble?"

"Why are you asking me?" she said. "Like I told you before, I'm no Madonna. There aren't even that many of the Ten Commandments I haven't broken."

Falcon smiled. "But you know what the Ten Commandments are, so that just goes to show that you've read the Bible. I thought you might know."

Eleanor shook her head, but she smiled and even chuckled.

"You're an odd character, MacCallister," she said. "It's almost like you don't care that those killers are back there, close behind us on our trail."

"Oh, I care," Falcon assured her. "I want to keep you and the little one safe." He nodded toward the baby riding in the sling that was hung around Eleanor's neck, so that the baby was snuggled against her chest. She had buttoned her coat up over it to keep him warmer. "But like I've said before, we'll play the hand we're dealt."

"Unless you know a way to deal off the bottom," Twister said, "and I don't reckon anybody's ever figured out how to do that with fate."

Despite the banter, which was just an attempt to keep their spirits up, all four of the adults were exhausted. Deep lines of weariness were etched in their faces. They had been pushing hard for the past forty-eight hours, trying to stay ahead of their pursuers and reach Chugwater.

But the horses were about done in, too, Falcon knew. They were just about at the end of their rope, and if they didn't make it to their destination soon, there was a rapidly increasing chance that they never would.

The snowfall thickened as they pushed on. Falcon, Hardpan, and Twister had all smelled snow when they started out that morning. Eleanor hadn't been convinced of their ability to predict the weather, but now she said, "How bad is this storm going to get? Does that rheumatism of yours tell you that, Twister?"

"Well, I dunno," the old prospector said. "These ol' bones of mine are achin' like it's liable to be a pretty good snow. Six or eight inches, maybe. Which ain't really all that much for Wyomin', you understand. Why, I've seen it come down so hard, you couldn't see your hand in front o' your face, just swirlin' clouds of snow—"

"It won't be *that* bad," Hardpan interrupted. "I'm better at tellin' what the weather's gonna do than this old pelican is. Always have been. Did I predict that cloudburst down in Arizona a couple of years ago that nearly washed us away in a flash flood?"

"I said it was gonna rain."

"You said it was gonna *rain*. I'm the one who said it was gonna be a toad-strangler and a gully-washer—*Yipes!*"

Hardpan jumped in the saddle and clapped a hand to his ear. When he took it away, crimson was smeared on his fingers.

"My ear!" he yelled. "They shot off my ear!"

"Barely nicked it, looks like," Falcon said. "But I heard that bullet go past us like a hornet. Move! Light out for Chugwater!"

It wasn't quite dark enough yet to see the lights of the town ahead of them—if it actually was ahead of them. If they had veered off course somehow, then they were probably doomed, Falcon thought grimly as his companions heeled their horses into a run again. Probably the last run the valiant animals had in them . . .

He wheeled his mount and pulled the Winchester from its scabbard. The chamber already had a cartridge in it. Falcon lifted the rifle to his shoulder as he peered at the hills they had crossed earlier in the day. Stillwater's men had to be fairly close.

There they are! Three or four riders topped a rise a quarter of a mile back and gazed toward Falcon. No telling how far ahead of the others they were, but nobody else showed up right away. While he could still see them, he cranked off five rounds, firing as fast as he could. He thought one of the gun wolves jerked in the saddle, but he wasn't sure about that. They all seemed to slow down, though, as if they realized that charging right into the muzzle of his gun maybe wasn't a great idea.

As they did that, Falcon yanked his horse around again and pounded after Eleanor and the two old-timers. They just needed to make it to Chugwater ahead of Stillwater's hired killers.

It was less than two days until Christmas. That was close enough for a miracle, wasn't it?

Duff had never had his arms full of hissing, spitting, clawing wildcats, but he had a pretty good idea now of what that would be like.

The ground in the alley was already a little muddy from the snow that had collected there. At the moment, the temperature hovered around the freezing point, so some of the snow had melted. Duff tried to brace himself, so he could heave upright and separate Meagan and Fiona, but he slipped again and all three of them floundered.

Fiona tried to claw Meagan's face, but Meagan chose a more direct way of fighting. She balled her hand into a fist and punched Fiona in the jaw, landing the blow solidly enough to make Fiona sag backward. That gave Duff the chance to get his arm between them at last. Meagan tried to swing again, but Duff held her back.

At the same time, he used his other hand to snag the collar of Fiona's dress, and when Fiona attempted to surge toward Meagan, he was able to stop her.

"Quit it, both o' ye!" he said in a low but urgent voice. "D' ye want the whole town to ken that you're back here brawlin' like a couple o' stray cats?"

"I'll kill her!" Fiona said. "Aye, she's got it comin'!" She turned her hate-filled gaze on Duff and bared her teeth. "Ye both do!"

He felt a chill go through him that had nothing to do with

the weather. At that moment, Fiona looked mad. Not angry-mad, but crazy-mad, enough so that she ought to be locked up in an asylum. Duff wouldn't have thought that was possible, if he hadn't seen it with his own eyes.

That lasted only a second, though, and then Fiona just seemed disgusted and annoyed as she said, "Le' go o' me, ye gigantic oaf! I'll no' hurt your trollop."

Meagan said, "You couldn't take me on your best day, you spiteful little bi—"

"Here, now, tha' be enow o' that," Duff said firmly. "Why don't we all concentrate on gettin' up, so we dinna have t' roll around in this muck any longer?"

Meagan and Fiona still looked like they wanted to snarl and spit at each other, but evidently they didn't like wallowing on the alley floor, either. Clumsily they all clambered to their feet.

"Look at us," Meagan moaned. "We're filthy!"

"'Tis no' anything to worry about," Duff said. "We all ha' costumes for the play, so we'll just wear them the rest o' the evenin'."

"But our clothes are dirty now," Fiona said. "If we go back out on the street—"

"The town hall has a back door, ye ken. We'll see if 'tis unlocked. E'en if it's not, perhaps we can draw someone's attention inside." He looked back and forth between the two young women. "Now, will ye, for heaven's sake, call a truce again?"

Meagan sighed. "I suppose." Her eyes narrowed as she looked at Fiona. "But I'll be glad when Christmas is over so this . . . this delinquent will be gone from Chugwater with your cousins, Duff."

Duff didn't mention that he'd planned for Andrew and Rosanna to stay at Sky Meadow until after New Year's. If they did, that would get Fiona out at the ranch, too, and away from Meagan—but he didn't think Meagan would like the idea of Fiona being out there with Duff.

Just get through the night, Duff told himself. *Worry about the rest of it later.* Keeping a wary eye on them, he shepherded them around to the back of the town hall, where he tried the knob on the door. Night was closing in quickly.

"Locked," he said. He rapped on the door, not pounding on it, but knocking loud enough that anyone who was near it would hear him, he hoped.

A moment later, light spilled out through the door as it opened a few inches. A familiar face looked out at them. Rosanna said, "Oh, my word! What . . . what's happened to the three of you?"

"Just a wee bit of a mishap," Duff said. "'Tis nothin' to worry yourself about, Rosanna. We just didna want to come in the front door lookin' all . . . disheveled like this."

Rosanna swung the door back wider. "I can certainly understand that. Come on in. You can go ahead and get into your wardrobe for the play."

"Aye, 'twas just wha' I was thinkin'."

Duff hesitated, not sure how to go about ushering Meagan and Fiona inside, but they took that decision out of his hands by both stepping toward the door at the same time and bumping shoulders. For a second, he thought they were going to start fighting again, but then Fiona said in a voice well below the freezing point, "After you, Miss Parker."

"Thank you," Meagan said, matching the chilliness of Fiona's tone. She marched in with Fiona following her.

Rosanna looked at Duff and arched an eyebrow. He just sighed and shook his head. Some things were best left unexplained.

A short time later, Duff was cleaned up and wearing Bob Cratchit's suit. He was waiting backstage, which was actually the small kitchen in the back of the town hall. He was there with some of the other cast members when Fiona came in. She had washed her face, brushed her hair, and donned the simple dress she would wear as Bob Cratchit's wife.

"Don't ye look nice," Duff told her.

"Don't bother tryin' to pretend tha' ye like me now," she said. "I ken ye've eyes only for tha' blond hussy."

"Meagan is a very nice girl—"

"Dinna waste your breath, Duff. 'Tis over . . . or soon will be."

Duff's forehead creased as he looked at her. Fiona's eyes were hard, almost lifeless, like little green stones. He wasn't sure he had ever seen so little humanity in a pair of eyes.

But then she took her breath, smiled, and lightly touched his forearm.

"Let's just get through the performance, shall we?" she suggested. "I took a peek out front. 'Tis packed, the hall is."

Duff wasn't surprised to hear that. The steady rumble of conversation from the audience as they gathered and waited for the play to begin penetrated back here.

The talk among the cast hushed, though, as Meagan came into the room. She had altered the Ghost of Christmas Future's costume to be slightly more modest, as she had told Duff she would do, but she was still stunning. He had never seen her looking more lovely, and as he stepped over to her and caught hold of her hands, he told her so.

"Thank you," she said. She smiled bravely and murmured, "I'm trying not to let *that* woman ruin tonight."

" 'Tis going t' be a fine night," Duff said. "Wait and see."

Andrew bustled in, rubbing his hands together in anticipation. For his role as Ebenezer Scrooge, he wore a sober black suit and a bald cap with a gray wig attached to it. A pince-nez with clear glass lenses perched on the bridge of his nose.

"What a crowd we have out there," he enthused. "I think everyone who lives in Chugwater is here, along with half the county. It's standing room only, and precious little of that! The aisles are full. It's a fine audience, and we're going to give them the performance they deserve, aren't we, my friends?"

"Aye," Duff said. Several other cast members voiced their agreement.

Andrew turned to Biff Johnson, who, in addition to playing an innkeeper, would also serve as the offstage narrator of the play, introducing it and bridging scenes. As a former sergeant in the Seventh Cavalry, he had a voice that could carry easily to the back of the crowded room.

"You know your opening line?" Andrew asked.

"Of course," Biff replied. Lowering his voice to a solemn tone, he recited, "'Marley was dead, to begin with.'"

Andrew clapped a hand on his shoulder. "Excellent delivery." He turned to Duff and said, "You look a bit down in the mouth, cousin. Are you not excited about the performance?"

"Aye, 'tis lookin' forward to it I am," Duff replied. "But I was hopin' tha' your brother would have arrived before now. 'Twould be good if Falcon was here t' see the play."

Andrew nodded and said, "Yes, I hoped he would be here, too. But that's the way it is with Falcon. He has a way of attracting excitement, and sometimes that delays him."

"Attractin' *trouble* might be a more accurate way o' puttin' it."

Andrew laughed. "Well, yes, that's true. But the show must go on, whether he's here or not." He shook hands with Duff. "Give it your all."

"And you as well, cousin."

Andrew turned to the others, took his watch out, and checked the hour. "All right, everyone," he said as he snapped the watch shut and replaced it in his vest pocket. "It's almost curtain time. Are we all ready?"

Murmurs of assent came from the cast.

"Very well. I'll take my place and we'll get started."

Andrew would be the only one on stage as the curtain was

drawn back. The others left the kitchen behind him and moved to wait on either side of the stage, where they would be behind the curtain when it was opened, and out of the audience's view.

Duff stood with Meagan, catching hold of her hand and squeezing it for a moment, then glanced around to see where Fiona was. He frowned as he realized that she wasn't in sight. He looked across the stage at the group on the other side and didn't see her there, either. With that bright red hair of hers, she should have been easy to spot. He wasn't sure where she could have gotten off to, right before the performance was supposed to begin.

Andrew positioned himself in the middle of the stage, shook his shoulders a little as if preparing himself, and then looked over at the side where a townsman was holding the rope, ready to draw the curtain back. Andrew poised his head to nod . . .

And guns fired somewhere nearby in the snowy night.

Chapter 34

Darkness fell almost as if a candle had been snuffed out as Falcon, Hardpan, Twister, and Eleanor galloped toward Chugwater—or what Falcon hoped was Chugwater. He had approached the town from this direction before, on previous visits, and usually, once Falcon MacCallister had ridden a trail, he instinctively knew it from then on.

Tonight his life, and the lives of his newfound friends, might depend on that ability.

Before the night closed in around them, however, Falcon saw that the snowfall was increasing. The flakes were bigger, heavier, and coming down faster. Gusts of wind whipped them around and made visibility difficult. Then darkness dropped on them like a hammer, and they really were riding blind. Falcon wished they had had a chance to tie all the horses together so they wouldn't get separated—but that wouldn't have worked, once they had to kick the mounts into a breakneck gallop, he realized.

"Stay close behind me!" he shouted to the others. "Don't veer off!"

Anybody who wandered off on their own was likely doomed, either by the elements or by the hired killers pursuing them.

Suddenly he leaned forward even more in the saddle. Was that a light he had just caught a glimpse of in front of them? A tiny, ephemeral yellow wink? It was there and gone so quickly, he couldn't be sure that he hadn't imagined it.

Then he saw it again. The light vanished just as swiftly the second time, but he was certain that it wasn't a figment of his imagination. It was small enough he could tell they still had a ways to go to reach it, but at least they had something to aim for now.

Somewhere behind them, guns banged. The reports were audible only because snow was piling up on the ground now and muffling the hoofbeats from their horses. Falcon felt as much as heard something hum past his ear. Stillwater's men were shooting blind—they couldn't be doing anything else in weather like this—but they were throwing enough lead that one of the bullets had missed him narrowly. Bad luck could be just as fatal as good aim.

Falcon grimaced and called on his exhausted mount for more speed. The horse responded gallantly. Falcon turned his head and shouted over his shoulder, "Come on! Not much farther now!"

He didn't know if that was true. But if it was, they had a chance.

Then, so abruptly that it almost took his breath away, they passed between buildings with lit windows. Enough of that warm yellow glow penetrated the swirling snowfall that Falcon was able to discern the outlines of a broad street with buildings on both sides. Up ahead was a larger structure, brightly lit. Falcon aimed for it, galloping between a large number of wagons and buggies parked along both sides of the street. They were in Chugwater, he realized, and something was going on, something centered around that lit-up building in front of them.

Before they could reach it, riders surged out of a side street, and Colt flame bloomed like crimson flowers as these unexpected enemies opened up. Falcon just had time to think that none of Stillwater's men could have gotten ahead of them. Then more bullets were screaming around his head as muzzle flame stabbed toward him.

A few minutes earlier, Nick and Logan Jessup, Kent Spalding, and the rest of the gang closing in on Chugwater had reined to a sudden halt as Spalding ordered in a low voice, "Hold it." It was too dark to see any hand signals.

"What is it, boss?" one of the men asked. "What's wrong?"

"Listen," Spalding said.

The night was quiet. A wind was blowing, but not hard, just enough to kick up the snow that was settling on the ground, now that the temperature had dropped well below freezing.

This snowy evening wasn't exactly tranquil, though. Somewhere not too far away, guns blasted again and again. The snow in the air muffled the sound a little, but not enough to keep the outlaws from hearing it.

"What in blazes!" Logan exclaimed. "Sounds like somebody's fightin' a small war up there!"

Nick tensed and tightened his grip on the reins. "I hope Fiona's all right," he said. "You reckon MacCallister or somebody else found out what she's been up to?"

Spalding said, "I don't think that would cause such a ruckus. That's quite a fight going on." The boss outlaw turned in the saddle. "Come on, boys! No matter what's happening in Chugwater, the town's ripe for picking! And we don't have any friends there, so anybody who gets in your way . . . gun 'em down!"

A pang of fear for Fiona's safety went through Nick. With all that lead flying around, he hoped she was keeping her head down.

*   *   *

Fiona pulled her coat tighter around her and pressed her back against the wall of the town hall. She felt the snowflakes brushing her face. Some of them collected on her eyelashes and melted, forcing her to blink the moisture away as if it had been tears. She moved along the wall until she reached the spot where she had hidden the tin of coal oil earlier. She'd planned to spread it all around the hall, once she barred the doors.

Now something had happened that threatened to ruin all her plans. She didn't know what it was, but she knew she wasn't going to give up her vengeance on Duff MacCallister without a fight.

She bent down and fumbled in the opening under the building, where the town hall sat on thick beams that served as its foundation, until she found the coal oil. She took it with her as she stole toward the mouth of the alley that fronted on Clay Avenue. She had to see if she could figure out what was going on, before she could decide what to do next.

As she reached the street, she looked along it toward the western end of town and saw the gun flashes darting this way and that. A man rode past a lit window not far away, and even though the snow partially obscured him, she recognized Nick Jessup. That meant the crowd of riders with Nick—and they were all blasting away at some other people on horseback down the street—had to be the Spalding gang. *They've charged into town too soon,* Fiona thought with wild dismay. The audience wasn't trapped in the town hall, and neither were the performers—including Duff.

Unless she acted fast, he was going to get away with his sins against her clan!

Inside the town hall, chaos and panic threatened to take hold. As the commotion built, Andrew thrust the curtain aside and stepped out on the stage. His powerfully commanding voice rang out.

"Calm, please! Stay calm! We'll find out what's going on! Everything is under control!"

His cousin meant well, Duff knew, but Andrew was wrong. With so many guns banging outside, everything clearly wasn't under control.

Meagan clutched his arm. "Duff, what is it?"

"I dinna ken, lass, but I intend to find out." Even though he wasn't wearing a gun belt and holster, he had the .45 stuck behind his belt at the small of his back. He'd been carrying it in his waistband during the tussle in the alley earlier, and when he changed into his costume for the play, he had checked the gun to make sure mud hadn't gotten into the barrel before he tucked it away again.

Now he swept his coattails aside, reached behind him, and palmed the gun. "Stay back where ye'll be safe," he told Meagan as he thrust the curtain aside to follow Andrew.

"Duff, be careful!" she called after him.

"Always, lass!" he replied, but failed to see the grimace that crossed her face. Duff wasn't reckless, but when trouble beckoned, he didn't hold back, either.

Men were already crowding into the doorway to get out of the town hall and find out what was going on. Marshal Ferrell and Deputy Burns bellowed for them to get out of the way, without much in the way of results. When Duff added his formidable size to the effort, though, the three men were able to clear a path and emerge onto the boardwalk, along with some of the other men who had been inside the building. A number of men from the audience were already in the street, and quite a few of them had guns.

Through the swirling snow, Duff saw unknown riders whirl and charge toward them, flame spouting from their guns as they did so. "Take cover!" he shouted to the playgoers who had ventured out. They scrambled to follow his suggestion as bullets began flying around them. One man grunted, clapped a hand to his chest, and pitched backward, knocking a couple of other men off their feet. They all fell in a tangle. Screams came from inside the town hall as slugs thudded into the walls and shattered windows.

Duff dropped to one knee and lifted his Colt. One of the attackers spotted him and swung a gun toward him. Duff fired first, drilling the man in the chest. The bullet knocked him backward off his mount, which ran on without him.

Duff twisted and looked for another target. A rider came straight at him and he was about to squeeze the trigger when he heard a familiar voice yell, "Duff!"

Duff saw the man's face then and exclaimed, "Falcon!"

Falcon kicked his feet out of the stirrups and dived from the saddle. He landed, rolling, the impact lessened somewhat by the layer of snow on the ground. As momentum carried him back to his feet, he threw himself flat on the boardwalk beside Duff. Falcon's gun was already in his hand, and as it roared and bucked, the music it played from a deadly duet with the blasts from his cousin's revolver.

"Howdy, Duff!" Falcon shouted over the gun thunder. "Merry Christmas!"

"Merry Christmas your own self, ye madman!" Duff replied as he swung his gun to the side and triggered again, blowing another of the mysterious marauders out of the saddle. "Have ye any idea what's goin' on here?"

"A bunch of hired killers chased me and my friends into town! I don't know who those other fellas are!"

"Neither do I," Duff said, "but 'tis clear they've no desire t' be friends!" He and Falcon fired at the same instant, but in different directions. Two more raiders pitched from the saddles.

Between the snowstorm and the melee going on, Falcon had lost track of Eleanor, Hardpan, and Twister. The two old-timers could take care of themselves, or at least put up a good fight. Falcon hoped Eleanor had reached some safe haven with the baby, though. If she got inside one of the buildings and kept her head down, they might be all right.

Assuming whoever these marauders were didn't lay waste to the whole town . . .

An unholy screech made Falcon twist around. A woman with red hair and a crazy expression on her face charged along the boardwalk toward him and Duff. She might have been pretty under normal circumstances, but right now she just looked loco.

"I'll kill ye, ye damned MacCallister!" she howled as she drew back her arm to hurl whatever it was she held at Duff.

The terrible cry made Duff think of the spirit creature known as the *bean nighe*, what the Irish called a *banshee*, whose shrieking meant imminent death. As he jerked toward the sound, he didn't know what he was going to see, but he wasn't expecting Fiona. She was almost on top of him, though, and was about to fling something at him.

Before she could, a vision in white appeared at the corner of Duff's eye. Dressed as the Ghost of Christmas Future, Meagan lunged across the boardwalk, tackled Fiona, and knocked both of them into the street. Whatever Fiona had been trying to wield as a weapon slipped out of her hand and sailed through the air.

With all the horses charging and bullets flying, the street was no place for the two young women to be. As they started rolling around in the snow, wrestling and slapping, Duff surged to his feet and said, "Come on and gi' me a hand, Falcon!"

They ran toward Meagan and Fiona, intending to separate them and drag them out of harm's way. Before they could get there, three riders swept up and reined in sharply; one of them dropped from his saddle to the ground as his horse was still skidding to a stop.

"Fiona!" he yelled. Then he looked up, spotted Duff, and spat, "MacCallister!" as his gun streaked up.

In that moment, Duff knew the man looked familiar, although he couldn't place him. Then the memory of the attempted bank robbery a couple of weeks earlier burst from his brain. The young man trying to kill him had been holding the horses that day, and one of the men with him that day was behind him on horseback now.

That thought took only a shaved fraction of a second. Duff pulled the trigger in that same amount of time. Flame licked from the muzzle of his gun as he beat the outlaw to the shot. The young man's finger jerked on the trigger, but his gun hadn't come level yet. His bullet plowed into the snowy ground as Duff's slug punched into his chest. He went backward.

"No!" the other would-be bank robber cried. He and Falcon fired at the same time, but the outlaw's shot went wide, while Falcon's drilled the man through the heart. He toppled off his horse, but his foot caught in the stirrup and the panicky animal bolted away, dragging the now-dead raider.

Duff and Falcon triggered again, the shots so close together that they sounded like one, and the third man slewed back in the saddle under the twin impact, but managed to stay mounted. He wheeled his horse away, firing wildly, and tried to escape, but he made it only a few yards before he tumbled to the ground and landed in a limp sprawl, too.

"Duff, look out!"

That was Meagan's voice. Duff whirled to see that Fiona had broken away from Meagan and was coming at him again. She had picked up whatever she'd dropped earlier and slung her hand at him, splattering him with liquid. He recognized the reek of coal oil.

"Now ye'll burn in hell for your crimes agin the Somerled clan, ye damned MacCallister!" Fiona screeched. "Angus Somerled was me uncle, and I've come all this way to avenge him and me cousins!" She must have been prepared with matches, because one of them suddenly flared to life in her hand as she stalked toward Duff. She drew her arm back to throw it. "Ye'll burn, MacCallister—"

A shot blasted. Fiona gasped and staggered to the side. The match slipped from her fingers and hissed out as it landed in the snow. She looked down, eyes widening in pain and horror, at the blood on her dress. Her knees buckled as she forced out, "No! I'll no' be denied . . . my vengeance . . ."

She fell forward on her face and didn't move again.

Duff looked over at Meagan, who was on her knees with a gun held in both hands and thrust out in front of her. He knew the outlaw he had shot must have dropped the weapon. Meagan lowered it, looked at him, and said, "You would have hesitated too long, Duff, and you know it."

"Aye," he breathed. "Ye may be right, lass . . ."

The battle in Chugwater's main street appeared to be mostly over. A few pockets of gunfire were scattered along Clay Avenue. Falcon said, "I've got to find Eleanor."

Duff had stepped forward to lift Meagan to her feet. He didn't know who Eleanor was, but as he folded his arms around Meagan, he asked, "Do ye need my help, cousin?"

"No, you stay here and tend to things," Falcon said. "This is my responsibility."

He stalked off into the snowy night, thumbing fresh cartridges into his Colt as the swirling white curtains enveloped him.

John Henry Stillwater clutched an expensive double-barreled shotgun as he moved along the boardwalk. He had hired people to carry out most of his unpleasant tasks for many years now, but he hadn't forgotten how to get his own hands dirty when needed. And he'd discovered that tonight, he needed to.

Of course, he wasn't a fool. He had Jed Pearson with him, in case he needed a hand from the professional gunman.

"Are you sure you saw 'em come this way, Mr. Stillwater?" Pearson asked.

"I saw them," Stillwater declared. "Even after all this time, there's no way I'd mistake that beanpole and his fat fool of a friend. They ducked down that alley up ahead . . . Look, there are their horses and pack mules!"

The four animals milled around in the alley mouth. Stillwater raised the shotgun as he stomped toward them. Nothing was going to prevent him from ridding himself of this threat to his fortune, once and for all.

A rifle cracked up ahead. The whine of a bullet passing over their heads made Stillwater and Pearson crouch lower.

"Back off, John Henry!" Twister McCoy called. "We don't want to hurt you. Me and Hardpan just want to go on with our lives!"

"Then why did you try to steal everything I have?" Stillwater yelled back. "I can never trust you two old thieves! You'll always be thorns in my side!"

He turned his head, nodded to Pearson, and took one hand off the shotgun to signal that the gunman should circle around and get behind their quarry. Pearson faded back along the boardwalk.

Hardpan spoke up this time, saying, "It's true, John Henry. We were wrong to try to take away what you worked for. Just leave us in peace and we'll never bother you again. You have our word on that."

"Not good enough! I have to be sure." A sudden wailing made Stillwater frown in surprise. He listened for a moment and then asked, "Is that a *baby* in there with you?"

"That kid's got nothin' to do with anything," Twister said.

"Maybe not," Stillwater said, sensing a way to turn this unexpected development to his advantage, "but that alley's going to be full of flying lead in a minute, so if you don't want the child hurt, the two of you will step out in the open, *now!*"

Tense silence followed that demand, then Stillwater heard a swift, whispered exchange of words, including what he thought was a woman's voice. That had to be the blond whore who had been traveling with the old desert rats. Stillwater didn't care what happened to her—her life was trivial in the bigger scheme of things—as long as Hawkins and McCoy died.

"All right!" Hardpan called. "We're comin' out. Hold your fire."

He and Twister stepped out of the alley. They still held their Sharps and Winchester, but their arms were raised.

Stillwater straightened and told them, "Throw those guns down!" He stalked toward them with the shotgun leveled.

Hardpan and Twister hesitated, obviously believing that if they dropped their guns, Stillwater would blow them away with the scattergun. In fact, that was exactly what Stillwater intended to do.

A sharp cry came from the alley, followed by Pearson calling, "Boss, I've got the girl and the kid!"

Hardpan's head jerked around. "Leave them alone! Blast it, John Henry, they never did anything to you!"

"But I'm willing to bet that you told her about that paper you have," Stillwater grated. "That means she's a threat, too."

"No, she ain't," Twister insisted. "We burned that paper, John Henry! It don't exist no more. None of us can threaten you."

Slowly, Stillwater shook his head. "Too bad, but I don't believe you, Twister." He raised his voice and called, "Pearson, kill the girl!"

Hardpan spat a curse and jerked the Sharps down. At the same time, Twister took a fast step to the side and tried to bring his Winchester to bear. The Sharps and the shotgun boomed at the same time. Stillwater felt the hammer blow of the slug as one load of buckshot ripped into Hardpan and spun him off his feet. Stillwater fell to his knees and the shotgun, with its second barrel unfired, clattered on the boardwalk in front of him.

With pain flaring through him, Stillwater reached for the shotgun. Twister leveled the Winchester and cried, "Don't do it, John Henry!"

Stillwater grunted, closed his hands around the shotgun, and tried to lift it from the planks.

Twister fired, slamming out one, two, three, four shots in less than four seconds. The bullets smashed into Stillwater's chest and drove him over, backward. He lay there for a second, blinking as he felt snowflakes landing on his face, and then he didn't feel anything anymore.

Falcon wheeled around the rear corner of the building as shots roared from the street. He had spotted Stillwater and one of those hired guns stalking Hardpan and Twister and had seen the gun wolf peel off to circle around behind the old prospectors. Moving fast, Falcon went after him.

He made it to the alley in time to see the gunman holding Eleanor and forcing her toward the street. He couldn't see if she had the baby, and with danger looming over her, he didn't know whether to hope that she did or did not. But either way, all he could do was call, "Hey!"

The gunman twisted around, maybe intending to use Eleanor as a shield as he fired at Falcon, but at that moment she was able to break free of his grip and pitch away from him, out of the line of fire. Falcon and the gun wolf triggered at the same instant. Falcon felt the hot breath of the other man's bullet against his cheek, but the gunman's head rocked back as the slug from Falcon's gun bored through his brain. He was dead when he hit the ground.

Falcon's instincts told him he had scored. He rushed forward and helped Eleanor to her feet from where she had tumbled to the ground. "Eleanor!" he said. "You're—"

"I'm . . . all right," she gasped. "And so is . . . the kid."

The leather-lunged wail from the blanket-wrapped shape in the sling hung on the front of her body confirmed that. The baby was all right, but he sounded mad as a hornet from all the jostling around. That was a good sign, Falcon figured.

"Eleanor!" Twister called. "Eleanor, come quick! Hardpan's hit!"

Falcon and Eleanor hurried to the boardwalk in front of the

building. Twister had lifted Hardpan so that the scrawny prospector was sitting with his back propped against the wall.

"Will you quit fussing over me?" Hardpan said. His irascible voice sounded almost as strong as ever. "I told you, most of that buckshot missed me. John Henry never was much of a shot, even with a scattergun. I've just got a couple of scratches."

"But you're bleedin'!" Twister said.

"And we ha' a good doctor here in Chugwater to tend to those wounds," a new voice said. Falcon looked over and saw Duff and Meagan approaching, followed by Elmer Gleason, several of the Sky Meadow hands, and . . .

"Andrew!" Falcon exclaimed. "Rosanna! You're all right."

"We're fine," Andrew said. Rosanna hurried to embrace Falcon, while Andrew clasped his hand and pumped it.

Falcon looked at Duff. "The fighting . . . ?"

"Appears t' be over," Duff reported. "As best we can figure from what some o' the fellows who gave up are sayin', there were two bunches o' miscreants attackin' Chugwater tonight, a gang o' outlaws and some hired guns workin' for a man named Stillwater. Would ye be for knowin' anything about tha'?"

"It's a long story," Falcon said, "but we can hash it all out later, as long as most folks are all right." He grinned at his brother and sister. "I was hoping you two would be here. But Andrew . . . what happened to your hair?"

Andrew ran his hand over the bald cap with its attached wig. "We were putting on a play," he explained, "an adaptation of *A Christmas Carol*. I was supposed to play Scrooge."

"Ah. Now I understand . . . I reckon." Falcon next looked at Meagan. "And you'd be . . . ?"

"The Ghost of Christmas Future, of course," she said. "I just hope all the Christmases to come don't turn out like this one!"

"If there be MacCallisters involved, I fear there's a good chance they may be," Duff said.

Chapter 35

Sky Meadow, Christmas Eve

The storm had moved on, dumping nearly a foot of snow on Chugwater and the surrounding vicinity. The thick overcast remained most of Christmas Eve, with the clouds finally breaking up late in the afternoon so that brilliant blue sky appeared in the gaps. By Christmas morning, it was clear, cold, and still.

A number of the townspeople and visitors who had come into Chugwater to attend the play had suffered injuries during the double raid on the settlement, but no one had been killed except members of the Spalding gang and the group of hired guns working for John Henry Stillwater. The survivors from both groups were locked up securely in the jail, waiting for deputy marshals from Cheyenne to arrive and take them back there after Christmas. Prison terms would be in store for most of them, but a few were wanted on murder charges and likely would have a date with the hangman in the new year.

Andrew's production of *A Christmas Carol* had been postponed until Christmas Eve. He had been willing to cancel it, but the town leaders had insisted that the show must go on. A battle royale with outlaws and gun wolves wasn't enough to make Chugwater forget about celebrating the holiday. People in these parts were made of sterner stuff than that.

Meagan had taken over the part of Bob Cratchit's wife. Eleanor had been prevailed upon to play the Ghost of Christmas Future, despite her protests that it wasn't fitting.

"Nobody cares where ye came from or wha' ye did in the past, lass," Duff assured her. "The only thing tha' matters is wha' ye do from now on, so 'tis most fittin', indeed, tha' ye play the Ghost o' Christmas Future."

What she planned to do was stay in Chugwater and adopt the baby. Some folks might disapprove of that because she didn't have a husband, but the bond that had formed between Eleanor and the little one didn't need to be broken. Duff and Falcon agreed on that, and not many people would want to argue with the MacCallister cousins.

Dr. Urban had patched up Hardpan's minor wounds and declared that the old prospector ought to be all right. During the day on Christmas Eve, Hardpan and Twister had spent a couple of hours consulting with Richard Norton, the local justice of the peace, and Jim Robinson, the prosecuting attorney, who were the most astute legal minds in Chugwater. Duff and Falcon sat in on the meeting. The old-timers *hadn't* destroyed their partnership agreement with John Henry Stillwater, despite what Twister had said during the showdown, and the two lawyers agreed that the document was valid and ought to stand up in any courtroom in the country.

"You'll have to go to Denver, where Mr. Stillwater's company is headquartered, to advance your claim on his assets," Norton had advised the old prospectors. "Do you know if he has any heirs?"

"I don't believe he ever married or had young'uns," Hardpan said. His torso was taped up with bandages under his clothes. "I don't know about any other relatives."

"You'll need good legal representation," Norton had said, nodding. "But I think there's a substantial chance that you two gentlemen are going to wind up quite wealthy."

"If we do," Twister said, "some of the money ought to go to Eleanor to help out her and the kid."

"That's right," Hardpan agreed. "And we'd like to donate some of it to the town of Chugwater, too, since we brought our trouble here and nearly ruined Christmas for everybody."

That sounded like a good idea to Duff. Hardpan and Twister might even want to invest in some of the businesses here. Chugwater was growing, and they might wind up growing their money even more.

With those things taken care of, everyone was able to turn their attention to the play, which went off without a hitch and drew a standing ovation from the audience when the cast and crew took their curtain call.

Even so, a shadow of sorts hung over the production, although no one talked about it. By now, thanks to information spilled by members of the Spalding gang when they were questioned, everyone knew who Fiona Gillespie really was and what her plan had been. Her warped need for vengeance could have caused scores of deaths if she had gotten her way.

Instead she was one of those unceremoniously laid to rest in the Chugwater cemetery on Christmas Eve morning. But her spirit might take some measure of satisfaction from the knowledge that what she had planned would not soon be forgotten in these parts, even if nobody talked about it.

After the play, a convoy of wagons had rolled through the snow to Sky Meadow, bearing not only the members of the crew who had attended, but also a number of visitors. Andrew, Rosanna, Falcon, Eleanor and the baby, Hardpan and Twister, all would spend the rest of Christmas Eve and Christmas Day on the ranch, as well as probably staying for a few days after that. After all the trouble, everyone was ready to relax and enjoy the holiday—and the Christmas feast that Wang was planning. Even though the holiday wasn't part of the culture he came from, he seemed to have adopted it with gusto.

Christmas morning

While they were waiting for that midday meal, the others sat in the big parlor, enjoying each other's company and the roaring blaze in the fireplace. Frost clung to the outside of the windows.

"I've been thinking," Eleanor said as she bounced the smiling, gurgling baby on her knee. "This child needs a name."

Falcon said, "If you're going to adopt him, then you ought to be the one to pick that." He laughed. "I'm glad I didn't start calling him Oscar or Wilbur or something like that."

"You could call him Harold," Twister said. "That's Hardpan's real name."

"You just hush up about that . . . Vivian," Hardpan snapped at his partner. Twister flushed and looked uncomfortable.

"That's a man's name, too," he protested. Hardpan just blew out a breath.

"Actually," Eleanor said, "I've already made up my mind. I'm going to call him Falcon."

"Now wait just a minute," Falcon said. "You shouldn't do that. If you do, folks are likely to think—"

"What? That you saved his life, and mine, too? Because that's true. If it weren't for you, Falcon MacCallister, this child and I wouldn't be here, and if that doesn't make you deserve to be his namesake, then I don't know what does."

Meagan said, "I think Eleanor is right."

"Aye," Duff agreed. "The bairn should be called Falcon, now and forevermore."

Falcon sighed, grimaced, and said, "All right. And I won't deny, it's an honor to have such a fine boy named after me. I guess there'll be a Falcon around Chugwater for a while."

"But 'twill no' be you," Duff said.

"No, I reckon I'll be driftin' on, once Christmas is over. You know me, I never like to stay in one place for too long."

"It's a MacCallister trait," Andrew said as he raised the cup of coffee he held. "Here's to being *skittish*, as Pa called it."

"And to Jamie Ian MacCallister," Falcon added as he lifted his own cup.

"Aye," Duff agreed.

Elmer came in wearing a heavy coat and stomping snow off his boots. "I got the wagon hitched up like you asked, Duff," he said.

"What's this?" Andrew asked.

"I thought ye all might like to take a ride around the ranch before we have our Christmas feast," Duff explained. "Falcon, ye've seen Sky Meadow, and, Meagan, you're very familiar wi' the place, since you're a partner an' all, but the rest o' ye havena seen my home, and I'd like to show it off!"

"That's sounds like an excellent idea," Rosanna said. "From what I've seen of it, the scenery around here is magnificent."

"Well, bundle up, folks," Elmer said. "The sun's shinin', but the air's still got a bite to it!"

A few minutes later, the big ranch wagon rolled away from the house, with Elmer at the reins and Duff sitting beside him. Riding in back, on benches placed there by the hands and cushioned with blankets, were Meagan and Eleanor, Andrew and Rosanna, and Hardpan and Twister. Falcon rode alongside on his saddle horse. The baby was sleeping in the house, and Wang had promised to look after little Falcon if he woke up.

The snow was deep enough to have coated everything with a thick white layer that was dazzlingly beautiful in the sun, but the wagon with its sturdy team of draft horses and high wheels handled it with ease. Elmer knew every foot of Sky Meadow as well, so he was able to follow a route that was easy on the passengers and didn't jolt them around too much.

The snow-covered vistas of hills and valleys and distant

mountains were sweeping and breathtakingly lovely. Rosanna and Eleanor both exclaimed in awe at the beauty of the countryside.

"I can see why you love it here, Duff," Rosanna said. "Andrew, when we retire from the stage, perhaps we should find a place like this to live in."

"Speak for yourself, my dear," Andrew said with a smile. "I intend to trod the boards until I breathe my last."

"The two o' ye will always be welcome here," Duff said. "'Twas ye who introduced me to the American branch o' the MacCallister clan, and for tha' I'll always be grateful. And to ye as well, Falcon, for helpin' me get started here."

"I was glad to do it," Falcon said from horseback. "And if you ask me, Wyoming's lucky to have you as one of its citizens, Duff. You've done a heap of good for folks around here."

Hardpan said, "What I'm wondering is if there's ever been any gold found around here?"

On the driver's seat, Elmer turned his head and said, "Don't go gettin' any ideas. There's an old gold mine in these parts, but it's on Sky Meadow range."

"We wouldn't jump anybody's claim," Twister said. "But we might poke around some on unclaimed range. We'll need somethin' to do, once we're gentlemen of leisure, won't we, Hardpan?"

Hardpan grunted. "Don't go weighing the gold dust before we've panned it," he told his partner. "We don't know we're going to wind up with any of John Henry's money, no matter what those lawyers said."

"Well, whether we do or don't, I figure we'll still go on prospectin'. I mean, after all these years, what else do we know how to do?"

Hardpan nodded slowly and said, "You've got a point about that."

Elmer made a big circle several miles in diameter and let the visitors get their fill of the landscape; then Duff said, "We'd best be headin' back to the ranch house. We wouldna want all tha' food Wang is preparin' to get cold."

Elmer turned the wagon and flicked the reins against the backs of the team. The horses surged forward, snow flying up around their hooves as they high-stepped toward home.

A short time later the ranch house came into view, looking peaceful and idyllic in the snow-covered countryside. Smoke curled from the chimney. No one was moving, but as the wagon drew closer, a frown creased Duff's forehead.

"Elmer," he said quietly, "are ye seein' what I'm seein'?"

"Hoofprints leadin' up to the house," Elmer replied, keeping his voice low, too. "Looks like half a dozen or so. We got more visitors."

"Aye." Duff turned his head. "Falcon."

"I see 'em," Falcon said from horseback. He had nudged his mount closer to the wagon seat. "You expecting anybody else, Duff?"

"Nae. But that doesna mean they're unfriendly."

"Then why'd they hide their horses?" Falcon asked. "I don't see them anywhere, do you?"

"Nae," Duff said again. The newcomers must have put their horses in the barn, out of sight. Again, that wasn't actually suspicious behavior, but Duff felt wariness stirring inside him, anyway.

He went on to Elmer, "Be ready to turn this wagon and light a shuck, as ye say. I dinna want anything t' happen to our friends."

"If there's a ruckus, I'd rather be in the thick of it," Elmer growled.

"Aye, but I'll be for countin' on ye to keep everyone else safe."

Elmer muttered reluctant agreement. Duff unbuttoned his sheepskin coat and pushed it back a bit, so he could reach the gun on his hip easier.

The six passengers were still chatting happily among themselves, unaware that trouble might be looming. Duff hoped he was wrong about that, but every instinct he possessed was setting off alarms now.

Nothing happened, though, as Elmer pulled the wagon up in front of the ranch house porch and brought it to a stop. The front door opened. Wang stepped out onto the porch with a welcoming smile on his face.

Then Duff caught sight of the man standing behind Wang and knew why his friend's stance was rather stiff. His reflexes made his hand move toward his gun.

"Hold it!" the man behind Wang called. "Touch that gun and I'll blow a hole through this Chinaman of yours!"

The chatter behind the wagon seat ceased abruptly at that harsh threat. Meagan leaned forward and said, "Duff, what—"

"Stay where ye are, lass," he broke in without turning his head. "And be ready t' get down if I tell ye to, all o' ye."

To the man standing behind Wang, he said, "'Tis his own man Wang is, he doesna belong to me or anyone else. And I tell ye now for your own good, ye shouldna be threatenin' him."

From the horse beside the wagon, Falcon said, "Telling him that won't do any good, Duff. I recognize that varmint. He's a hired hard case from a place over in Utah called Carlsburg. Claims to be a deputy, but he's really just a killer."

"His name is Briggs, Anse Briggs," Eleanor said from the first bench seat. "And he's no good, just like the rest of Kramer's bunch."

"Aw, honey, that's no way to talk," Briggs said. His face, barely visible past Wang's head, had a smirk on it. "After all the good times we had together, and all."

"Good times for you, maybe," Eleanor said tightly. "Not so much for me."

"Doesn't matter," Briggs snapped. "You're comin' back with us, anyway. The boss doesn't let anybody run out on him." He raised his voice a little. "We don't have any quarrel with the rest of you, except for that big galoot on the horse. MacCallister, we've got scores to settle with you."

"Anytime," Falcon said. "Just stop hiding behind Wang and we'll get to it. I'm curious where the rest of your friends are, though."

"Check the windows," Elmer said. "Reckon I see rifle barrels behind 'em. There's probably somebody in the bunkhouse, too, with a gun on the crew. Wouldn't've been too hard to get the drop on 'em, it bein' Christmas mornin'. They wouldn't be expectin' any trouble."

Duff said, "Aye, 'tis Christmas mornin'. No time for killin'. This is a day for celebratin' life, lads. Put your guns up, get on your horses, and ride away. We'll call it no harm done, and ye can go back home."

"Not hardly," Briggs growled. "We've got a job to do, and we aim to do it."

Duff sighed and nodded slowly. "Well, then . . . ye canna say we didna gi' ye a chance."

He nodded again, this time a curt signal to Wang.

The slender Chinese moved so fast, it seemed like magic. One second, he was standing there with Anse Briggs's gun pressed against his back, and less than an eyeblink later, he had whirled to the side and launched a spinning kick aimed at the gun wolf's head. If Briggs had just pulled the trigger, he might have done some damage to someone in the wagon, but instead he tried to swing the weapon and draw a bead on Wang again.

Before that could happen, Wang's foot smashed into the side of Briggs's head with all the power of Wang's wiry body behind it. A sharp crack sounded in the cold air as the kick broke Briggs's neck.

"Kill them! Kill them all!"

The hoarse shout came from behind the wagon. Falcon jerked his horse around and saw Otto Kramer himself charging toward them from the bunkhouse, with another of his hired guns. Both men held pistols that roared and spurted flame.

"Get down!" Duff shouted to the passengers in the wagon as he dived off the seat. Glass shattered and sprayed outward from the front windows in the house as the men hidden there opened fire. Elmer hung on to the reins with one hand and pulled out his old hogleg with the other to return the shots. Duff landed agilely, rolled over in the snow, and came up with his gun blasting.

Meagan, Eleanor, Andrew, and Rosanna all hunkered behind the benches, while Hardpan and Twister, who had brought their Sharps and Winchester with them, stood up in the back of the wagon and joined the fray. One of the hired killers had just charged out onto the porch, trying to get a better shot, when a slug from Hardpan's Sharps hammered into his chest and flung him backward through the open door. Twister's Winchester joined the fusillade from Duff's and Elmer's guns.

At the same time, Falcon hauled his horse around and the animal reared up on its hind legs as Falcon triggered shots at Kramer and the gunman behind the wagon. The hired killer went backward, arms and legs flailing, as Falcon's bullets chopped him down.

Kramer, his face twisted with unreasoning hate, advanced stolidly on his thick legs. One of the man's shots slapped past Falcon's head, just before Falcon squeezed the trigger again. Kramer jolted back a step, then plodded ahead again as a crimson flower bloomed on his shirtfront. More flame geysered from his gun muzzle. Knowing that he needed to end this fight before some of the flying lead found an innocent person, Falcon aimed his next shot between Kramer's eyes—and blew the man's brutal brains out. Kramer went down and started turning the snow red around him as the echoes of gunfire dwindled.

"Is that all of 'em?" Elmer said into the silence that followed.

"Aye, appears t' be," Duff said as he got to his feet. He kept his gun ready, though, just in case.

"Little Falcon!" Eleanor cried. She jumped down from the wagon just ahead of Meagan's attempt to stop her and dashed toward the porch steps.

Wang intercepted her. "The young one is unharmed," he assured her. "None of the men bothered him. They wanted only to set their trap for when all of you returned."

"I've got to see for myself," Eleanor said. She pushed past him. He didn't try to stop her this time, because by then, Duff and Falcon were right there, too, and they both went into the house with guns bristling.

The two gunmen who had been shooting from the parlor windows were both dead, riddled by the heavy fire from Duff, Elmer, Hardpan, and Twister.

Duff shook his head at the damage to the house. "We'll be for havin' some work t' do," he told Elmer.

"I can board up them windows for now, to keep the cold from freezin' us out."

"And I will build up the fires in all the fireplaces," Wang said. "Plus, there is plenty of hot food to help keep everyone warm."

"And little Falcon is fine," Eleanor said as she came into the parlor carrying the baby. The others came in from outside, too, followed by the cowboys from the bunkhouse, who weren't happy about being held prisoner the way they had been. They were happy to haul off all the carcasses and dump them on the other side of the barn, where they would keep in the frigid temperatures until the undertaker could get out from Chugwater to claim them.

In the meantime, the door to the parlor was closed tightly to keep the cold air from penetrating to the rest of the house—and to keep the smell of gun smoke from permeating the air too much as everyone gathered around the big table in the dining room.

Duff stood at the head of the table, which was practically

groaning from all the food Wang had prepared. He gazed around at his friends and family, smiled, and said, " 'Tis only one thing I can be for sayin' at a moment such as this . . ."

" 'God bless us every one'?" Twister guessed.

Hardpan turned and glared at him. "If I had my hat, I'd be swatting you with it right now, you lunkhead! Duff was about to say that. What'd you have to go and interrupt him for?"

"I'm sorry," Twister said.

" 'Tis nothin' to worry about, my friend," Duff told him. "Actually, I was about t' say . . . 'Happy Christmas to all!' "

Epilogue

Dunoon, Argyll, Scotland, present day

" 'An' t' all a good night!' " Graham McGregor declared.

"But . . . it was the middle of the day, wasn't it?" Richard van Loan asked with a slight frown.

"Oh. Aye, 'twas, I suppose. Odd, all the times I heard me grandfather tell me tha' story, I never thought about tha'." The old man frowned. "You practical Americans! Always tryin' t' ruin a good story wi' logic an' such."

Richard shook his head and said, "Oh, no, I love a good story. Forget what I just said, Mr. McGregor. 'Happy Christmas to all, and to all a good night.' That's what Duff said, and what better way to end such a rousing tale."

"Aye, 'tis a good one."

"Is any of it . . . you know . . . true?"

McGregor drew himself up again. "Would ye be for callin' me old grandfather a liar?"

"No, of course not," Richard responded hastily. "I just know how these Old West tales, they're usually full of exaggerations and things that never could have happened."

McGregor cocked his head to the side and squinted. "An' were ye there, lad?"

"What? No, certainly not."

"Well, then, ye dinna ken wha' might ha' happened an' what might no' have, do ye? Th' past is full o' things beyond our ken, and all we can do is dream of them."

"You're right," Richard said slowly. "And what's the point of life, if not to dream?"

"Spoken like a true Scotsman. Ye must ha' a drop o' good Scots blood to go wi' that Dutch." McGregor pointed. "An' yonder comes tha' lass o' yours, wi' her arms full o' packages. Will ye tell her the story I just told ye?"

"You know, I believe I will. I think she'll enjoy it."

"Then 'twas time well spent in the tellin' of it. Good day to ye, lad."

Graham McGregor leaned back against the wall, started to pack his pipe again, and smiled as he watched the young American go to meet his beautiful redheaded lassie. Later, he thought, he would stroll down to the White Horse Pub and get himself a drink.